Kate was

one foot tucked bene[illegible], the other poised over a metal basin on the floor. She was washing her feet with slow, graceful, almost sinuous movements, drawing the washrag past her trim ankle, halfway up her slender calf, then down again to the very tips of her toes.

A heavy wave of hair draped one fragile shoulder, while the rest of it spread over her back like a shawl of spun gold. And the golden lamplight filtered through her thin white cotton gown to silhouette the perfect curve of one breast.

The scene was so lovely, so intimate, so utterly feminine. Race could hear his own ragged breath as he struggled to control the flashfire that ripped through him. If this was what going barefoot brought to pass, he'd see that this beauty never wore shoes again....

Dear Reader,

Welcome to another great month of the best in historical romance. With summer just around the corner, Harlequin Historicals has picked four titles sure to heat up your spring nights.

The *Royal Harlot* is Lady Leonie Conniston, a British spy whose assignment is to keep the enigmatic Prince Klaus from danger. However, when Klaus discovers her true identity, who will save her from his growing passions? A big book from author Lucy Gordon.

Newcomer Merline Lovelace gives us a sweeping tale set in ancient Britain. Lady Alena has no love for men after a brutal first marriage, but then why does she find passion and comfort in the arms of a *Roman? Alena* is the first installment of the Destiny's Women trilogy by the author.

In *The Fourth of Forever* by Mary McBride, Race Logan is looking for a harmless roll in the hay with "Kate the Gate," but is shocked to discover the woman in question is not at all what she seems.

And rounding out May, Kathryn Belmont's *Fugitive Heart* tells the story of Jeremiah Sloan and Sarah Randall, who pose as man and wife in order to pull off one of the biggest slave rescues of all time. Yet will their feigned marriage make them yearn for the real thing?

We hope you enjoy these titles. Next month, look for a big book by medieval author Claire Delacroix, and the next installment of the Warrior series by Margaret Moore.

Sincerely,

Tracy Farrell
Senior Editor

MARY McBRIDE

THE FOURTH OF FOREVER

Harlequin Books

TORONTO • NEW YORK • LONDON
AMSTERDAM • PARIS • SYDNEY • HAMBURG
STOCKHOLM • ATHENS • TOKYO • MILAN
MADRID • WARSAW • BUDAPEST • AUCKLAND

ISBN 0-373-28821-2

THE FOURTH OF FOREVER

This edition published by arrangement with Harlequin Enterprises B. V.

Printed in U.S.A.

Books by Mary McBride

Harlequin Historicals

Riverbend #164
Fly Away Home #189
The Fourth of Forever #221

MARY McBRIDE

Mary McBride can't remember a time when she wasn't writing. Before she turned her talents to fiction, her poetry was widely published in "little" magazines and college quarterlies.

Her husband is a writer, as well. "It's wonderful," she says. "I have my own live-in editor and proofreader. The only problem is our combined libraries are threatening to crowd us and our two boys out of the house."

They live—and buy bookcases—in Saint Louis, Missouri.

In loving memory of my parents,
Barbara Bulman Vogt and Herbert O. Vogt,
who met on the Fourteenth of Forever,
Valentine's Day, 1943

Chapter One

Leavenworth City, Kansas
July 4, 1862

Race Logan had never seen so much red, white and blue in his life. The Stars and Stripes flew everywhere, snapping in the warm morning breeze that came in off mile after mile of flat Kansas prairie. The whole damn town was draped with bunting—the mercantile, the bank, the feed and grain. He didn't care much for towns, he thought, and he liked them even less when they were prettily wrapped.

"Looks like an explosion in a flag factory," Race muttered, angling a lean hip onto the hitching rail in front of Cassidy's Mercantile.

"It's Independence Day, Horace."

Race grinned slantways at Isaac Goodman, his longtime partner, a man as big and as black as a bear. "Well, now, you know me, Isaac. I'm all for independence."

"'Specially when it applies to you." The black man laughed as he crossed his arms over his barrel of a chest.

"Most especially when it applies to me." Race's grin darkened to a scowl. He looked over his shoulder at the door of the flag-draped mercantile, catching a brief glimpse of himself in the plate glass window. Buckskin tunic. Flat-crowned hat. The frown of a man who wasn't where he wanted to be. "Where's that pasty-faced storekeeper? He said he'd open up for us right after first light. What the hell was his name?"

"Cassidy," the black man said, nodding toward the bank and then several other solid brick buildings around the town square, all of which displayed that name along with swags of red, white and blue. "He didn't strike me as any too healthy, Horace. Maybe he's done taken to his bed."

Race sighed roughly. "Better not have. I've got better things to do than wait around outside his store all day."

Isaac's gaze cut toward the far end of the street, where silk bunting fluttered above the door of the fancy house. "Those ladies'll keep."

A raised eyebrow was Race's sole acknowledgment of his partner's remark. He was thinking once more how he hated towns. It seemed the minute he set his feet inside city limits, he was already searching for an exit. Too much noise. Too many people asking too many questions. Too many shoulders rubbing up against his. And, today, way too much red, white and blue.

Too set in his ways, Isaac kept telling him. Maybe he was. But what else was there? He'd been working the Santa Fe Trail his whole life, traveling with his father and Isaac Goodman as soon as he was old enough to walk without falling down, without wandering off from the wagons and getting lost in the tall grasses. Race was thirty-two now and instead of getting lost in the prairie grasses, he towered over them.

Towns, on the other hand, made him feel cramped and restless. Towns were for picking up freight, for buying supplies, for hiring crews—rootless men like himself—to drive his wagons southwest. And today, this town was also for partaking of the pleasures of a sweet-scented female in a big, soft bed. Tomorrow, as always, he would be gone.

A tug on his pant leg broke his reverie, and Race looked down into the bright eyes and smudged faces of two small towheaded boys. Each one clutched a Union flag in a grimy hand.

"We're looking for Race Logan. Are you him, mister?"

Race tipped his hat back a notch. "I'm him."

"Our pa says you killed about a hundred redskins. He said you've got the scalps to prove it," the smaller one said.

The older boy rubbed a toe in the dirt. "We was wondering if we could see them."

Crooking his knees, Race lowered himself so his eyes were level with theirs. He planted each big hand on a small, bony shoulder. "Tell you what, boys. I've got plans for today, but if you want to come by my wagons tomorrow at first light, I'll show you a genuine redskin scalp." He angled his head toward Isaac and shot the older man a wink. "We still got that Apache arrow, Isaac? The one that struck old Simon Tate through the heart?"

"I expect I could find it," Isaac said.

The boys' eyes were huge and bright as Race continued. He rubbed his jaw as he said, "'Course that arrow's a mite bloodstained so I don't know if you fellas would want it."

"We want it," they exclaimed in unison.

"Thanks, Mr. Logan," the older one said. "Here. This is for you." He pressed his flag into Race's hand then turned to run after his brother.

Race straightened up. "What are you chuckling at?" he asked Isaac.

"You gonna drag out that old skunk pelt one more time and pass it off as a genuine scalp?"

Race angled his hip back onto the hitching rail. "I just hope to hell I can find it come morning."

Isaac laughed. "How's it feel to be a legend in your own time, Horace?"

"You wait and ask me that after I've been to the fancy house, partner." He stuck the flag in the leather band of the older man's hat. "Happy Independence Day."

Cyrus Neely's head came up from the scrubbed oak table when the cannons boomed at Fort Leavenworth three miles away. He blinked his bloodshot eyes.

"It's all right, Papa. They're celebrating the Fourth of July over at the fort. Here. See if you can keep this coffee down." Kate placed a tin cup on the table in front of him. "Go on now," she urged as she watched her father stare at the steaming liquid as if it were a witch's brew.

He raised his red eyes slowly, from the cup to his daughter's face. "Caroline?" His voice was thick and uncertain.

Kate reached out to touch his whiskery jaw. "It's me, Papa. It's Kate." She watched as a glimmer of recognition seemed to pierce the cloudiness in her father's eyes. A glimmer and then the murky dark returned.

"I thought you were my Caroline." He brushed her hand away, then pushed his chair away from the table and rose on unsteady feet. "I'll be out back."

"We're pretty near out of food, Daddy," she said quickly, "and there's just ten cents left in the sugar bowl."

He muttered an oath as he stepped out the back door then shambled toward his still.

With an oath of her own, Kate took his place at the table. Sometimes, she thought, she wished she had favored his side of the family instead of bearing such a striking resemblance to her mother. It seemed the older she got, the more her hair took on the reddish cast of Caroline Neely's glorious tresses, the more her eyes deepened in their green, and the more her figure turned into Caroline's ample curves. At seventeen now, Kate was the spitting image of the woman who had died five years ago. And the more she looked like her mother, the more her father drank.

She lifted the tin cup, blew on the hot coffee and took a sip. She could put lampblack on her hair, she supposed. Perhaps wear spectacles to dull the color of her eyes. There wasn't much she could do about her voice though. That was her mother's, too—that deep velveteen tone. "Like an angel calling from the bottom of a barrel," her mother had always said.

"Some angel," Kate muttered aloud.

She stood up and smoothed the wrinkles from the front of her white muslin dress, then checked the hem she'd let down the night before. It just touched the floor now, concealing the tips of her bare toes. If she didn't take long strides, nobody would ever notice she wasn't wearing shoes.

Picking up the coffee mug, Kate walked to the front door and gazed out at the tall weeds in the front yard. Some of them were up to her knees now. Trumpet vine was twining through the broken front wheel of their wagon, just above the spot where a mockingbird was building a nest. She frowned, wondering how they'd ever repair the rim without disturbing the delicate construction of twigs. But then she told herself it was useless to worry about that. If they didn't have money for food, why worry about hiring somebody to fix the wagon?

Kate leaned hesitantly against the post that supported the porch roof. It shimmied a little under the weight, then creaked a warning. She quickly stood up straight. She'd be lucky if the whole house didn't fall down around her ears soon. One of these mornings, she'd wake and find herself wearing the roof for a hat.

From the back of the house she heard her father uttering a string of curses. She fought the urge to go to his assistance. She wasn't helping him anymore. The sight of her would only make whatever was wrong much worse. If he even looked at her, she thought glumly. He didn't do that much anymore.

Instead she set the tin mug down, then cupped her hands and called to him. "Daddy, I'm going into town for the celebration. Will you be all right while I'm gone? And will you keep your promise not to take any of that hooch into the fort?"

There was no answer, just another string of curses and the dull crash of crockery against stone. With a sigh, Kate picked up the basket she had located in the barn the night before. She looped it over her arm and stepped carefully down the rickety front steps, then headed east toward town.

Race and Isaac watched the slow progress of the storekeeper and the woman who accompanied him. The lanky, wheat-haired man would halt every dozen paces or so, then bend forward, hands on his knees, coughing, while his companion busied herself with her parasol and tapped an impatient foot.

"Do you suppose he'll get here by sundown?" Race asked.

"That's one unfortunate man, Horace. And if that yellow-haired gal on his arm is his wife, then I'd say he's truly cursed."

"She's a fine-looking woman, Isaac."

"Yup," the older man replied. "And all the way down the street she's been eyeing you like a heifer regards a prize bull. Or hadn't you noticed?"

Race had noticed. He would have to have been blind not to, he thought. He had few rules where the fair sex was concerned, but the ones he did have he adhered to steadfastly. He never dallied with another man's woman, and he avoided entanglements like the plague. The little blonde now approaching him signaled caution on both scores.

After a final racking fit of coughing, the storekeeper and his companion arrived.

Ned Cassidy extended a pale, long-fingered hand. "Sorry I'm late, Logan. Mr. Goodman." The storekeeper nodded to Isaac just as the woman beside him gave him a stiff nudge in the ribs. "I'd like to present my sister, Miss Althea Cassidy."

Race's mouth eased into a grin. Well, now, a sister was a whole new ball game. He reached up to touch the brim of his hat, at the same time taking her damp little hand into his.

"Miss Cassidy."

"How do you do, Mr. Logan." Her light blue eyes came up to his, and locked. "I've heard a great deal about you, and I must say I'm looking forward to hearing a great deal more. I hope you're planning to attend the supper basket auction this afternoon. My basket's the double-handled willow and it'll be just brimming over with treats."

Ned Cassidy coughed again, but this time it sounded more like a warning than an illness. "Mr. Logan's here to arrange for supplies, Althea. I'm sure—"

The blonde's eyes never strayed from Race's as she cut her brother off. "I'm sure he'll have an appetite later on this afternoon, Ned. Any man his size undoubtedly works up a ravenous hunger."

Her damp hand was still in his, and it moved now. Or rather it slid, slowly, deeper into his grasp. Her blue eyes widened perceptibly. "You do have an appetite, don't you, Mr. Logan?"

More than he'd had a moment ago, Race thought as he replied, "I'll keep an eye out for that basket, Miss Cassidy."

"Please do." She smiled at her brother then. "Well, Ned, I'll just leave you men to your important commercial enterprises." Then, with a twist of her parasol and twitch of the bow strings at the back of her skirt, she walked away.

Ned Cassidy's pale face was flushed now as he gestured toward the front door of the mercantile. "This way, gentlemen."

Behind the storekeeper's back, Isaac lifted a grizzled eyebrow in Race's direction as he silently mouthed the words "prize bull."

Race merely glared at his partner as he followed him into the store. Towns and women! He'd be lucky if he survived them, he thought.

On her way into town, Kate had turned off the road and sneaked into the Stringfellows' orchard. She was standing on tiptoe, reaching for a good-size apple when she heard a voice yowling her name.

"Kaaate!"

Ignoring it, she proceeded to pluck the apple, then reached for another.

"Kaaate!"

Kate bent down and gently placed both apples in her basket.

"Give me a little smooch, Kate, and I won't tell my old man you're stealing his apples."

She whirled in the direction of the voice. "Get away from me, Hank Stringfellow, or I'll march right up to your front door and tell your mama what you're up to."

A gangly boy with close-cropped red hair and freckles jumped down from a nearby tree. He licked his lips, then grinned. "Go on and tell her, Kate. And then I'll tell her how I paid you that basket of apples for your favors. Who do you think she'll believe?"

He took a long step toward her, and Kate pitched an apple at his head.

"Get away from me, Hank."

"Aw, come on, Kate. Just one little smooch." The boy advanced another step, his hands ready to deflect the next piece of fruit that sailed in his direction. "Come on, Kate. Just one little bitty feel."

This wasn't the first time Kate had been accosted. It had happened so many times—on the road, down by the creek, even on her own front porch—that she was ready when he lunged for her. Gripping the apple-laden basket tightly with both fists, she swung it. Hard. Hank Stringfellow went down with a howl, his hands covering his face.

Kate lobbed two more apples—one at his head, another at his crotch—then took off running down the road, her bare feet kicking up the dirt behind her.

Chapter Two

The fancy house sported a striped silk swag, as well as a sign tacked up on the locked front door: Closed Due To Patriotic Sensibilities. Race knew it was locked, because he had tried the knob, twice. He had pounded on a window, too, to no avail. He hurled a curse at the gaudy silk banner that flapped just over his head, gave the door a kick for good measure, then headed back toward the town square. If whores had any patriotic sensibilities at all, he thought, they'd keep the damn place open.

Well, hell, he was as patriotic as anybody, especially on this Independence Day with a war going on. But he had his priorities, dammit. And he was going to be out on the trail for the next few weeks with fifteen wagons, sixty oxen, two dozen stubborn, dusty mules with men to match, and not a female in sight.

He was tempted to blame that sickly Cassidy fellow. The man had had such a hard time breathing and talking at the same time that it had taken half the day to accomplish what should have taken little more than an hour or two.

To really put the capper on it then, his walk to and from the fancy house had made him miss the beginning of the basket supper auction, and the double-handled willow basket brimming with treats had already been bought by some young swain who was making calf eyes at the Cassidy girl while she was staring hot daggers at Race.

In fact, now, as he leaned a shoulder against one of the town square's big oaks, he noticed that up on the bandstand there was only a single basket left. With the luck he was having, Race thought, it was probably put up by the schoolmarm or the minister's wife.

The mayor, whose straw hat was banded in red, white and blue, hooked the basket over his arm as he called out to the crowd assembled in the grassy square. "Last chance now, folks. Let's just take a little look-see, shall we? What do you suppose we've got here? Fried chicken? Roast pork?" He lifted a corner of the red-and-white-checkered cloth and peered at the contents. Once. Twice. With a bewildered expression then, he gazed out into the crowd.

"Well, come on, Mayor," somebody called. "What's inside?"

"Yeah, what is it?" others echoed.

"Apples," the mayor said.

"Apples an' what?"

The mayor ran a finger under his high collar. "Just green apples." He scanned the crowd again. "Kate Neely, are you out there? Is this your basket?"

Laughter rippled through the gathering. Elbows shot out to nudge neighbors. Tongues clucked and bonnets wagged in disapproval as a slip of a girl stood up, her shoulders square as a major's, her chin at a fierce angle, and her hands fisted at her side.

"It's mine," she said.

Race, who had been slouched against the tree trunk, contemplating his pitiful, holiday-imposed celibacy, leaned forward now and tapped one of the boys sprawled on the grass in front of him. "Who's that?"

The boy leered over his shoulder. "That's Kate."

"Kate the Gate," the other one echoed. "You know what a gate does, don't you, mister?"

"Yeah, I've got a pretty good notion," growled Race, who couldn't abide such public mockery of a female but certainly wasn't about to let his last chance at a little slap and tickle go by even if it meant eating half a dozen green apples for his supper. After another quick appraisal of the girl's rich red-gold hair and her shapely little body, he opened the bidding at four bits, figuring he'd go as high as five dollars, the price a night in the fancy house would have cost him.

The mayor acknowledged his raised hand. "I have a bid of fifty cents from the gentleman in buckskins. Who'll make it a dollar?"

In the silence that followed, Race saw at least a dozen women skewer their menfolk with their eyes, daring them to open their mouths. And he saw the girl's shoulders sag a notch and her chin dip another. She was such a tiny thing. Young, too, he realized. He'd seen men five times her size and twice her age buckle and run under less humiliating circumstances.

"A dollar," he shouted.

The mayor looked perplexed. "I have a bid of a dollar. Any more bids?"

The silence was dense now, thick as a noose around the girl's neck, and sufficient to twist Race's gut as he watched a hot flush dapple her cheeks. The boy in front of him leaned toward his friend to whisper, "Ain't nobody gonna pay for what he can get for free."

"Five dollars," Race yelled.

"Mister, you're bidding against yourself," the mayor sputtered.

Race straightened to his full six feet two inches and fished a five-dollar gold piece from his pocket, then flashed a broad grin in Kate's direction. "Well, hell, Mayor. I guess I'm just partial to apples."

Partial to apples, my Aunt Mathilda's ass! Kate was seething. She wished the Fourth of July had never been invented. She wished every inch of bunting along Main Street would go up in flames. And, more than anything, she wished a hole would open up in the earth and she could drop through it.

All she had wanted to do was be a part of the celebration on this special flag-waving, heart-drumming, patriotic day. She'd already lost a brother in the war and she had figured if anybody was entitled to participate in the festivities, she was.

She would have put up a fine basket, but all there was in the kitchen this morning was flour and salt and the ten cents lying in the bottom of the sugar jar. In the cellar, there was only a dab of salt pork and a crock of plum jelly. So, on the way into town, she'd filched the apples from the Stringfellows' orchard, fighting off bugs and bees and Hank Stringfellow in the bargain. It seemed like such a good idea at the time.

Now, though, as she watched big, buckskin-clad Race Logan coming in her direction, she realized it had been a dreadful mistake. And not just the apples. The whole notion that she could be a part of the celebration had been stupid and misguided, based on fond hope rather than good sense. Why she ever believed the town drunk's daughter would be accepted into the warm, patriotic bosom of the community was beyond her now. She must have been running a fever last night when she had decided to attend the festivities.

It was a cinch she was running one now though, because her face felt hot as a stove top. Race Logan! Everybody knew who he was...just the most legendary man who ever rode the Santa Fe Trail. The little boys had been yammering about him all day...about how he took over his father's freighting business when he was just fourteen after watching his old man scalped by Apaches...about how he took a hundred scalps himself in retribution...about how he tried to enlist with a volunteer detachment at Fort Leavenworth when the war started and how General Sturgis wouldn't let him, claiming he was more useful to his country making sure supplies got through for the army out West.

Kate had heard the girls talking about him, too. Althea Cassidy had made a perfect fool of herself all day wagging her tongue about his being sweet on her. Why didn't he buy *her* supper basket, for heaven's sake? The answer was obvious as she watched the man walk toward her with that cocksure, about-to-flop-in-the-hayloft grin on his face. Race Logan had heard about Kate the Gate.

None of it was true, of course, but that didn't stop the gossip once it had gotten started. It only made sense that Hank Stringfellow wasn't going to admit Kate had clobbered him when all the other boys were crowing about their conquests. And the Branson boys, Riley and Clay, sure weren't going to say who gave them both black eyes and nothing else. Or the others who'd tried one way or another, one time or another these past few years. Keeping her virginity, in light of her long-lost reputation, was getting to be just plain tiresome. No matter what she did, the stories came out different.

And here came Race Logan, with a reputation of his own. He was handsome, Kate supposed, with that wild dark hair that nearly touched his shoulders. He was broad of shoulder, narrow of waist, and his legs looked about six miles long. She liked his loose-limbed walk even though it smacked of a tomcat on the prowl.

The late-afternoon sun cast his long, dark shadow before him. The shadow kissed the hem of her skirt before it engulfed her. She raised her face to his. Nobody told her about his eyes. They were pure turquoise, rimmed with dark lashes, softened at the corners by deeply etched crow's-feet. They fairly took her breath away.

"Miss Kate," he said in a voice that was as warm and lazy as summer itself. Then he took her hand, and Kate felt a sudden shimmer of heat all the way to her shoulder.

She swallowed hard, trying to force her heart back down into her chest, trying to put out the sizzle along her spine, to ignore the sensuous grin that told her Race Logan had every intention of celebrating this Fourth of July by creating fireworks with Kate the Gate. Dazzling fireworks. Like the ones that had already begun inside her while her mind went suddenly and inexplicably blank—after allowing as how she might as well be hung for a wolf as a sheep.

The buggy wheels squealed for grease and the sorrowful bay gelding should have been put out to pasture five years back, but it was the best the livery stable had to offer under the circumstances. Leaning back in the seat now, Race had to admit the circumstances were very much to his liking. He even found himself glad—well, almost glad—the fancy house had been closed.

Little Kate was more than pretty and proud; she was a bright girl and well-spoken, too, now that she had calmed down a mite. Back in town, when he had lifted her up into the buggy seat, he could feel the tightness under the soft female curves. Just to please her and to show his good intentions, he had eaten an apple right off the bat. Its juice had been warm and sweet even though the fruit wasn't quite ripe. It probably wasn't such a bad comparison to Kate herself, who struck him as just a tad shy of ripeness. If she was much over sixteen, he would have been surprised.

Race turned his head to look at her now. The hands clasped in her lap were delicate, but hardworking, nevertheless, with rough patches and short nails. Her dress was of cheap, unbleached muslin, but it appeared well fashioned and skillfully sewn. If he had to guess, he'd say that her petticoats and underwear were made of the same fabric, without a flounce or a ruffle. Her clothes were hardscrabble. There were no two ways about it.

But the rest of her! Her strawberry blond hair was pinned up, but he suspected it would fall in heavy waves over her shoulders and ample breasts. He couldn't remember ever seeing such an interesting face on a girl so young, but maybe her experiences as Kate the Gate had added that knowing light in her green eyes and that arrogant little tilt to her chin. Only God himself could have given her that lush and inviting mouth. He felt his body tighten at the mere sight of it, and he turned his head forward again, where the view of the bay's ragged, tick-infested rump brought him back to his senses.

She was half his age. He was practically old enough to be her father, and considering the carousing he had been doing by the age of sixteen, Race considered himself definitely old enough. Maybe even too old. She looked at him now, her green eyes not yet round with trust, but not as slatted and wary as they had been back in town.

"Where are we going?" she asked, unclasping her hands briefly before linking her fingers together again and letting them drop as nonchalantly as possible in her lap. They were still shaking and she didn't want him to see how nervous she was.

He nudged his hat back, allowing a dark curl to escape onto his forehead. "I thought it might be nice to see a little green. I was getting pretty tired of all that red, white and blue. How 'bout you?"

Kate nodded then idled her gaze on his strong, sun-darkened hands. His thumbs were smoothing back and forth over the leather reins. She imagined his touch—as she had felt it when he spread his big hands at her waist and lifted her so easily up into the buggy—and her heart did a little flip-flop in her chest. Whether it came from fear or desire, Kate wasn't at all sure.

"I know a place," she said softly, then watched as one of his eyebrows lifted as if to say "I'll bet you do." She fussed with the folds of her skirt for a moment. "There's a turnoff about a quarter mile from here. Wilson's Creek runs through an orchard there. It's a pretty spot for a picnic dinner."

It was, in fact, where she had stolen their supper just this morning, though it seemed like a lifetime ago.

"It wouldn't be an apple orchard, would it?" he asked, a rich chord of humor in his voice.

"What's wrong with that?"

"Oh, nothing's wrong with it. I'd just be a little more careful around apples if I were you, Miss Kate."

She looked into his vibrant turquoise eyes. They were as deep and clear as a lake, and for a moment she swore she could see her own reflection there. "More careful? Why?"

This time his dark eyebrow quirked even more rakishly. "They didn't do a whole hell of a lot for Eve, did they?"

Kate laughed. "I guess not." And then her mouth settled into a thoughtful pose as she recalled her narrow escape from Hank Stringfellow's amorous intentions and wondered whether she would have run so fast if it had been Race Logan who had jumped down from the apple tree this morning. "Which would you rather be, Mr. Logan, an angel or a devil?"

Race chuckled low in his throat. "I don't believe I have much choice after all these years, Miss Kate. Old Lucifer's probably already got my name inked in his book. What about you? Which would you rather be?"

He felt a definite shifting within his chest when she raised her face to his, when her eyes opened to him, round and verdant and trusting.

"I don't believe I have much choice, either," she said somberly, following her words with a wistful little sigh and then leaning ever so slightly against his arm.

The sun was long gone. They sat by the fire he had built of apple twigs and branches, listening to the cool churning of creek water and the high whine of locusts. Race had eaten more apples than any human being ever had in the course of a single day. And sometime between sundown and the present moment, sometime while he was looking at Kate and listening to her deep smoke-and-velvet voice, he had decided to see her safely, and chastely, home.

It wasn't because he didn't want her. In fact, as the evening wore on, he wanted her more than ever and his intentions, quite frankly, baffled him. Worse, they irritated him. The itch he'd meant to scratch itched more than ever now. And what was he doing about it? Nothing except making himself sick on apples and shifting uncomfortably on the hard earth beneath him while he savored the devilish expressions of her face and the deep, angelic music of her voice.

Kate pitched an apple core over her shoulder. Her face glowed in the firelight and there was a bright glint in her eyes. "Where'd your mama ever come up with a name like Race?"

"She didn't," he said as he poked a stick in the fire. "I was named after my father, Horace Logan, Sr."

Her hand flew to her mouth to stifle a near explosion of laughter. "Oh, Race, I'm sorry. It's just that...Horace?"

He scowled, thinking there probably wasn't a man alive who would dare tease him the way this saucy little tart was doing now. Suddenly, though, he was in no mood to be teased. "It's a perfectly good name. What's wrong with it?"

Kate bit her lower lip. "Nothing's wrong with it. It just doesn't fit you somehow. Horace is...oh, I don't know...old and bald and bespectacled."

"All of which I'll probably be one day. Old, anyway. Provided some redskin doesn't put an arrow through my heart. Hell, I'm old already."

"How old?"

"Old enough to know better," he gruffed.

"Tell me." She nudged his shoulder with hers. "How old?"

He sighed. "I'm thirty-two, Kate. What are you? Fifteen? Sixteen?"

"Seventeen," she said adamantly.

Race unwound his long legs, stood, and walked to the other side of the campfire. "I don't even remember being seventeen." He tried but couldn't hide a certain callousness in his voice. By the time he was seventeen, Horace Logan, Jr. had killed more men than he ever wanted to. There was no pleasure in looking back at that kind of youth. It had held no pleasure for him then.

Kate stood and brushed the dirt from her skirt. As she angled around to tend to the back, Race noticed she was barefoot. She must have kept her feet tucked under her dress all evening, he thought, for surely he would have noticed those shapely toes and that little glimmer of slim ankle. Surely his body would have reacted to the sight as it was doing now. Kate turned then and saw the direction of his gaze. Immediately her bare toes disappeared beneath the hem of her dress and, even in the dim firelight, Race could see the color rise in her face.

"Doesn't your father keep you in shoes, Kate?" It came out more accusation than question.

Her chin lost a bit of its perpetual tilt. "It's summertime, Race. There's no need..."

He cut her off, coming around the campfire to pull her into her arms. His breath was warm against her temple. "You deserve better. Don't you know that, Kate? Good God, what kind of a man would let his daughter go without shoes?"

She arched her head back to meet his piercing, firelit gaze. "You don't know anything about it. About my father. About me."

"I know enough," he gritted. "All I need to."

Her green eyes narrowed fiercely. "You mean you've heard all the gossip around town. All the stories about Kate the Gate. Is that what you call enough?"

Race's grip tightened on her. "It doesn't matter what I've heard. And I don't give a good goddamn what you've done. That was the past. It's all over now."

Kate blinked. She didn't understand.

He didn't, either. One minute he was older and infinitely wiser than she was, and the next he was a snot-nosed kid so in love with her he didn't know what he was saying anymore. "Katie, I..." His mouth closed and tautened as he moved back a step, away from the searing contact with her flesh. What was the point? He'd said far too much already. It was time to go.

But then they heard the slow clomping of a horse, accompanied by the clank of crockery and a raspy, off-key rendition of "John Brown's Body."

Kate stamped her foot. "He promised me," she snapped as she turned away from Race, grabbed up her skirt and ran toward the road, calling, "Daddy, wait up."

Race stayed where he was. He thought if he even caught a glimpse of the misfit who let this beautiful girl go barefoot, he'd be hard-pressed not to lay him out cold. But he could hear the quiver in Kate's voice as she begged him to go back home, told him there was no more money for food. And then Race's blood ran cold when he heard her cry, "Oh, Daddy, I need shoes."

"Leave me be, girl," her father bellowed. "I'll do as I damn well please, and no slut of a girl's going to tell me otherwise. You want shoes? Then you go ask one of those young bucks in town to give you shoes along with whatever else they're giving you."

Race was about to change his mind about knocking the bastard's head right off his shoulders even though he didn't like to tangle with drunks. They were too unpredictable. And this particular drunk would be easy to hurt real bad. He had almost decided to do it when the horse snorted and galloped away.

Kate came back into the circle of firelight, looking for a moment like a whipped pup—but just for one unguarded moment, which he knew he wasn't meant to see.

He sighed roughly. Comfort didn't come easily to him. He was used to being with men who didn't want it and women who didn't need it, at least not from him. All he knew to do was take Kate in his arms and press his lips to her sweet-scented hair, holding her as if he'd never let her go, whispering her name again and again, and telling her it would all be fine, that he was with her now. Lying, he thought. It wouldn't all be fine, and the fact that he was with her now said nothing about tomorrow. But her silence led him to believe she knew it as well as he did, had probably heard it all a hundred times before.

Her arms curled around his waist as she lifted her face to his. Race cupped her chin in the palm of his hand. His thumb traced the sensuous curve of her lips. "You'll have your shoes, little Kate," he whispered. "I'll see to it."

She closed her eyes a moment, shaking her head. "It's not shoes so much," she said. "I want...I want..."

"What? What is it you want, love?" Softly he kissed each corner of her mouth, tasting the salt of tears she hadn't allowed him to see. "Tell me, Kate. Tell me what you want."

Her tongue touched her lips just before she formed her reply. "I want people to stop laughing at me and boys to stop grabbing at me. I want people to treat me like a lady, the way they treat Althea Cassidy. I want..." She finished with a long, quivering exhalation. "I want respectability."

With his heart hammering in his chest, he realized he had been expecting a far different answer from those moist pink lips. You, he thought she'd say. I want you. Now. Tonight. Disappointment flicked in the pit of his stomach like the tongue of a snake. He could give her shoes, or a decent meal, or money. He could give her his body, his hands and his mouth and his manhood to slake any craving, to satisfy completely any need. But where respectability was concerned, he had nothing to offer her. And no time. He was leaving tomorrow.

He stepped back from the circle of her arms. "It's time to take you home, Miss Kate. Let's go."

They'd hardly spoken on the two-mile ride to the ramshackle place Kate called home. It was dark, but she could still see Race's gaze taking in the weed-choked yard, the empty, unpainted chicken coop, the vacant hog pen, and the tumbledown front porch. His mouth flattened in a tight, grim line as he lifted her down from the buggy.

Sensing his harsh appraisal, she forced a note of brightness in her voice. "Where else would a barefoot girl live?"

His face remained impassive as he walked her up the rotting steps, over the warped boards of the front porch to the door that her father had left ajar. Once inside, Kate scraped a match and lit a small lamp.

"Thank you, Race, for a fine Fourth of July," she said, turning to him, lamp in hand. "I enjoyed your company."

He nodded stiffly. "My pleasure, Kate. I enjoyed your company, too." His lips quirked in a quick little grin. "And the apples."

Hard as she tried, she couldn't coax her lips into a smile to match his. "Good night, then," she said softly.

The color of his eyes was a deep sapphire in the lamplight, dark and hard as gemstones as he bent to touch his lips to the crown of her head. He turned then and walked out the door, closing it behind him.

Kate just stood there and listened until the squeak of the buggy blended with the raspy noise of crickets, then she walked aimlessly around the room, picking up odd socks and crumpled papers, which she dropped into the empty picnic basket. That was how she felt, she thought—empty—except for odd and crumpled feelings deep inside.

It's your own damn fault, she told herself. Blubbering about an old drunk hell-bent on killing himself and then corking it with all that whining about respectability. Somehow Race had pulled the truth out of her like a bucket from a deep, cool well. She never would have confessed that to anyone else. Well, nobody else had ever asked.

The trouble was he hadn't asked more, hadn't reeled the bucket up quite far enough. The trouble was—and the awful truth—she craved Race Logan just as much as she did respectability. More. Given the choice tonight of devil or angel, Kate the Gate would have opened wide, swung happily into hellfire and brimstone for that big, loose-walking, low-talking, heavenly eyed man.

The trouble was, Race thought as he eased up on the sorry bay, he had promised her shoes. Now how was he going to accomplish that without knowing what size?

"Nothing worse than a pair of shoes too tight," he said out loud to the bay. "Worse than no shoes at all."

The horse heaved his great head back over his shoulders, then shook it.

"Right," Race said. "We get a big pair and then she can stuff the toes with cotton." He pictured those pretty toes peeking out from the hem of her skirt. Now Race shook his head. "Blisters," he said to the horse as he pulled back on the reins.

The bay sighed as he came to a standstill, withers rippling and one hoof pawing the ground.

"I am not looking for excuses," Race proclaimed to the horse, to the sky overhead, and most of all to himself. He'd promised her shoes and he'd be goddamned if he'd gift a lady with a pair that didn't fit.

The problem was, though, Kate was no lady. Why that galled him he couldn't quite say. After all, he was about as far from a gentleman as New York was from San Francisco. Still, he always figured that someday—about a hundred years from now—if he ever fell in love, it would be with a woman of quality. Not some damn barefoot girl who spread her legs for anything and everything in pants.

In love! That was a joke. He'd been looking for a little willing flesh, that's all, and he'd suffered a setback because the available flesh was so young and tender. That didn't seem to bother anyone else, though, did it? Apparently it didn't bother Kate the Gate. To earn a reputation like hers, she'd probably been giving it away for years.

"Respectability!" he muttered. "That'll be the day, Katie girl." She'd been doing it with boys. Let's just see how she liked it with a man.

The horse started at the quick tug on one rein. "Your night's not over yet, you flea-bitten bag of bones. Come on."

And your night's not over by a long shot, Kate the Gate, he thought as he pulled the bay around. *You best oil your hinges, little girl.*

Chapter Three

He looped the reins over a rickety hitching rail and threw the bay a sidelong glance. "This won't take long," Race said, then he took the front porch steps in a single stride and went to the window where he had seen a square of yellow light as he approached the ramshackle house.

Kate was sitting on the bed, one foot tucked beneath her, the other poised over a metal basin on the floor. She was washing her feet—not with a quick lick and a dab, but with slow, graceful, almost sinuous movements, drawing the washrag past her trim ankle, halfway up her slender calf, and then down again to the very tips of her toes.

A heavy wave of hair draped down one fragile shoulder while the rest of it spread over her back like a shawl of spun gold. And golden lamplight filtered through her thin white cotton gown to silhouette a perfect curve of breast.

The scene was so lovely, so intimate, so utterly feminine. Race could hear his own ragged breath as he struggled to control the flash fire that ripped through him. My God, if this was what going barefoot brought to pass, he'd see that this beauty never wore shoes again.

Had he groaned out loud? He wasn't sure, but suddenly her head snapped up and her gaze shot to the window. Her green eyes were cold with fear for an instant before recognition warmed them. Recognition and welcome.

"You came back," she said, without surprise, without even a catch in her voice to betray any doubts she might have had.

He raised the window farther to accommodate his height, then slung his legs over the sill and eased his shoulders through the frame. Without a word, Race walked to the bed, took the washrag from her hand, dropped it into the basin, then drew her up into his arms.

Slowly, so slowly, he let her slide down his body until her toes just touched the floor. Kate could feel unyielding muscle under soft buckskin and smell the musky, purely male scent of him. She could feel his heart beat hard against her cheek and the straining ridge of his manhood against her abdomen as her arms circled his waist. Warmth rushed through her. And a strange ache. An unfamiliar emptiness longing to be filled.

Race took her face in both hands, his fingers spread through the rich silk of her hair. There was no anger in him anymore. That had dissipated at the sight of her the way a morning fog dissolves in sunshine. Now there was only need, hot and piercing. He dipped his head and laid claim to her lush mouth.

Instinctively she opened for the stunning caress of his lips, for his sweet marauding tongue. The deep, drugging kiss sent flickers of heat through her, melting her bones and making the rest of her liquid as warm molasses.

Race lifted his head. "You taste like apples," he murmured into her hair. "And your hair smells like pure moonlight." As he spoke, his hand was working up the thin fabric of her gown. His fingers drifted across her ribs, feathered over her abdomen, then curved beneath her breast, letting its warmth and weight fill the palm of his hand as his thumb traced lazy circles around the hardened peak.

A little moan broke from her throat as his mouth moved back to hers with a spate of small, nipping kisses that made her wild inside as she tried to capture his teasing lips.

"Tell me that you want me, Kate," he rasped. But before she could answer he was drinking deeply from her mouth. "Tell me." Gathering a fistful of her hair, he brought her head back. His eyes were dark and fierce, demanding. "Tell me."

"Yes."

"Yes what?"

"I...I want you."

He whisked an arm beneath her knees and lifted her high against his chest, his other arm cradling her shoulders. "I want you, too, little Kate." He set her gently on the bed, then stepped back to remove his clothes, eyes locked on hers all the while he unbuckled his belt, unlaced the neck of his buckskin shirt, then wrenched it over his head.

His chest was a hard curve of muscle beneath a mat of fine dark hair that thinned over firm, flat cords of abdomen. Kate thought she had never seen such beauty before. No man had ever struck her as beautiful. Until now. There was a frightening beauty in the sculpture of his shoulders, in the long ropy musculature of his arms, in the suggestion of dormant power those muscles contained.

The mattress canted as he sat to pull off long boots and socks, and Kate listed against his warm back a moment. The touch of that bare, heated skin on her arm sent a shock of desire through her. Along with a shock of awareness of what was about to happen. Here. Now. To her.

He leaned back, raising his torso slightly to unlace his trousers, and took them off along with his underwear in a quick sweep of his hands. Kate watched, then looked away, then looked back. Having spent her life in close quarters with a brother and a father who hadn't bothered with modesty, she knew what to expect, more or less. Race Logan, in his passionate condition, was more rather than less. Much more. Kate only had a vague notion of what went where, but she was fairly certain there was no part of her that could accommodate him.

A thread of panic stitched through her now. It might be a good idea, under the circumstances, to let him know she'd never done this before, that she wasn't all that sure she wanted to finish what she had so foolishly and feverishly begun, that...

Before she quite realized what was happening, he had taken the hem of her gown in both hands and lifted it over her head then tossed it aside. Naked now to his hot gaze, Kate was speechless.

"Lord, you're a beauty, Kate," he said, sighing. He slipped one arm around her waist while one hand braced her neck as he slowly forced her back with the weight of his own body, all the while dropping tiny kisses onto her eyelids, her nose, her chin.

"Race?" Her voice sounded small, thin as a wisp of smoke.

"What, love?" He traced his warm tongue over her lower lip.

"There's something you should know. About me, I mean. Something—"

He cut her off by drawing her lip between his teeth, sucking gently.

Kate managed to wriggle away from the sensuous prison of his mouth. "You have to know about..."

He raised his head, angling hers so their eyes met. When Kate tried to avert her gaze, he forced it back. "Listen to me. I know all I need to, Kate. It doesn't matter."

"But it..."

His eyes burned blue as the heart of a flame. "Shh. Yesterday doesn't count, Kate. This is now. This is you and me."

As he spoke, low and gravelly, his hand moved to her breast, slowly and gently kneading the firm flesh, sending waves of want through her. His lips drifted over her cheek, her chin, her collarbone, over the swell of her breast. His tongue flicked hot across its aching peak before he drew her into his mouth. An unbidden cry of pleasure escaped her, and her fingers clasped in his dark hair. When he left her, a current of air chilled the flesh his suckling had moistened, and Kate felt momentarily bereft, abandoned, until his mouth sought the other breast to instill the same intense tug of pleasure there.

She was so sweet, so warm. Her lovely body sprang to life everywhere he touched her. And Race touched her, letting his fingers glide up the silky inner curve of her thigh to the hot velvet place where she was slick and ready for him. So soon. But then she was no stranger to this act. The mere thought was torture now as he touched her. He would have liked to have been her first lover, the one to guide her, to lead her to the shimmering place where she had never been before. She moaned softly as his finger eased inside her, and her response drove all other thoughts out of his head.

Those deft, ardent hands had kindled such heat in her that she almost forgot her fears. Still, somehow between the kisses and the caresses, Kate felt compelled to let him know what this moment was, for her, new and wondrous and like nothing she had ever known before. She needed to tell him, ached to tell him that all the others had lied about her, that there had been no others, that all the stories were no more than some brutal fairy tale the town kept telling itself.

The words kept fashioning themselves on her lips, and then he would do something new to her, move his hand somewhere else, or his mouth, and the words would only come out as soft animal cries. But he had to know.

He came back to her mouth now to taste the deep sweetness, to consume her soft, strangled sounds of passion.

"Race," she uttered breathlessly.

"What, love? Tell me."

"I never... I don't... oh, Race, all the others..."

He didn't want to hear it so he stopped her lips with his, but she wrested her mouth away.

"You have to know," she breathed against his ear. "About the others. It was all just..."

Something ripped in him then. It was more than his male pride, more than his wish to be the first, the only, the last. He could live with what she was, what she had been, but he didn't have to hear it. He didn't *want* to hear it. It drove him wild with a rage that had no place to go. A rage he could only release by stilling her mouth with his, parting her legs with a rough, impatient hand and entering her—hard, with the force of his anger rather than his desire.

It was too late when he felt the brutal tearing deep inside her. And too late when her cry of surprise and pain shivered against his lips. Too late.

He left her mouth with a savage curse, and left her body gently, although the damage had already been done. "Damnation, Kate!" Race sat up and dragged the fingers of both hands through his hair, trying to catch his breath, to stop the pounding of his heart and the hard tensing of his body. "Why the hell didn't you tell me?" he shouted.

Kate, swept up in her own storm of emotions, yelled back. "I tried! You wouldn't listen to me."

He slung his legs over the side of the mattress, his back to her and his head shaking in bewilderment. He cursed again.

"I'm sorry," Kate said, pulling the sheet up to cover herself. She didn't know what else to say. She didn't really know what had happened, or what was happening now for that matter. "Was...was that it?" she asked him hesitantly. "Is it over?"

He closed his eyes a moment, muttering another curse, and then, with a glance in the direction of his deflated ardor, he sighed. "Yeah, Kate, it's over. For now, anyway."

"Oh." She hugged the sheet more tightly to her bosom.

"Oh," Race echoed in a tone more sarcastic than he intended, but then he couldn't seem to manage even his voice right then. "I've got to get out of here for a minute," he said, grabbing his pants.

Gnawing on her bottom lip, Kate watched as he slammed her door, then a second later she heard the back door slam, and after that the privy door. She felt irritated, more than a little disappointed, and on the edge of tears. She felt, in fact, like slamming a few doors herself.

When he came out of the privy, his pants back on and his wits a little more about him, Race lifted the lamp he had brought with him and looked around the desolate rear yard. Walking carefully through weeds and broken crockery and rusty tools, he approached a curious-looking collection of wood crates. Good

God, Kate's old man had a still here. Right out in the open. It was a wonder he wasn't in jail already.

Race picked up one of the corked crocks and, carrying it loosely by the neck, ambled around to the front of the house where he sat on the steps. The bay was nose deep in weeds, but he lifted his head at the sound of the cork thunking out of the jug. Race raised the container in his direction in a toast. "Here's to women," he said. "God bless 'em." He took a long, bracing swig as the horse shook its head then returned to cropping weeds.

Women. He'd known his share, that was for sure. For years, at each end of the trail, in Westport, in Independence, and in Santa Fe. Soft, pale Missouri girls and fiery, dark-eyed *señoritas*. Over the years they came and went. Or, more exactly, they came and he went. He wondered sometimes if he really trusted the opposite sex, and often thought perhaps his distrust had something to do with the fact that his mother had walked out on him and his father both not long after Race was born.

Basically what he trusted was the Santa Fe Trail. It was truly his only home. And his only possessions were the wagons and oxen and mules to do the job. He'd made the trip so many times he knew each trickle of creek, each tall blade of grass, every rut and swale for eight hundred miles.

He had worked as hard as any of his oxen for his whole life, and despite the fact that he had more money in the bank than he knew what to do with these days, he was basically a saddle tramp whose life had settled into a sweet rhythm. The heightened activity and danger of the trail was punctuated at each end by the relaxed and relatively safe pleasures of the flesh. That was how it had always been, and how he always imagined it would remain. He wasn't the marrying kind.

Or was he? Race tipped the jug again and stared out at the moonlit slats of the chicken coop. This was a hell of a place, a hell of a life for a girl like Kate.

He leaned back against the rickety roof post, cocking one knee, the crock of cider balanced on his extended thigh. Race closed his eyes a moment, then opened them to stare at nothing in particular. A virgin! Well, not anymore. He'd seen to that. Dear God, if he could just go back and have those moments to live again. He had taken something so precious from Kate, and there was nothing he could do to undo the damage. Glumly he realized he had gotten his wish—to be her first lover—and he'd really done a bang-up job.

If only his head would clear. If only he could sort things out: how this Fourth of July had begun one way and ended so different; how a little girl had stood up in a mean crowd with her shoulders stiff and her chin high; how she had strangely altered the course of his life, for better or for worse.

Kate had turned down the wick in the lamp then dug herself as far as possible into the mattress with the sheet over her head. She wanted to cry, but she wouldn't allow the tears to start. If they began, they might never end.

She had no idea if Race had any intention of coming back. She wasn't sure she cared right then, one way or the other. Then the latch clicked on the door. She heard the soft brush of bare feet over the floor and felt the mattress dip as Race sat beside her. His big, warm hand settled on her hip.

"It's too late to hide from me, Kate," he said softly.

Her response was a sniff, a wriggle of her hip in an effort to dislodge his hand.

"The next time will be better for you, honey. I promise."

"There's not going to be a next time, Race Logan," she said from under the sheet.

He lit the lamp and turned the wick so the light was low and golden, then he reached for the washrag in the basin. "Turn over on your back, Kate," he said, tugging the cover from her.

"Don't." She yanked the sheet back. "Leave me alone."

"You're worse than a mule, little girl. Come on now. Don't be stubborn, Katie. I want to take care of you."

She whipped the sheet back to uncover her head—the better to stab him with her eyes. "You took care of me, all right," she snapped. And then the tears she'd been keeping in check burst forth, cascading down her cheeks. Race lifted the damp rag to her face, but she batted his hand away.

"All right," he said through clenched teeth. "Now look. I'm doing the best I know how here. I know I hurt you. Believe me, if I could have it to do all over again, I'd do it different. Or I wouldn't do it at all."

He raised his hands in a helpless gesture, then let them drop. His voice thickened. "I'm sorry, Kate. I'm just so damn sorry."

Before she even knew she was doing it, Kate sat up and slid her arms around him, pressing her cheek against his warm, bare chest. "It's all right," she whispered. "It doesn't hurt anymore. And it wasn't that bad. Not all of it, anyway. I liked the kissing and touching part."

Race stroked her rich red-gold hair. He'd meant to comfort her, now here she was comforting him, easing his conscience and trying to lighten the burden he bore, turning the tables on him as surely and as completely as any experienced woman of the world might have done.

Earlier, outside on the porch with the sympathetic horse and the consoling jug, he had decided to simply apologize and then leave without touching her again. Maybe he'd measure her feet so he could at least see that she got a good pair of well-fitting shoes. Not much in return for what she'd given him, he admitted, but what else could a saddle tramp do? He had a contract with the army. There were fifteen wagons waiting at the railroad siding, all of them loaded and ready to roll to Fort Union in New Mexico Territory. Tomorrow. There were two dozen men whose livelihoods depended on him, not to mention his own life, his well-established routine, a way of living that precluded any long-term relationships. As soon as the war was over, as soon as the railroad pushed the head of the trail farther west, Race knew he'd never see this town, or anybody in it, again.

Kate was nuzzling her face against his chest now and letting her hands roam over his back, making his heart pick up speed and his bloodstream surge. Her arms encircled him as surely as a rope. She was taking all his good intentions, stringing them out and tying them in complicated knots. And then she raised her pretty little face to his, and she reeled him in with her big green trusting eyes.

"I hope we don't both regret this." He sighed raggedly as he leaned her back onto the mattress.

He reached down for the damp cloth he had dropped to the floor and then spoke softly as he eased the sheet away from her and slid her gown up her legs. "There's some blood the first time, love. I'm not going to hurt you now. Open your legs a tad."

A tad. It was the most she could manage, and Kate had to grit her teeth to do that. But his touch was so gentle and his eyes were so warm and his voice was so soft. And as he continued to draw the cloth over her most intimate part, she began to think it almost felt good. Very good. The fires that had been doused so abruptly before now began to stir in her again.

Her eyes roved over his broad shoulders, the dark expanse of his chest, the hard musculature of his torso, marveling that a body so potentially lethal in its power could also be so gentle, that a man who had seen and done all that Race Logan had could still be capable of such great tenderness.

She closed her eyes and gave herself up completely to his infinitely delicate ministrations. It wasn't long before the cool touch of the cloth had been replaced by the warmth of his hands. Moving over every inch of her, they fanned the flames inside her to new and powerful heights.

"Open your eyes, Kate."

It wasn't easy. Her lids were heavy, as if drugged. But when she did, it was to encounter a pair of deep blue-green eyes beneath a dark fringe of lashes and a mouth that slid into a slow smile.

"You're going to like what I'm going to do to you, little Kate. The place I'm going to take you," he whispered hoarsely. "A place you've never been before."

She blinked, not understanding at first. Not until his hand began to move, slowly at first, teasingly, and then as the fire climbed inside her, more insistently. He caught each of her soft moans with his mouth, murmuring words of passion, urging her, pushing her relentlessly toward a peak of ecstasy where her whole body seemed to disintegrate into a myriad of sparks and shooting stars. Fireworks. Her own dazzling celebration.

And then he moved over her, whispering his promise not to hurt her, but only to follow, to join her in that special place. He entered her slowly, so achingly slowly it seemed now that she longed desperately to be filled, to take him deep within her, to capture and keep him there. She arched her back and slid her legs around him, heard her name tear from his lips as he let go of caution and control, and sank deeply within her. Kate clung to him tightly, her body moving with his, matching his, meeting his, until, with one final, soul-wrenching thrust, he joined her in that spangled place.

* * *

Lying on his side, Race pulled Kate into him, crooking her knees with his, nestling her backside against him. He rearranged the wealth of golden hair that separated his lips from her delicate ear, her warm cheek. Satiated, depleted now, he couldn't keep his hands from drifting over her or keep his lips from touching her face. He couldn't stop wanting her. Worse, he couldn't bear the thought of leaving her in this ramshackle place.

"Come with me, Kate," he murmured as he stroked her hair.

She sighed lazily. "I did."

"No. I mean tomorrow. When I take my wagons south to Santa Fe. Come with me."

She didn't respond for a long moment, and then, very quietly, she said, "What are you asking me, Race?"

"I don't know what the hell I'm asking you," he muttered. "I only know I can't leave you here. And I..." His voice dropped off into a frustrated sigh.

"What?"

"Nothing. Just come with me, Kate."

Again she was silent for a while. "Are you asking me to marry you?"

He levered himself away from her. Lying on his back, fingers splayed to the ceiling as if for heavenly guidance, he said, "I don't know." Then his hands dropped helplessly to the mattress.

Kate flipped over and cocked an elbow under her head, studying the frown lines that creased his fore-head and the grim set of his mouth. "Well, that's an honest answer, anyway. I appreciate that even though I never expected to be anyone's mistress."

"I never expected to get married," he shot back, rolling his eyes in exasperation. "This is just plain crazy."

Kate laughed. "Well, nobody's twisting your arm, Race. Don't do it then if you don't want to."

"I don't."

"Well?" She laughed again.

Race speared her with his gaze. "Seems to me you're finding this all pretty funny."

"It is funny. You're buzzing around in one place like a horsefly with a pin stuck through his middle." She bunched the sheet up to stifle her laughter.

He rose from the bed and stabbed his legs into his pants. "I'm glad you're amused."

Kate didn't respond, but merely watched as his fingers tried to deal with the lacings on his fly. She couldn't quite suppress a grin. This was not a clumsy man, yet he could barely manage to fasten a pair of pants right now.

He glared at her, then dropped onto the bed to shove his feet into his socks and boots. He wrenched his buckskin shirt on over his head then just sat there silently, his forearms on his knees, his head bent forward.

Kate reached up to touch a lock of soft, dark hair that curled over his collar. "My daddy's all that's keeping me here," she said softly.

Race turned to her, his turquoise eyes melting into hers. "I'll be your daddy. I'll be good to you, Kate."

Kate was caught in the liquid warmth of that gaze, not certain whether she was drowning in a pool of deep green water or swirling in a cloudless blue sky, but knowing she was spinning irrevocably toward this man. Her heart held still as her lips moved. "Yes."

Chapter Four

From the moment she first saw him with his hip planted on a hitching rail and a rakish grin playing at his lips, Althea Cassidy wanted Race Logan. Never, in all of her eighteen years, had she wanted a man more. And never, ever, had she been on the wrong end of an infatuation.

Her brother, Ned, had opened the mercantile especially for him this holiday morning, so Race Logan could get the supplies he needed for his trip to Santa Fe. He'd been waiting for them outside—one long leg swinging lazily as he leaned against the rail with his arms crossed, pulling his buckskin shirt tight across the muscles of his back. He slung himself off the hitching rail with one smooth, fluid motion that had called to mind a tawny mountain lion. He shook hands with Ned, and then Race Logan had turned his turquoise eyes on her, causing an amazing burst of pyrotechnics in the pit of her stomach and palpitations the likes of which she'd never known.

She had spent most of this Independence Day with just one thing on her mind. Even now, after midnight, as Althea sat by the window of her family's big brick house on Main Street, she was thinking about Race Logan as she waited for him to return from his tryst with Kate the Gate.

Every once in a while her naturally pouty mouth would become even more so, and her light eyebrows would draw together with displeasure and distaste when she allowed herself to think about that damn basket of apples and the grin on Race's face when he rescued that little strumpet from embarrassment and disgrace.

Well, Althea knew why, of course. Who could blame a man—especially one as virile as Race Logan—for wanting to spend a while with the town tart? Men were men, after all. But he'd been with Kate more than a while now. It was seven going on eight hours by Althea's calculations as she looked once more at the china clock on the mantel. When was that buggy going to come back?

As if the Lord himself had sought to provide her with an answer, she heard the brisk clip of hooves, then saw the vehicle as it turned onto Main Street. She caught a glimpse of long legs as the buggy passed the house on its way to the livery stable down the street.

"Well, now," she breathed against the windowpane, then rushed to the hall mirror to pat her blond sausage curls into place and give a little downward tug to the already low neckline of her best watered silk dress. She thought briefly about pinching her cheeks to raise a spot of color, but Althea doubted that was necessary, because her face felt hot and flushed already.

She slipped soundlessly out the front door, then rucked up her skirts, and hurried after the buggy and its driver.

It did nothing for Race's mood when he realized there was nobody at the livery stable at this hour of the night to tend to the horse and buggy. He couldn't just leave the sorry bay hitched all night after the animal had listened to him so patiently on the ride back into town. With a beleaguered sigh, he climbed out of the buggy, gave the horse a pat on his flank and began to unfasten the traces.

A fine way to spend his last night of freedom, he thought. The ride back to town had chilled his feet considerably. After virtually having promised Kate the sun, the moon and most of the stars, Race was beginning to weigh the consequences of his rash proposal, if indeed that's what it was.

He hadn't exactly asked her to marry him. Not in so many words. She was the one who kept mentioning marriage. But then he hadn't exactly said no, either. It struck him now as sadly ironic that, on Independence Day, he had practically tossed his own away. And for what? A barefoot girl with big green eyes and a basket of apples.

Hell, the apples weren't even ripe, he fumed as he yanked on the shaft tug. Then his mouth quirked sideways into a grin as he thought of the firm weight of Kate's breasts and how they filled his hands so plentifully and how they tasted sweeter and more ripe than any apple ever could.

He held still a moment, just staring at the horse's red-brown back. Kate Logan! He liked the sound of it. Kathryn and Horace. No. Kate and Race. Dear Lord, what was he doing? He was not, he told himself again, the marrying kind.

He tossed the harness at a nail on the wall, then led the bay into a stall. As he was taking the bridle from him, it dawned on Race that he hadn't bothered to give the poor old nag an apple, so he retrieved the one that was still on the buggy seat, along with the half-empty crock of cider.

"Here you go, fella," he said. The bay took the offered fruit greedily. Race tipped the jug for a long swig of the potent homemade liquor.

"Oh, Race," a sultry voice breathed just behind him.

He swallowed, lowered the jug, and turned slowly. And just as slowly his gaze dipped to a flushed, upturned face. "Miss Althea," he murmured in a tone nearly as sultry as her own. There was a sudden quickening in him, a little flicker of pleasure and warmth and desire. And then it was gone. Gone as surely as if a bucket of cold water had just drenched him. The feeling, or rather its sudden absence, rocked him. My God, he thought, is that what it meant to love just one woman? Would he forever find everyone dull and uninspiring compared to his Kate? Was he truly as doomed as he felt?

Althea took his bewildered, hooded gaze for passion. She slipped her arms around his waist and moved against him. "Oh, Race," she breathed again. "I've been waiting so long."

He began a hesitant retreat, but his heel hit the door of the stall. The bay whinnied behind him. He was trapped, and his eyes lifted heavenward for assistance. He'd never said no to a female before. In the realm of denial, Race Logan was a virgin. Pure as a newborn babe. Placing a hesitant hand on the blonde's bare shoulder, he said, "Now, now, Miss Althea. Don't go getting all worked up."

She tightened her embrace and moved closer to him, though Race didn't think that was possible. She was already practically climbing over him. A cold sweat prickled between his shoulder blades as she whispered something about getting him worked up, and one of her hands traveled from his back to his hip to the lacing on his trousers.

He dropped the jug of cider and clamped her firmly around the waist, setting her away from him. "You're in an awful big hurry, aren't you, Miss Althea?"

Pale lashes fluttered over blue eyes. "Well, I..." She floundered for a brief moment, her hands fidgeting with the watered silk of her skirt, her pouty pink mouth drawing into itself. Then, as if finding her stride once more, she gave a little yank to her bodice then planted her hands on her hips. "Well, I guess a lady is hardly a match for Kate the Gate."

You're no lady, honey, he wanted to say, but he bit his tongue. Her sickly brother had done him a favor this morning by opening the mercantile especially for him, and then had given him a handsome discount to boot. Insulting Althea wasn't exactly the way to thank Ned. You never knew how protective brothers were with sisters, Race thought. But then, if Ned Cassidy was at all concerned about his baby sister's reputation, he was probably a very busy man. There had to be a way to get this female off his back—in a manner of speaking—and, at the same time, return the brother's kindness.

She was looking up at him now with those big baby blue eyes and that puckered little mouth, just waiting. Anticipating Lord only knows what. And suddenly Race knew what to do.

He took her dimpled chin between his thumb and forefinger to hold her poised for a fairly convincing kiss—a kiss during which her tongue darted out to sample his, then retreated teasingly. He left her mouth and pressed his lips to her ear.

"Where do you live, Miss Althea?"

"Why?" she asked with a little moan as his tongue briefly touched the shell of her ear.

"Do you have a big, warm bed?"

She tipped her head back. There was shock in her expression, then curiosity, and then outright glee. "Just down the street," she said, eyes glittering with the promise of desire and the prospect of deceit. "We'll have to climb in through a window, though. My mama and papa are very strict. And they're light sleepers. My brother, too."

Race bent to pick up the jug, relieved to see the hay-strewn floor had prevented it from shattering. He held out his hand to Althea then. She grabbed it and led him briskly out of the stable and down the dark, quiet street.

A little breeze played with the red, white and blue bunting on the front of the bank—the Cassidy bank—

as they passed, reminding Race of the holiday. He wondered vaguely if the fancy house had reopened, then wondered why he wondered since he was pretty sure he'd never see the inside of that or any other fancy house again.

He was marveling that a single day could change his life so completely, and cursing his bad luck, when Althea brought him up short on the sidewalk.

"This is it," she said, her voice tinged with excitement.

Race looked at the big, dark house. He nodded.

"You'll have to help me up the trellis," she said breathlessly. "I left my window open. Come on. Let's hurry."

He swept her up into his arms and locked his gaze on her wide blue eyes. "Miss Althea," he drawled, "didn't anybody ever tell you that hasty little girls can get in very big trouble?" Saying that, Race strode toward the front door.

"What are you doing?" she cried as he took the porch steps two at a time. "Are you insane?"

"No, ma'am," he said, and raised his fist to knock on the heavy oak door.

"Stop it! You'll wake up everybody in the house."

"Think so?" He pounded again, harder this time.

Althea wriggled in his tight grasp. She pushed against his shoulders, butted against his belt line and slammed her fist into his chest, all to no avail. Finally she crossed her arms vehemently over her bosom. "You'll be sorry for this, you son of a bitch," she snarled. "Put me down."

"Now, now, Miss Althea," he purred. "Ladies don't swear."

"What would you know about ladies? All you know about are tramps like Kate the—" She sucked in her breath as he began to let her drop, forcing her to grab hold of his neck with both arms to keep from crashing to the porch boards.

The front door jerked open just as Race was about to pound on it again. He was met by an ice blue pair of eyes in a beefy, red face. Father Cassidy, Race presumed, looking as if he were about to spit out a mouthful of nails. Standing just behind the big man was the sickly Ned, looking baffled rather than angry beneath a shock of wheat-colored hair that strayed across his forehead. His eyes were still half-closed with sleep and he seemed to be having trouble catching his breath.

Neither one of the men seemed particularly surprised to see Althea at this hour or in such a predicament. Race was quick to conclude that she had been running them both a ragged chase for quite a while.

Suddenly he felt bone tired. His head was beginning to throb from all the cider he had consumed. Althea Cassidy was beginning to feel burdensome in his arms. Nobody seemed happy to see her, the wayward daughter-sister, returned without so much as a scratch. The father was sputtering and Ned, it appeared, was trying to speak, but he couldn't get enough breath to form words. Althea took advantage of the moment of confusion to launch a sharp elbow into Race's sternum.

That did it. He thrust her into her father's arms. "Your cat got out," he said, then turned on his heel and stalked away.

Her father nearly threw her to the floor. "That does it, young woman. I've had all I can take of this. You're going to marry Colonel Sikes whether you like it or not. I'll inform him first thing in the morning. Let him worry about you from now on."

Althea wrenched herself from her father's grasp, then pushed Ned out of her way as she stormed to the edge of the porch. "I'll get you for this, Race Logan," she screamed at his departing back. "That's a promise, mister. You're going to remember this day and what you did to me. Do you hear me?"

He did. Her voice was shrill and sharp in the dark night. She sounded like a gypsy hag aiming a curse at his soul. Good luck, Colonel Sikes, you poor devil, he thought.

He headed for the wagons, which were camped at the edge of town and, once there, he crooked his legs, settled to the ground and leaned back against a wheel. What a night! What a day! Race tipped the jug he'd managed to hold on to through the whole altercation with Althea. He took a long pull. And then another. He wondered bleakly how his life might have been different if he'd come here on the third of July instead of the fourth. He wondered what would have happened if the fancy house had been open for business. He drank a great deal of cider, speculating foggily about apples.

* * *

The lantern cast a wavering light across the littered backyard where Kate, wet, soapy hands pressed to the small of her back, straightened up from the washboard. It was useless, she thought, like trying to wash the red out of a sunset. Those telltale bloodstains on the sheets were permanent. Grimly now, she reminded herself of her rash decision to be a devil rather than an angel, to be hanged for a wolf rather than a sheep.

"Your sheep days are over, girl," she muttered as she lifted the soggy sheet from the washtub and proceeded to wring it out with a vengeance. She carried the damp bundle to the privy then and stuffed it down the hole. The door creaked on its loose hinges as she closed it behind her, and suddenly a chilly breeze blew up, sending leaves and scraps of paper skittering across the yard. A long, pendent branch of willow swept over the bare flesh of Kate's arm and across her back. The touch made her turn.

"Race?" she called out. There was a tremor in her voice as her eyes scanned the backyard. No one was there. There was nothing but weeds and broken crates, overturned crocks, and her daddy's confounded still.

Back in her room, Kate snapped a new sheet over her mattress and tucked in the corners with military precision. She stood back—arms crossed, head tilted, a satisfied expression on her face—then promptly burst into tears.

"Come with me, Kate. Now. Tonight." Race Logan's warm, whiskey-deep voice echoed in her brain the way his touch still lingered on her skin. Hard as she

tried, she couldn't comprehend what had taken place today, could barely understand what she had lost and what she had found.

Most certainly she had lost her virginity. But, even before that, she had lost her heart. To Kate's way of thinking that was the more significant loss. The fragile tissues of her womanhood had torn with a pain that had lasted only a moment or two, but her heart was still as susceptible to Race Logan as that frail barrier had been, and any damage done to that would last a long, long time.

She flopped down onto the bed now, burying her face in the pillow, breathing in musk and buckskin and cider. A strange, beguiling combination. A stranger's scent. She didn't know the first thing about Race Logan.

She didn't know the first thing about falling in love, either, yet apparently that's what she'd gone and done. Her brother, Charley, saw a girl at the Baptist church picnic once, and though he hadn't even had the nerve to strike up a conversation with her, he had come home swearing she was the girl he was going to marry. He would have, too, if Charley had survived the war. How had he known, Kate had wondered, after just that first glance?

But somehow she had known, as well, that first moment when she had gazed into Race's eyes, when she had dived headlong into their lake-colored depths. There had been a sense of recognition, as if her heart had whispered, "There you are." He had seemed to sense it, too. Or maybe not. Maybe he was warm and gentle with every woman. Maybe he made every woman feel the way Kate felt now—as if she belonged to him for all time.

Maybe, she thought as her heart began to skitter with panic, she should have gone with him earlier, the way he'd wanted her to do. He had said, his turquoise eyes blazing, he'd be damned if he'd leave her in this dump a moment longer. *"Come with me, Katie. Now."*

She had wavered once more. *"But my daddy—"*

"—doesn't give a tinker's damn about you. Can't you see that?" Race had kissed her again then, a kiss that said hello and goodbye in the same searing moment. *"You settle up with that miserable excuse for a parent. You tell him there's somebody now who wants to take care of you the way you deserve. Somebody to see that you have shoes. I'll be back for you tomorrow, Kate. I'm not leaving you here."*

Calmer now, Kate sat up and wiped her eyes. Perhaps, she thought, leaving was the best thing she could do. Perhaps if she wasn't always around to remind him of his Caroline, her father would stop drowning his sorrows in cider. Maybe, with her mother's ghost gone, he would eventually pull himself together. Maybe.

Maybe she was just singing a pretty song to make herself feel better about leaving. Because that's what she was going to do. Right or wrong. Barefoot or in shoes. Devil or angel or both. She was going to go with Race Logan—south, west, anywhere. It was, after all, the Fourth of July. High time she declared her own independence.

And on the morning of the fifth of July, Kate sat demurely in a straight-backed chair, her legs crossed at the ankles, her hands clasped in her lap. She was wearing her blue calico, having folded her white muslin dress and her spare set of underwear, and tied them in a checkered tablecloth along with her only prize possession, a leather-bound copy of *Great Expectations.* Her father wouldn't miss it. Nor, she acknowledged at last, would he miss her. He might, she thought sadly, even be glad she was gone.

Once again, she cautioned herself not to run like some excited little child when Race arrived. He was thirty-two years old, after all. He would expect her to conduct herself like a grown woman. She would walk to greet him. She would. Well, she'd try, anyway.

Kate sat. And she sat. The morning shadows in the front yard disappeared as the sun climbed up to noon. Afternoon shadows began to slant, longer and longer. Her small sighs of impatience turned to stony silence. The corners of her mouth no longer twitched into unbidden grins, but pulled down with worry and dismay. Her eyes, little by little, lost their excited light. He wasn't coming.

And then she heard hoofbeats thundering down the road and the light sprang back into her eyes, along with the color to her cheeks. Her mouth widened in a glowing smile. She couldn't have stayed in the chair one second longer. Her feet fairly flew to the door. "Race!" she cried happily.

But it wasn't. It took her a long, heart-withering moment to comprehend that it was Hank Stringfellow, not Race Logan, who was riding so hard toward the house and calling her name.

He hauled his mare to a stop at the porch, pushed his hat back from his damp red hair, and wiped a plaid sleeve across his sweat-streaked face. "Doc Stanza sent me for you, Kate. Your papa's had a terrible accident. It don't look so good and the doc says you best get to town right quick."

The color flowed from her face.

Hank held out his hand. "Here. Put your foot in that stirrup, Kate, and swing a leg around behind me. Come on."

Her gaze was guarded, like a wounded animal.

"I ain't gonna hassle you, Kate, if that's what you're thinking. Not today. Now come on. The doc said hurry."

"Yes. All right."

"Hang on," Hank Stringfellow said when she plopped onto the saddle behind him. He dug his boot heels into the mare, turning her back toward town.

Kate hung on, her arms linked around his ribs, her cheek pressed against the back of his wet shirt. Wet with the sweat of his ride. Wetter now with her tears.

But, by the time they reached town, Kate wasn't crying anymore. Her face was grim and gaunt, and her eyes were dry and dull as she walked up the outside stairs to Doc Stanza's office.

The white-haired doctor looked up from the chair in which he had been slowly rocking. He shook his head. "I'm sorry, Kate," he said. "Damn fool fell off his horse and broke his neck. There wasn't much I could do. He expired about an hour ago."

She opened her mouth to speak. There were no words.

Doc Stanza stood up, pulled down his rolled-up sleeves and began to button his vest. "I had them take him over to Wister, that new undertaker. I said you'd be by to make arrangements."

"All right," she said, turning toward the door.

"You'll be fine, girl," the elderly doctor said. "You'll see. You're better off without him, Kate." He clucked his tongue. "Damn fool's been trying to follow after your mama for years. He finally went and did it right."

"I'll be fine, Doc," she echoed tonelessly. "I'll see you get paid, but it might take a while."

"Don't you worry about that now. You give me what you can when you can."

Kate started down the stairs outside, but her knees buckled and she sat, hard, on a step. Just sat. Staring. The sun was dipping behind the cottonwoods at the edge of town, and the locusts were beginning to greet the end of day with their husky chants. No matter what Doc Stanza said, she wasn't better off without her father. She was just alone.

Kate could see the dusty place where the wagons had pulled up for the hundreds of crates they were hauling to New Mexico. They were gone. Race Logan was gone.

No. Don't even think abut him now, she told herself. Don't let him cross your mind. At best, he was a dream, and dreams didn't come true for the likes of her. At worst, he was a cad and a liar. She probably should be grateful he had left her here rather than abandon her somewhere down the road. She ought to get down on her knees right now and thank her lucky stars. Only she didn't have any lucky stars. None at all. Not even a damn little twinkle.

Somebody was slamming a board against the side of his head. Over and over. Race opened his eyes. Sudden light shot him through with pain, sat him up and slammed him down again. A rough curse tore through his clenched teeth.

The board that had been beating him was the side of a wagon, he realized, as his head thudded against it once more. A moving wagon. He wrenched himself up, held his head in his hands a minute, trying to remember who had slugged him. It must have been a hell of a brawl, he thought. All his ribs felt broken. His stomach felt as if he'd been poisoned, as if he'd eaten a bushel of green apples, as if...

Oh, damn! Apples! Kate!

"Isaac," he bellowed through the rear opening of the canvas cover. "Isaac."

He heard muted laughter then and the wagon came to a stop. A dark face appeared, framed by the canvas arch. The dark face split with a big, white grin.

"Well, lookee who's not dead," Isaac Goodman said as he climbed inside the wagon.

"What happened?" Race lowered his head to his hands again, his fingers pressing to keep it from exploding like a grenade.

"You been sicker than any dog I ever did see. What was in that jug you had? Kerosene?"

"Cider," Race groaned. "Where are my clothes?"

"Oh, you don't never want to see those clothes again after what you done spewed on them." The big black man had been bent at the waist beneath the canvas arch. He squatted now, dandling his hat between his knees. "I'll get you something to put on if you're sure you're all done with that spewing. I don't relish being a wash lady, you know."

"Yeah, I know," Race said guiltily. He lifted his gaze to his old friend. "Thanks, Isaac." He shook his head mournfully. "I guess I really tied one on last night."

"Last night! Ooo-eee. You been out about thirty-six hours. We're almost to the Arkansas River. Lead wagon ought to be getting there now. I been keeping back real slow so you didn't get tossed around any more'n necessary."

Race's head snapped up. "Kate!"

A slow smile spread over Isaac's face. "There you go again. Who's this Kate anyhow? She must have been some sweet treat the way you been going on about her."

Sweet as an apple, Race thought. And bruised now. Badly bruised. What had she thought yesterday when he didn't come? He didn't even want to think about it, didn't want to picture what disappointment did to that pretty face or what anger could stir up in her green eyes. "Get me some clothes, will you? I've got to get back there."

Isaac sighed and stood as much as the canvas would permit. "I'll get you the clothes, but you aren't going anywhere tonight. Sun's about gone. Besides, you're still looking a little on the puny side to me. You best—"

"Just get the goddamned clothes, will you?" Race said, cutting him off.

"Well, now, Horace, you try asking me nice and maybe I will," the older man purred. "Or maybe I'll just let you drag your sorry ass back to Leavenworth without a stitch."

"Please," Race ground out. "Please get my goddamned clothes."

Isaac grinned as he backed out of the wagon.

It occurred to Race then that he'd escaped his closest brush yet with matrimony. He told himself he should be breathing a deep sigh of relief right about now and thanking the Almighty on bent knees. Only he wasn't. He kept picturing pretty Kate in that pitiful shack, waiting for him.

All right, Race thought, she'd be bruised. She'd be madder than hell. But he'd make it all up to her. With kisses and tears if necessary and a dozen pairs of shoes. And he'd never—not if he lived to be a hundred and five—let a drop of cider pass his lips again. And maybe by the time their grandchildren were grown, he'd have the nerve to taste another apple.

Chapter Five

When Kate walked out of the undertaker's establishment, her eyes stinging with unshed tears, Ned Cassidy was down on all fours on the sidewalk, breathing in great gasps of air like a man who had just washed up out of a storm-tossed sea. She rushed to see what was wrong.

"I...I'll be fine in just a minute, Miss Kate," he managed to say between breaths.

"Do you want me to fetch Doc Stanza?" she asked as she knelt beside him, her hand smoothing his back as he strained to breathe.

Ned shook his head. "No. Thank...thank you though for offering. I'll be all right. It's just one of those...those spells I have. It'll pass."

Kate stayed beside him until it did. Thin, pale Ned Cassidy had always been kind to her when she traded at his family's store. He had extended credit to her more than once. More often than not, he sold her items for less than they had cost the mercantile. She helped him to his feet now and stood by while he brushed off the knees of his checked wool pants and tightened his cravat.

"You're sure you're all right now?" she asked. "I can walk you over to the mercantile if you need me to. Not that you can't make it under your own steam, of course, but I'm going that way anyway and I..."

He brushed a hank of hair from his high forehead. His face was round and soft, with eyes as pale as a robin's egg. His lips were thin, but he smiled at her with a warmth that made his face almost handsome. "It's supper time," he said. "I just closed up. Was there something you needed from the store, Miss Kate?"

Her fingers played nervously with the collar of her blue calico dress. "Yes. No. Well, I..." She was already knee-deep in debt to the Cassidys, and she figured she might as well wade in up to the hips, if he'd let her. Knees or hips, it was going to take her forever to pay him off. "My daddy passed away this morning, Mr. Cassidy. I'd like to bury him in a clean, new shirt, but I haven't any money."

Ned put his hand on her shoulder. "I'm sorry. I hadn't heard. You have my deepest condolences, Miss Kate."

He said it as if he truly meant it, she thought. Then he pulled a long key chain from his vest pocket and twirled it once before drawing her hand through his arm.

"You come along with me. I have a white linen shirt that's probably just your father's size. And whatever else you'd like."

Kate lifted her chin. Her eyes met his. "I can't pay you. Not today anyway. And my debt is already a considerable one."

He patted her hand. "We'll work something out," he said. "Come along."

Ned stepped forward, but Kate didn't budge. "If 'work something out' means you believe you can have your way with me, Ned Cassidy, you can put that out of your head right now. I expect to pay you," she said firmly. "And with cash. Is that understood?"

He looked almost stricken, as if she had slapped his face. "I do understand," he said quietly, then began to step forward again. This time Kate went with him.

They had to stop twice for Ned to catch his breath. "This is such an imposition," Kate said as she patted his back once more. "I can come back tomorrow."

"Nonsense," he wheezed.

When they reached the door of the mercantile, Ned extended the key chain from his pocket, unlocked the door and held it open as Kate stepped inside. It was cool and dim, and the smell, as always, nearly overpowered her. New leather. Fresh, folded bolts of fabric. Toilet waters. Flowery talcs. The sweet-smelling ink of newspapers and books. Peppermints and licorice. Patent medicines. The elegant smell of new shoes. If heaven had a fragrance, she thought, it must be this ethereal blend.

"It always smells so good in here," she said, and sighed. "It truly lifts my spirits."

Ned was searching through a drawer behind the high glass-and-walnut counter. "That's kind of you to say,

Miss Kate. You should come in more often then. Just to sniff. You wouldn't have to make a purchase.'' He raised his head to offer her a small smile. ''Air's free. Even in Cassidy's.''

Kate smiled back.

''What will you do now?'' Ned asked her as he stood wrapping the shirt in brown paper and tying it with twine.

''I haven't had time to think about it,'' she replied, watching his long, pale fingers crease the paper and twist the string. ''I should have been more prepared for this eventuality, I suppose.'' Kate bit her lower lip as it began to tremble. ''I'll have to find work. A livelihood of some sort. And somewhere to live. Do you know of anyone who needs a girl for housework?''

His hands stilled over the package. ''I need someone, Miss Kate.''

Her eyes flew to his. Ned Cassidy blinked then and stuttered as he tied several more knots in the twine. ''What I mean is, I—I could use some help here in the store now that my sister is getting married.''

''I didn't realize Althea was engaged,'' Kate said, trying to sound pleasant as she recalled how Ned's sister had stuck her prim little nose in the air yesterday when Kate had said hello, and how Althea had gushed to the other girls about Race Logan.

Race! Oh, God. A gaping hole seemed to be opening in her heart and a lump brewing in her throat. Kate swallowed hard, trying to banish him from her thoughts.

''What kind of help?'' she asked Ned, hoping to change the subject back to possible employment.

Anything not to think of him, of Race, of how he hadn't come back.

"Somebody to dust. Keep the place clean and neat. Maybe even help out with the customers when it's busy."

"I could do that," Kate said.

His face shone like a newly minted coin. "Oh, I know you could. I think you'd be quite good at it. Otherwise I wouldn't have made the offer." Ned ran a finger under his collar now as if it were suddenly too tight. "Would you . . . would you consider it?"

Kate looked around. She took in a deep breath, filling her senses again with a whiff of heaven. After what'd she'd done with Race Logan, she thought, this might be as close to heaven as she'd ever get. She turned back to Ned Cassidy, her hands on her hips and her chin lifted into his face. "I'll do more than consider it, Mr. Cassidy. I accept your offer. When do you want me to begin?"

"Tomorrow?"

She chewed on a fingernail. "I'll need to find a place to live," she said, almost thinking out loud.

"There's a room you could have in back," he murmured.

"What?" She noticed the pink flush on his cheeks, wondering if he were coming down with a fever.

He cleared his throat. "I said there's a room in back with a chair and a bed. I . . . uh . . . I go in there sometimes when I'm having one of my spells. I don't see any reason why you couldn't use that. Temporarily, anyway. Until you find something more to your liking. It isn't fancy or anything, but . . ."

"I don't know what fancy is, Mr. Cassidy. If you're offering me a place to stay, I'll take it."

"Well, then—" he sighed as he pushed the package across the counter "—tomorrow, Miss Kate."

"Thank you," she said. "Yes, indeed, Mr. Cassidy. Tomorrow."

Grudgingly Race had taken Isaac's advice and remained with the wagons while they camped overnight on the bank of the Arkansas River. After a swim in the river and a plate of bacon and fried potatoes, he felt like a new man. A man with a brand-new future.

Long after his men had left their card games and whittling and quiet campfire talk to settle in their bedrolls, Race and Isaac pitched a few extra logs on the fire and sat staring into it. The big black man handed Race one of his cigars.

Race bit off the tip, then picked a fleck of tobacco from his lip. "You got enough of these to last you the whole trip, Isaac?"

"Plenty," Isaac said, touching the end of his cigar with a burning stick then passing it to Race, who lit his then tossed the stick back into the fire.

"You won't have any trouble. Nothing you can't handle anyway." Race angled his head in the direction of the sleeping drivers and outriders. "This is a good crew. You won't have to ride them too hard."

Isaac shrugged and blew out a thin stream of smoke. "Won't be the first time I've made this trip alone. Used to do it when your pa was alive. And who do you think made that round-trip after the Kiowas turned your backside into a pincushion?"

Race sighed. "That was a long time ago. What? Ten years?"

"Something like that," Isaac grunted. "Why don't you spit it out, Horace?"

"What?"

"Whatever it is that's splicing your guts and making slipknots with them."

Race watched the smoke from his cigar rise and disappear against the black canopy of sky. He never could hide much from this man. At the same time, there were things about Isaac Goodman he felt he would never know, dark things buried deep. "You ever been married, Isaac?" he asked him now.

"Once."

He could have said "tell me about it," but Race knew it wasn't necessary. If Isaac wanted to talk, he would, without prompting. If not, he'd be still as a jet-black stone.

"Her name was Girl," Isaac said quietly. "Her mama had so many babies that by the time she whelped her last one she'd just plumb run out of names. Patience and love, too, I expect. Girl was a wild one. On her own from the start. When she came to Starling Plantation, when Master Starling bought her, she was skinny as a stick of licorice. Lord, but she was pretty." Isaac smiled. "Only a child still. I had to wait a few years for her."

Race raised an eyebrow. "You knew right away?"

Isaac's smile deepened. "I knew all right. Girl did, too, even though she was too sassy to admit it." His lips tightened then. "We didn't marry exactly. Master Starling was partial to Girl himself and he wouldn't allow it. But we made promises, to each other, to the Almighty. It didn't last long, but what we had was good." His dark eyes settled on Race. "You pondering marriage, Horace?"

"Maybe."

Isaac nodded solemnly.

"Maybe not," Race added brusquely. "I don't know."

"It'll change things. Didn't for me. Things don't change when you're a slave. But you. Well, you'll have to stay put. You given that much thought, have you?" Isaac grinned. "You given much thought to all the female hearts that are gonna crack right down the middle when they hear that Horace Logan's taken himself a bride?"

Race drew on the cigar. "She probably won't have me. Not now. Not after I stood her up."

"She love you?"

"Hell, how do I know?"

Isaac leaned back on his elbows, his boots toward the fire. "You love her? Enough to change your life? To settle down?"

A few days ago the mere notion would have struck terror in Race's heart. Now the idea of staying put had a certain appeal. Kissing Kate good-night. Sleeping with her golden head tucked into his shoulder. Making slow midnight love. Waking with her. Seeing she had shoes. Without realizing it, he was nodding his head.

Isaac nodded, too, and pitched the stub of his cigar into the fire with finality, as if some kind of unspoken agreement had been reached. "What time you planning on taking off in the morning?"

Race hooked a thumb toward the river. It had flooded earlier in the spring, making both banks steep now and a treacherous tangle of debris. "I'll stick around until we get the wagons across." He saw the black man give him one of those looks that said "Still think you have to do everything yourself to get it done right, don't you, Horace?"

"I don't suppose a couple hours will make a whole hell of a lot of difference at this point, Isaac," he murmured, though his lips twitched into a grin at the man who knew him so well.

The former slave shook his head slowly and sucked his teeth. "You never know, Horace. That's one thing I've learned. You just never know." He stood up and walked to his bedroll, leaving Race alone by the fire.

Damned if that wasn't the gospel truth, Race thought. One minute he'd been a free and happy man, looking for nothing more than a quick roll in the hay. Then he laid eyes on a little barefoot strawberry blonde, and everything seemed to change. He wasn't free anymore. And he wasn't happy, either—not without her.

But he did know one thing, he thought. Even though marriage was still a notion that stuck in his craw, he was going back to get her. As soon as he saw his wagons safely through the crossing, he was going to be on his way back to Kate. He'd stop in town just long enough to buy a pair of soft black kidskin shoes with smooth soles and long black laces. He'd ride out to her shanty then and put them on her and do up the laces himself. And then he'd unlace them...slowly....

Water poured from the brim of Race's hat as he yelled to make himself heard over a cannonade of thunder. After weeks of blue skies and relentless sun, the clouds had rolled in that morning, dark as November, and the heavens had opened without mercy and without a sign of letting up.

They had gotten fourteen wagons across in spite of the steep, rough slope and the additional hindrance of the downpour. But then, as Race was leading the last team of oxen toward the river, the lightning began in earnest and the earth itself seemed to shake with the thunder. Somebody had once told him that Arabs lit fires under the behinds of recalcitrant camels to get them going. He was sorely tempted when the four animals stomped and bellowed but refused to move an inch forward. Lucky for them it was too wet to even strike a match.

The driver, young Oliver, was hunkered down in the high seat as if making himself as small a target as possible for the lightning. Race couldn't tell if it was rain or sweat pouring off the boy's face.

"You hang on tight to those reins, now, Oliver," he shouted to him before calling over his shoulder. "Isaac, I need you over here."

When the lightning slackened, he knew they had to move fast. Isaac, black as night in his big rubber poncho, was quick to respond to his shout.

"The lightning's stopped for now," Race yelled. "Let's get them moving."

"You go on," Isaac said, squinting against the lashing rain. "You already lost all day this side of noon."

"Isaac, I've got the rest of my life to be married, but I've only got about a minute or two before the damn lightning starts again." He pulled hard on the yoke of the lead team and they took a tentative step forward. Race gave the black man a grin. "See! Now are you going to help me or are you just going to stand there like a big black mule?"

It was slow going down the bank. The four oxen, made skittish by the storm, balked again and again. Together, Race and Isaac managed to shove and pull and bully the huge buff-colored beasts, until the lead team was standing in the river with the heavy wagon still sharply angled on the steep bank.

Then the sky split with a jagged bolt of fire. Another one arced to the ground close by. The panicked animals lunged to the left and the wagon began to cant precariously to the right. Oliver, the driver, slid the length of the wet seat and landed hard on the ground. He lay there motionless.

Race, seeing the dangerous slant of the wagon and the body lying beneath it, let go of the yoke and hauled himself back up the bank to pull the fallen driver to safety. But Oliver's wet slicker was slippery and Race couldn't get a good grip on him. He had to move in right beside him, slide his arms around the boy's chest, and . . .

The lightning bolt and the piercing thunderclap were instantaneous. The oxen lunged again, and there was a sickening snap as one of the wheels cracked beneath the heavy, shifting load. The wagon came down with a slow, agonizing groan on Race, who instead of rolling out of the way, had rolled, at the last second, over Oliver's limp body to protect it.

While the storm raged on, it took close to an hour to bring a team of oxen back to hitch up to the four who had remained behind in panic. Half a dozen men swam back across the river to unload the tonnage from the toppled wagon, rig it with ropes, and finally—with eight oxen straining on the slope of the riverbank—lift it enough to allow Isaac to pull Race out.

"It's about time," Race said through clenched teeth. His pain-shrouded eyes sought his friend's. "You're a sight for sore eyes, Isaac. Help me up, will you?"

"You just lie still," Isaac said quietly, pressing a hand on his shoulder. "I'm going to get some of the men to help rig up something to keep the rain off you till we can get the wagon righted and get you in it." He started to rise, but Race caught a handful of his wet poncho.

"I don't want to get in the wagon, Isaac. I want to get up. Now help me, will you?"

The older man grimaced. "I would, Horace, but I don't think you'd stay up more'n a second or two. Your leg's busted."

"What?" Race shifted around and looked down at the leg he didn't even feel. His pants were soaked with blood where his thigh bone had poked through. The sight made his stomach turn over. He was cold suddenly and his teeth wouldn't stop chattering no matter how hard he gritted them. His head dropped wanly back to the wet ground.

The next thing he knew, he was choking and Isaac's face was floating above him in lantern light like a dark, scowling angel.

"Here," the big man said, pouring something foul down his throat. "Swallow it this time. Don't go spitting it out. It's laudanum. I'm gonna set your leg in a little while and I'd appreciate it kindly if you wouldn't scream, Horace."

Race swallowed the tincture and grimaced, as much from the taste of it as the pain in his leg. "How's Oliver?" he asked in a voice that sounded sandy.

"Dead. Probably the minute he hit the ground," Isaac replied.

Race closed his eyes. "We've got to get word to his family. They're in Albuquerque. He's got a mother and three sisters. They—"

"Four sisters," Isaac corrected him. "I'll see they get word." He leaned closer, inspecting Race's eyes. "You feeling the least bit woozy yet, Horace? I'd like to get on with this so's I can eat my supper."

Race laughed, which brought tears to his eyes the pain was so great. "Listen to me, you old codger. I want to get a message back to Kate. You send one of the boys to tell her I'm coming back to marry her just as soon as I can. Will you do that?"

"'Course, I'll do it. Maybe you best tell me your lady's last name. Bound to be more'n one Kate in a town that size."

He didn't know. If he ever knew, Race thought, he'd clean forgotten it. Aw, shit!

"Horace?"

Race rolled his head, as much in pain as disgust. "Tell him…tell him to ask for Kate…Kate the Gate."

Isaac's face swam in his vision then and his voice seemed to come from far away. "Consider it done, Horace. You hold on tight now 'cause this ain't gonna be fun for either one of us."

He held on tight, clamping his teeth on whatever it was that Isaac put between them. He held on tight until he just couldn't hold on anymore.

A week after the death of her father, Kate was convinced of two things. Race Logan wasn't coming back and Ned Cassidy had had no ulterior motives when he'd offered her the job and the room, nor when he had insisted she use two fresh bolts of poplin for her new dresses, nor now, when he was slipping another pair of shoes on her feet.

"They're too expensive," she said as she looked at the soft black leather that covered her foot.

"They're perfect," Ned said. "The others were too big. Walk around, Miss Kate. See if they pinch you anywhere." He rocked back on his heels to allow her room. His face shone brightly as he watched her walk from the fitting chair to the counter and back. "Well?" he asked.

"Well, they feel fine, but they're much too expensive," Kate protested.

"Nonsense. Consider them an employee benefit." He stood up and beamed down at her.

Kate frowned in return. She should feel so happy, she thought, but she only felt glum. The shoes made her think of Race, of his promises and all his pretty talk. They reminded her that not only had her feet been bare, but so had she—body and heart and soul.

"You don't like them," Ned said now, an almost childlike note of disappointment in his voice. "Well, sit. We'll find another pair."

"I do like them," she insisted. "It's just that..."

The bell on the front door tinkled then and Althea came in, or rather wafted in, on a cloud of orange blossom toilet water and in yards of pink dimity.

"Ned, I have to have some of that Belgian lace for my trousseau. Seven or eight yards ought to do, I should imagine." The blonde leaned against the counter, tapping her nails on the glass top. She skewered Kate with her pale eyes as she said, "Unless you're too busy flirting with the help."

Ned's face flushed. He had just gotten down on his knees again, preparing to remove the shoes, when his sister came in. Now he jerked upright and appeared to struggle for breath.

"Oh, dear," Althea said, rolling her eyes. "Another spell. Well, I'll just hunt through some of these drawers and find the lace myself." She batted the hoop of her skirt around the counter and began opening drawers.

Kate touched Ned's sleeve. "Are you all right?" He looked panicky, as if he wanted to breathe but didn't quite know how to go about it. Like a fish out of water. "Would you like to go in back and lie down for a minute?"

He nodded frantically.

Kate took his arm and led him through the curtain into the back where she helped him down onto the narrow cot, but as she turned to leave he caught her hand.

"Stay. Please," he gasped.

"But the customers..."

"My... my sister's there. Please."

"Well, all right." Kate sat beside him, smoothing her skirt over her knees with her free hand, feeling helpless because she didn't know how to aid or comfort him, or how to return all his kindness, or how to tell him politely he oughtn't hold her hand.

Out in the front of the store, the bell tinkled on the door. Althea straightened up and turned, a ready smile on her lips, but when she saw that it was a young man in dusty denims and a stained hat, her smile flattened out into a businesslike pose.

"Yes? May I help you?" Her tone was crisp to the point of rudeness.

The young man swept his hat from his head when he saw her. "Yes, ma'am. I've been asking around town and I was told I could find a certain Miss Kate here."

"She's busy," Althea snapped. "What do you want with her?" As if she didn't know. With Kate working in the mercantile now, boys were continually loitering outside the door. Like hounds after a bitch in heat.

"Well, I've brought a message for her," he said, sweeping the floor with his gaze. "From my boss. That'd be Mr. Race Logan."

Althea's face took on an entirely new expression. Sweeter. Softer. "Really," she purred as she came around the counter in a swoop of pink. She linked her arm through the young man's then and leaned against him. "You know, I'm just about to perish from the heat in here. Why don't we step out on the sidewalk. You can give me the message and I'll be only too happy to pass it on to our Miss Kate."

"Well, thank you, ma'am. That's right nice of you."

Kate was back, straightening shelves behind the counter when Althea returned. "Who was that?" she asked her with mild curiosity, for somehow Ned's sister seemed enormously pleased about something. Her normal expression was one of displeasure, but her prim pink lips were almost smiling now.

Althea sniffed. "Only some dirty cowboy looking for tobacco. I sent him on down to the feed and grain. How's my brother?" Her mouth resumed its perpetual pout.

"I believe his spell has passed. He's resting now."

"Well, I'll just let him do that." Althea gathered up eight yards of Belgian lace, stuffed it into her handbag and floated out the door without even a backward glance at Kate.

Chapter Six

After working for eight weeks in the mercantile, sleeping in the back room and spending every day but Sunday with Ned Cassidy, Kate began suffering "spells." She wondered if whatever he had was catching.

This particular morning was the worst yet. She thought she would have another twenty minutes or so to recuperate from the dizziness that had pitched her back onto the bed, but the bell tinkled softly out front informing her that Ned was early. Again. It seemed as if he shaved a minute or two off each day.

"Miss Kate," he called softly through the curtain. "I've brought your coffee."

Still hot and steaming, she was sure. He must have poured it in the kitchen of the big house, then loped halfway across town with the cup and saucer in his hands. There was no other way the brew could have stayed so hot. It gladdened her that he was able to cover the distance between the Cassidys' big house and the store in such a short time. Two months ago he wouldn't have been able to do that—with or without coffee. Along with the steaming brew, he always brought her a biscuit slathered with butter. Kate's stomach lurched now at the mere thought of food.

Ned stuck his head through the curtain. His light blue eyes rounded with concern. "You're not up. Are you ill, Miss Kate?"

Kate sat up, clutching the quilt around her, and offered him a weak smile. "I was just being lazy."

"And so you deserve to be," he said, coming into the little room and placing the cup and saucer on the crate that served as a table by her bed. He nudged his watch from his vest pocket. "It's barely eight o'clock. Why don't you be lazy until nine or so? I don't expect it to be busy this morning."

"No, I—"

"Who's the boss around here?" he asked with a mock gruffness that surprised Kate because she had never heard him use anything but gentle, diffident tones. "I order you to be a stay-abed, miss." Saying that, he put the coffee in one of her hands and the roll in the other.

Kate took one look at the dark liquid and the glob of butter on the roll, and her stomach turned over. She thrust the cup back into Ned's hands, dropped the roll, and lurched to the washbasin, where she emptied her stomach down to the tips of her toes.

"Not again!" she wailed, her head hanging over the bowl.

"Has this happened before, Miss Kate?"

She could feel Ned's hands, tenderly pulling her streaming hair back from her shoulders, gently smoothing over her upper arm. She nodded wanly.

"Every morning for the past week. I wonder if one of those patent medicines out front would help. I need to find something, anything, to make this go away."

His hand smoothed over her bent back, much the way she had comforted him during one of his attacks. "You need a husband," he murmured.

"What?" She straightened up and whirled around.

Ned touched his handkerchief to her wet lips. "I suspect you're with child, Miss Kate," he said softly.

No. That just wasn't possible, she thought. It had only been that one time. And her first time, too. It simply couldn't be. But then she allowed herself to remember the passionate heights to which she had soared and the overwhelming feeling of completion she had experienced when Race's hard body had shuddered with release. And with a dull ache deep inside her, Kate knew it was true. Oh, God! She was carrying Race Logan's baby.

She swayed slightly, and Ned steadied her then led her to the cot, where he sat beside her for a moment before slipping to his knees before her.

He gripped her hands. "I'm not a strong man, Miss Kate, though I must admit you make me feel that way often enough." Ned's self-deprecating chuckle diminished in a sigh. He drew in a deep breath then and continued with some urgency, as if he feared he'd lose his nerve, or his breath, or both. "Not strong, perhaps, but I'm steady. I would be very good to you. And to the child. I'd consider it my own."

Kate's wet green eyes lifted to his. Why weren't they turquoise? she wondered. Why wasn't his hair wild and dark? Why didn't his mouth slide into a devilish grin? Why didn't he smell like apples and buckskin and sweet summertime? Why...?

"I'd be honored if you would marry me, Miss Kate."

Why did she feel so cold, as if a winter wind were blowing through her soul?

"I'm asking you for the last time, Isaac," Race growled. "Will you please for God's sake get me a pair of crutches?"

"Nope."

"All right then." Race shoved up on an elbow. "I guess I'll just have to dismantle this bed then and use the rails to make them myself."

La Fonda del Sol, the inn where they always stayed in Santa Fe, was just off the plaza, and Isaac looked out the window now at the activity on the street below. He turned then, and crossed the room to place a black, bear-size hand on Race's shoulder, shoving him back onto the mattress.

"I'm about to lose my patience with you, Horace. You heard as well as I did what that sawbones said. You give that leg a good, long rest or else he'll be having to break it all over again and reset it."

Race grumbled a curse, glared at his splinted leg, then stared at the ceiling.

"You just try to think pleasant thoughts," Isaac counseled as he returned to his seat by the window. "Think about that little gal back in Kansas."

"I haven't thought about anything else for two whole months, old man," he snorted. "Why don't you go check the mail again?"

"Ain't none. Not a single wagon's come in today. I been watching. Besides, you ain't written her. How's she supposed to know where to send a letter?"

"She knows where I am. Anyway, I don't write letters."

"Well, maybe she don't, neither."

Race cursed again, then dragged the pillow out from under his head, punched it and shoved it back. He knew he was being just plain cussed, taking his frustrations out on Isaac, but he couldn't help it. Two months of being nearly hog-tied in this bed had made him crazy. The prospect of another two months made him a raving maniac.

If things had gone the way he'd planned, little Kate would be here now. Maybe they'd be married. Maybe he would have been able to convince her just being together was enough for the time being without taking that fatal step. But either way he'd be looking into her sweet green eyes now and not staring up at a stuccoed ceiling whose every blister and pore he now recognized as if it were his own skin. Hell, he should be looking at Kate's cream-colored flesh right now instead of a damn ceiling.

"Damnation."

"If swearing helps, Horace, then you just go on and scorch my ears. It don't bother me none. I'm glad to help by listening."

Race swore again, this time with a little less vigor. Then he sighed. "Since you're so damn smart, partner, how about answering a question for me."

Isaac crossed one leg over the other and looped an arm over the back of the chair. "Go ahead. Ask away."

"If you were a female—"

"—which I ain't."

"Just listen," Race grumbled. "If you were a female who dreamed of being respectable, how would you go about it? What would you do?"

"I'd get myself born into a filthy rich, respectable family and then I wouldn't have to do nothing else."

Race edged up on his elbows again. "But if you'd been born dirt poor, what would you do?"

The black man rubbed a hand over his jaw. "Well, lemme see now. First I'd get me a big, respectable house and all the trimmings. Maybe a fine carriage and a matched pair of dappled grays." Isaac closed his eyes now. "I'd walk with my nose in the air the way respectable folks tend to do. If I were a female, I'd carry one of those tiny beaded bags and a great big parasol." His eyes opened then, and a grin broke across his face. "And I sure wouldn't have anything to do with the likes of you."

Race met his grin with a scowl.

"Are we discussing Miz Kate, Horace?" Isaac asked. "The little gal with no last name? Now that wouldn't be the reason you ain't written her, would it? 'Cause whilst you were falling for her, ass over teacup, you didn't bother to find out her full name?"

"What do you want me to do, old man? Scrawl 'Kate the Gate' on an envelope and send it on its way?" Race crossed his arms over his chest and dug his shoulders into the mattress.

"Nope. I just want you to be honest with yourself, Horace. That's the reason you ain't sent word to her. Not 'cause you just plain don't write letters. And, since she ain't sent word to you, her knowing where you are and all... Well, I think you need to do some considering about that."

Race crossed his arms tighter. "Meaning what?"

"Meaning maybe she don't care about you the way you care about her." Isaac fell silent then and resumed his vigil out the window.

She cared, Race thought. Cared enough to let him be her first lover when the entire male population of Leavenworth City had tried and failed. Cared enough to consent to leave her misfit father. She cared. And he had let her down, badly. But, sweet Christ, he'd make it up to her.

He shot up to a sitting position. "Isaac, I want to buy a house. Today. You go out right now and find me the biggest, fanciest house in Santa Fe."

The black man turned slowly from the window. "That's crazy, Horace. I hear a fever talking."

"You hear a man crazy in love. Now if you don't go find me that house this minute, partner, I'm taking this bed apart for crutches and I'll go find one myself."

Isaac eased himself up out of the chair. "You don't listen to nobody but yourself, do you, Horace?"

"I know what I want, Isaac. I want Kate Whatever-the-hell-her-name-is. It doesn't matter what her name is because she's going to be Kate Logan as soon as I can manage it. And she's going to have more respectability than she ever knew existed. Starting with a fine big house. And shoes, dammit. More shoes than she ever dreamed."

Kate sat as demurely as she knew how in the Cassidys' formal parlor, despite the ovenlike heat of early September, despite the fact that she was nervous as an ant on a griddle under the stern gazes of both Edmund and Hortense Cassidy, and despite the fact that her feet were killing her so much that she had slipped her new shoes off underneath her petticoats and was now blissfully wiggling her toes on Hortense Cassidy's elegant Persian rug.

Mother and Father Cassidy hadn't wasted any time, she thought, once Ned had told them of their engagement. And they weren't mincing any words, either.

"To put it quite simply, Kate, we don't think marriage is in our son's best interest," Edmund Cassidy concluded.

Kate merely sat there, secretly wiggling her toes, waiting for Ned's father to drop the other shoe. She didn't have to wait long.

The portly man sucked in a serious breath and let it out slowly. "It isn't in your best interest, either, young lady. Should the two of you continue with this folly, I will be forced to disinherit my son."

"Ned won't have a penny," Hortense put in, as if to clarify a notion a girl with Kate's background couldn't possibly understand. "Not one red cent."

They both sat there then, regarding her expectantly, as if anticipating that Kate would throw up her hands and say she was sorry for the inconvenience and even sorrier to miss out on their enormous fortune.

Sorry, folks. I'll just have to find another sickly victim for my obvious greed.

As they watched her, Kate slid her blistered feet into her shoes. Ned, bless his heart, hadn't thought to give her stockings. But he had certainly been right about his parents. He had practically predicted their very words. Just as he had told her what to say in reply. The only thing she could say, considering the circumstances. She stood up now, hands clasped demurely at her waist.

"Mr. and Mrs. Cassidy, I'm carrying your grandchild."

Kate turned on her blistered heel and walked out of the Cassidy mansion and back to the mercantile.

Ned followed her into the back room, where she flopped facedown onto the cot.

"Was I right, Kate?" he asked anxiously. "Did they threaten to cut me off?"

She nodded as much as possible with her face in the pillow.

"I knew it! And did you tell them about their grandchild? What did they say?"

Kate nodded again, then twisted around to face Ned. "They didn't have to say anything, Ned. They just looked at me like I was dirt to be swept under their fancy carpet."

Ned drew in a raspy breath, then took both Kate's hands in his. "Dear, dear, Kate. I apologize. But it was necessary. Please trust me. I know them. And I promise you they'll never look at you that way again after what you told them today."

As if on cue, they heard Edmund Cassidy noi
clearing his throat out in the store. "Ned," he call
"I need to speak with you, son."

Ned winked and gave a little squeeze to Ka
hands. "You see?" he whispered, then called, "I'll
right out, Father."

After Ned left, Kate turned her face into the pill
again. She'd never been more miserable in her l
Was this how all fallen women felt? she wonde
miserably. A single hot summer night of loving, a
now she was not only soiled, but a liar to boot. E
worse, she was lying in order to marry a man
didn't love.

She buried her wet face more deeply into the p
low, wishing she could turn back time, wishing it w
Independence Day again, only this time she'd s
home, darning her daddy's socks, or doing wash,
just staring at the wall.

No, that wasn't what she wished at all. For e
now, even with her shame, she wouldn't trade a s
ond of the time she had spent in Race Logan's ar
Sometimes it seemed those precious memories w
what got her through the long days and the lon
nights.

That didn't say much for her intelligence,
thought, knowing she'd do the same fool thing all o
again if given the chance. It did, however, say sor
thing about her heart.

Kate sat up and swiped a fist at her eyes. She had
been sensible that hot summer night, but, by God,
was going to be sensible now. She figured she had t
choices. She could traipse off after Race and pro

bly wind up alone, having her baby by the side of the road somewhere. Or she could accept Ned's proposal, and give her baby a fine name and a better chance at life than she had ever had.

Chapter Seven

He had bypassed the town, urging his trail-weary horse farther west, past the apple orchard now heavy with snow, across the frozen creek. But the minute Race saw the ramshackle house, with its cold tin chimney and front door hanging by a hinge, he knew it was deserted. All around it the snow was deep and crusted, marked here and there with animal tracks but not a single sign of human life.

Just to be sure, he swung down from the saddle, pulled his cane from the rifle scabbard and made his way up the slippery front steps with an almost elderly caution. All he needed to do, he thought, was break his other leg now and get set back another five months.

Where the hell was she? Snow had blown in the broken windows and formed drifts and slick patches on the floor. The firewood was frozen in a solid stack, but the stove was gone. He could see the marks where it had been bolted to the floor. Somebody had pried it up, gouged the floor and the doorframe trying to get it outside.

Her bed was still there and he lowered himself onto it now, stiff legged and clenching his teeth against the cold, attempting to get his emotional bearings, to contend with his disappointment, and to tamp down the fear that was rising in his throat.

There were at least a dozen explanations, Race told himself as he brushed snow from the sodden mattress. The simplest and best answer was that she and her father had moved into town. Maybe the old man had changed his ways, given up drinking and moonshining, gotten work, and was finally providing for her. Maybe right this minute the two of them were sitting down to Christmas Eve dinner in a small cottage just off Main Street.

He stabbed his cane at the floor. What was he going to do, just sit out here telling himself pretty stories until nightfall? Trying to extinguish the panic that threatened to explode in his tight rib cage? Seeking to postpone whatever terrible truth accounted for this godforsaken place? His Kate was gone, and for a minute his life seemed to hang in the balance.

He should have taken her with him that night rather than allow her to remain behind. She had said she wanted to do some cleaning up, to write a letter to her father, to set things straight. But looking around now, Race regretted that he hadn't told her to forget it. The place was beyond help even then, and she could have sent her old man a letter from Santa Fe.

The sad truth of it was, though, he had been glad to go back to town alone that night, and when he had kissed her goodbye, he wouldn't have bet the farm that he'd be back the next day.

Good thing he didn't, he thought now with a twisted half smile. He looked around the little room where they had made love. What a dump! But all he had seen was Kate that night. Kate with her golden lamplit hair, her glistening satin skin, her trusting green eyes. She'd trust him again, Race told himself. He would treat her like a skittish mare—stroke and caress her, feed her from the palm of his hand if necessary, promise never to leave her again. And, by God, he wouldn't.

But first he had to find her. And before he went looking any further, he was going to stop in at the mercantile and get her those shoes.

"I can't imagine what's keeping Ned," Kate said, twisting the gold band on her finger, the band that seemed to fit more tightly every day as her body began to swell.

"Well, we've waited long enough," her father-in-law said from the head of the table. "Ned knows we have supper at five-thirty." Edmund Cassidy shifted his bulk to produce a pocket watch that he opened with a flourish and a scowl. "Five-forty-seven. Pass the potatoes, please, Mother," he said to his wife at the opposite end of the table. "Althea, start the vegetables around, if you will. I don't see why my son's tardiness should ruin Christmas Eve dinner for the rest of us."

Hortense Cassidy, in draped gray velvet that matched her upswept hair, gave Kate an apologetic glance as she handed her the bowl of mashed potatoes. "Don't worry, dear. Ned hasn't had one of his spells in weeks. If I know my son, he's kept the store open for someone who forgot tomorrow was Christmas."

"And then he'll take two bits for a four-bit purchase," sniffed Althea. "The fool."

Kate glared at her sister-in-law. With her big blue eyes and yellow curls, Althea had the looks of an angel. Her disposition, however, was the devil's own handiwork. She never missed an opportunity to say something unkind—about anyone. No wonder Frederick Sikes had chosen to spend the holiday eve with his regiment rather than his new wife. Even the colonel wasn't safe from her sharp tongue. It was difficult for Kate to believe she had once regarded the blonde with a measure of awe.

"Ned is a generous man," Kate said quietly now, coming once again to her husband's defense.

Althea's blue eyes glinted with malice. "Well, if anyone would know about Ned's generosity, Kate, I'm sure it would be you."

Kate sighed inwardly. She had tried so hard to please Ned's family, and, by and large, she had. But all of her efforts were wasted where Althea was concerned. Sooner or later she was going to lose the temper she had held in check for Ned's sake. Best not do it tonight though, she cautioned herself. She didn't want to spoil everyone's holiday.

"Perhaps Ned plans to meet us at church," Kate said when she had finished her dinner. She pushed her chair back from the table. "I believe I'll just go over a few minutes early and see if he's there."

"Very well, dear," Hortense Cassidy said. "Do be careful."

"You watch the snow, Kate," her father-in-law said, eyeing her thickened waistline and the slight swell of the silk pleats over her belly. "I don't want you falling down and causing any harm to that grandson of mine."

"Heaven forbid," crooned Althea to Kate's departing back.

Once out on the front porch, Kate took a deep breath of the cold December air as she fastened the clasps of her hooded woolen cloak. The Cassidy house, where she had lived since her September marriage, was always oppressively warm. And it wasn't just the temperature. Edmund and Hortense Cassidy, as Ned had predicted, had given the couple their blessings once told that they were going to be grandparents.

Apparently they had despaired that their sickly thirty-year-old son would fail to pass along the Cassidy name. After Kate had given them the news, the chilly couple turned warm, and their threats became endearments. Perhaps, too, Kate thought, the Cassidys were secretly pleased that their son had at last shown a little backbone. They had, for whatever reasons, rallied behind the newlyweds and opened their home to them.

Yes, once they knew Kate was pregnant, that their son had planted a Cassidy seed to see their name and their enterprises into the future, they drew Kate firmly into the bosom of the family and stood by her with an almost ferocious affection in public. Edmund Cassidy saw that her father had a proper granite headstone for his grave, while Hortense saw to it that Kate was properly and beautifully coiffed and shod and gowned.

If anyone called her Kate the Gate anymore, Kate was unaware of it. Now, when men passed her on the street, they tipped their hats and murmured, "Miz Cassidy," with their eyes directly downcast. The womenfolk of the town remained a bit chilly and stiff—like icicles, Kate thought—but most of them were melting, if only to earn the regard of Hortense and to avoid the blustering, and often blistering, disregard of Edmund.

From the front porch, Kate scanned the fresh cover of snow on Main Street. It looked so clean with just one or two wheel tracks through it. Blown by the brisk wind from the plains, it lay in feathery drifts against the sides of buildings and in soft pillows of white on rooftops. Windows glowed yellow and warm over sills where snow billowed like white bunting. Everything was so still. For a moment it seemed like a village in a fairy tale with Kate the princess in her flowing, warm, woolen cape.

Hardly a princess, she thought, as she felt the baby flutter inside her when she started down the porch steps. She wasn't slim and lithe anymore. She wasn't even young. Matronly was more like it. Getting ungainly. But above all else, she was respectable. Kate Cassidy now, not Kate the Gate. Never again Kate the Gate.

For a minute she wished...no, she had promised herself she wouldn't do that anymore. No more blowing on dandelion puffs or searching out the first evening star. No more wishing. She wasn't an innocent child after all. She had made her bed—with Race Logan—and now she had no choice but to lie in it—with Ned Cassidy, a good man. Ned's happiness about the baby was genuine and generous, and he sometimes made her forget—if only for a moment—that the child wasn't truly his. Ned was gentle and sweet and tender. He had made no demands on her physically. Whether that was due to his concern about her condition or his own poor health, Kate wasn't exactly sure. But she was grateful, nevertheless.

Not that she wouldn't have performed the duties of a wife, but it would have been just that. A duty. Her husband had earned her gratitude and her admiration and her respect, even a deep affection... but not her love.

Not her love. Kate had buried that last summer—along with the telltale sheet, her innocence and all her wishes and dreams.

The shoes felt as light as feathers in his hand. "What did you call these, Cassidy?" Race asked the man who once again had done him a favor by keeping the mercantile open after hours.

"Pumps," Ned said from behind the counter where he was straightening up, securing lids on candy jars, and realigning patent medicines on the shelf at his back. "Silk pumps. The soles are leather. Kid, I believe."

Race frowned. They didn't look very substantial. Dancing shoes, he would have called them. Or slippers. "You sure you don't have anything else? Real shoes? Something with laces?"

With a patient sigh, Ned said, "I'll look in back again, but I'm pretty certain that's it. Seems like everybody in town was buying shoes last week. I bought a pair myself to give my wife for Christmas."

Still studying the delicate footwear, Race said, "I didn't know you were married, Cassidy. When did you slip that particular noose around your neck?" Race lifted his head and grinned across the room then at the pale, lanky man, suddenly feeling a common bond. After all, if he had his way, he, too, would be subject to the same noose in a few days.

"September the twelfth," Ned said. "The happiest day of my life."

"Congratulations. To you and your bride." Race tried to picture the woman who would take the sickly Cassidy as a lifetime partner. Probably had a face like a hatchet or a figure like a rain barrel. Maybe not. Cassidy was sickly, but he was also a wealthy man from a prominent family. As catches went, he was probably considered better than most. "I'd like to meet her someday," Race said, not really meaning it but not knowing what else to say on the subject.

"Well, come on to the Christmas Eve service at the First Presbyterian with me after I close up," Ned said affably. "You can meet her and do your soul some good at the same time."

He disappeared behind the curtain once again as Race lowered himself into the fitting chair and leaned his cane against the arm. His soul, he thought, actually felt pretty decent. It had, ever since deciding to make his life with Kate. What bothered him now was his leg. It had started aching with the snowfall two weeks ago, and had slowed him considerably, making the long ride from Santa Fe even longer. Six hundred miles had seemed more like six thousand. Still, now that he was here, it seemed the perfect night. Christmas Eve. He and Kate had met on a holiday, after all. It was only fitting that they take up where they left off on another holiday. And a sacred one at that.

His thumb traced over the smooth silk of the delicate slipper. She couldn't wear these outdoors, that was for sure. But then he had no intention of letting her outdoors for a good long while. A little grin flared at the edges of his mouth.

For the past five months he'd done very little but think about Kate, about this day. The fever and the pain had beaten him down the first month; after that he'd been laid up with his leg in a splint. When he did finally get out of bed—against Isaac's protests and very nearly over his partner's dead body—his leg wouldn't bear any weight at all at first. But each day was a little better. Each day the leg got a little stronger and bore a little more weight. And each day brought him closer to the day he'd get back to his Kate.

The shoes were merely a token, a symbol. He had already bought her a house—a big rambling adobe just around the corner from the plaza. With Isaac's help, he had furnished it. He was prepared to make her one of the foremost citizens of Santa Fe. God knows he had the money to do it after so many years of hard work and nothing to do with the profits but watch them grow in the bank. Once he had made up his mind to settle down, he had pursued it with a vengeance—even when he was hog-tied in bed with his leg in a splint. Isaac said he was crazy. Crazy in love was more like it.

But his grin turned to a scowl now. He'd spent so long thinking about this, planning it, dreaming of lacing and unlacing shoes. And now the shoes were all wrong, and he was keeping Ned Cassidy late on Christmas Eve all because of some damn silly notion he'd nursed like a lovesick puppy. In addition to all that, he hadn't yet worked up the nerve to inquire as to the whereabouts of the girl he knew only as Kate the Gate.

There was a brassy tinkle then as the door of the mercantile opened. Frigid air wafted in, along with a small female nearly hidden by an enormous cloak. Race watched as a delicate gloved hand swept the hood back. He recognized the yellow curls instantly. And he was more than a little familiar with the ice-blue eyes that zeroed in on him.

"You've got your nerve showing your face in this town again, Race Logan, after what you did to me," Althea snarled.

"Merry Christmas, Miss Althea," he said. His leg was aching too much to get up, so he remained in the chair. Besides, he thought, if anyone least deserved politeness and a show of gentlemanly respect, it was this little chit who was coming down on him now like a winter storm.

"It's Mrs. Sikes, now," she snapped, "no thanks to you."

He grinned up into her sour face. "My condolences to the colonel."

If she weren't a lady, Althea thought, she would have spit right in his outrageously handsome face. If it weren't for Race Logan and his high-handed rejection of her last summer, she wouldn't be Mrs. Frederick Sikes today. She wouldn't have been married off to a cold-blooded, tightfisted soldier who made her nearly beg for anything he considered a luxury. And the colonel, damn his soul, deemed luxurious anything other than food and simple cotton frocks. Miserable as her existence was now, it promised to get even worse next spring when Frederick moved her to Fort Union, a hellhole of a military installation in New Mexico Territory.

And it was all Race Logan's fault. All of it. The man was responsible for every recent misery in her life, and Althea was going to make him pay. Dearly.

She was doubly glad now that she had conveniently forgotten to pass along the message Race had sent via the dusty cowhand last July. "I guess I know why you're back," she said, patting one of her perfect sausage curls. "What a pity you're too late."

His eyes flickered over her face. What was the little hellcat up to now? "Too late?"

Althea studied a perfectly shaped fingernail. "She's married." Her voice was cool, casual.

Race's voice, on the other hand, was not. It was low and lethal. "Who?"

"The little slut you came back for. Kate, that's who. She's just about as married as anyone can get, Logan. With a gold band on her finger and a bun in the oven to boot."

He stood up now, not out of politeness but sheer rage. Taking the blonde by the shoulders, he shook her, loosening her curls. "Don't play games with me, Althea."

"It's the truth, damn you. Let me go."

He didn't. His fingers dug into her shoulders through the heavy wool of her cape. "Who did she marry? Where is she?"

Althea raised her chin into his dark, hard face. How she was going to love seeing that tough exterior crack when she told him. "She married my brother. In September." A malicious smile spread across her lips. "Kate the Gate is Mrs. Cassidy now. A fine, upstanding citizen. Too good for the likes of you, I'm sure." She saw the jolt of pain in his eyes, though his mouth remained a brutal slash.

"I don't believe you," he said, thrusting her away from him and reaching for his cane, which he stabbed at the floor.

The blonde casually readjusted the misaligned shoulders of her cloak. "I don't give a tinker's damn if you believe me or not. It's true. Ask anybody."

Race's head was swimming. It wasn't possible. Kate was his. He was going to marry her. "I sent word," he murmured now, almost oblivious of Althea's presence. "I told her I'd be back. I asked her to wait."

Althea laughed. "Why would anybody wait on some saddle tramp when they could sink their claws good and deep into the son of the richest man in town? Kate got just what she set her sights on."

"Respectability." The word came unbidden from his lips as he heard it echoing inside his head.

"I don't know if anybody around here respects her, but they all sure keep their mouths shut now. Nobody'd dare risk my daddy's wrath now that Kate the Gate is carrying his grandchild."

"When?"

Althea picked a fleck of lint from her cloak. "When what?"

His mind was ticking off the months since the Fourth of July. "This baby. When's it due? How far along is she?"

"What are you asking, Race? Whose baby it is? Of all the insulting..."

"When, dammit?" he growled.

Another smile curled her lips. "Well, you know, I'm not all that sure. Why don't we ask my brother? He is the one responsible, after all." Her voice rose from a simper to a shout. "Ned? Are you in back?"

His round, pale face appeared from behind the curtain. "Well, Althea. I thought you'd be at church by now. Did you call me?"

"I was just telling Mr. Logan about your blessed event. When's the little darling due, Ned? I've quite forgotten."

"June," he replied immediately and with some authority while he lingered behind the counter.

"June," his sister repeated. "That's what I thought. Of course, it makes perfect sense. October—" she ticked off the months on her fingers "—April, May, June. Nine perfect little months." Casting a wicked sidelong look at Race, she added just above a whisper, "My brother is apparently quite potent... despite his appearance."

She knew it wasn't true, of course. Their bedroom was adjacent to hers, and Althea took every opportunity to listen through the wall. She had yet to hear anything but Ned's rasping and coughing and the couple's scandalously chaste good-nights. And, judging from her looks, Althea suspected Kate was five months along if she was a day.

Althea was lying through her teeth—guessing really—but the devastation it caused to Race Logan's face stoked the coals of malice in her heart. The man went absolutely pale. If it weren't for the dark growth of stubble on his chin and cheeks, he would have looked quite like a ghost, she thought. Damn him! He was truly wild for Kate. Head over heels. He might even believe he was the father of the little bastard in Kate's belly. Well, good. He'd hurt all the more for it. From his head to his heels, and, hopefully, in between.

Race turned his back on the blonde now, focusing all of his attention on that lanky and pale pillar of the community, that paragon of male potency, Ned Cassidy. "You're a lucky man, Cassidy." You respectable son of a bitch.

"That I am," agreed Ned with a smile. He drummed his long, thin fingers on the counter then and softly cleared his throat. "Those church services are about to start, Logan. If you've, uh, made up your mind about the pumps—"

"I'll pass," Race said, cutting him off. His knuckles were white as he gripped the cane and started for the door, barely in control of himself. If he didn't get out of there immediately, he was going to explode from the rage that was boiling inside him. Another minute and he would haul that moon-faced tower of respectability over the counter and beat him to a bloody, senseless pulp. Another minute and he wouldn't be able to keep swallowing back the bile that was rising in his throat, choking him.

"Merry Christmas," Althea chirped to his back.

The bell on the door jangled raucously as he slammed it behind him. It was all he could do not to turn and ram his fist through its oaken panels. It wouldn't matter if it broke every bone in his hand. Nothing would ever hurt worse than this. Race wanted to throw his head back and howl like a wounded beast at the cold white moon. Instead, he shoved his cane into the rifle scabbard on his saddle, heaved himself up and slammed his heels into the unsuspecting black stallion, which snorted and bolted into the snowy night.

The church was warm. Almost stultifying. It smelled of evergreen and tallow and wet wool coats. Sitting in the front pew—the Cassidy pew—between the bulk of her father-in-law and the rigid pose of her mother-in-law, Kate felt imprisoned. She held the hymnal protectively over the pleats that were beginning to strain over her stomach.

Next Christmas, she thought, she would be holding a baby in her arms. A Cassidy baby—a lucky child who would never be homeless or shoeless or abandoned. That was all that truly mattered. Her child would wear the Cassidy name like a shield to protect it from all the barbs and stings and bladed looks that had made Kate's own life so miserable so long.

Not that she was deliriously happy now, she thought, feeling the press of Edmund Cassidy on her right and Hortense on her left. Their respectability, the mantle of acceptance she had coveted so long, was cloying. Sometimes it felt like a tight noose around her neck. But she was trying to be content, for her child's sake if not her own. And she might have been if only Race Logan hadn't blown through her life on the Fourth of July. If he hadn't touched her like a hot wind, all full of pleasures and promises and passions. A tramp wind that left her scorched and needy and empty, save for the seed he had planted within her.

Kate sighed inwardly, castigating herself for thinking such thoughts, especially in church. She told herself she was lucky, after all. Her baby was lucky. Race wouldn't have made much of a father. Children didn't need wind for a parent. They needed to plant their feet in firm soil. Ned. Ill as he was, and weak in many ways, Ned would be that terra firma for her child.

The swirling snow outside one of the tall side windows caught her eye, and Kate glimpsed a lonely rider heading out into the storm, head dug deep into wide shoulders, upper body bent against the icy wind.

Poor soul, she thought. No one should be alone on Christmas Eve, much less be riding into the cold heart of a blizzard. She hoped he was pushing that big black horse toward somebody who loved him, somebody who would warm him once he arrived.

Chapter Eight

On Christmas morning in the spacious, silk-swagged front parlor of the Cassidy mansion, Kate sat on the Persian carpet with her legs tucked beneath her as her fingers traced the delicate spindles of a cradle. "It's beautiful, Ned. Thank you." She raised her eyes to her husband's soft blue gaze.

Edmund Cassidy snorted. "Ought to be. That came all the way from Grand Rapids, Michigan. Cost two arms and a leg to get it here on time."

"Nothing's too good for Kate," sniped Althea from the settee she shared with Colonel Frederick Sikes, who had surprised them by knocking on the front door just after breakfast.

The officer flicked a piece of lint from the knee of his dark blue trousers now and said, "Hopefully, my dear, Kate will loan it to you at some point in the future."

"Yes. Hopefully. As long as I can't have one of my own," Althea said to her miserly husband, then shifted her cool gaze to Kate. "I'm sure Race Logan could transport it safely between here and Fort Union. What do you think, Kate?"

Kate thought she'd like to break the beautiful oak cradle over her sister-in-law's blond head. Her references to Race had been more frequent this morning, more barbed than usual. Fortunately, no one else seemed to notice them. "You're more than welcome to use it, Althea," she told her. The reply earned her a warm pat on her back from Ned and a sniff from his sister.

Frederick Sikes leaned forward, his elbows braced on his knees and his bushy mustache twitching. "You might not have to transport it all that distance in order to borrow it, Althea." The colonel angled his head toward Ned. "Eh, Ned? Have you told them yet?"

Kate turned from her inspection of the cradle to see Ned's face flush a deep crimson.

"Told us what yet?" the senior Cassidy demanded.

"Ned?" Hortense asked uncertainly.

Ned cleared his throat and drew in a raspy breath. "Actually, Frederick, I..." His lips sealed closed a moment as he studied Kate's quizzical expression. He smiled—a wisp of a smile—and then stiffened his shoulders. "Father. Mother. Kate and I just may be accompanying Althea and Frederick to New Mexico in the spring."

His listeners, Kate included, responded in unison. "What?"

Edmund Cassidy followed his exclamation with a raucous gurgling in his throat. "Nonsense," he added with a definite sense of finality.

"What a foolish notion, Ned," his mother chirped. "I must say I'm surprised at you."

Kate simply stared in astonishment as Ned replied, "No, Father, it isn't nonsense. And, Mother, even if it is a foolish notion, I'm afraid it's true. It's very likely that Kate and I will accompany Althea and the colonel to Fort Union." His gaze flitted briefly to Kate. "We haven't reached a firm decision yet."

A firm decision! This was the first Kate had heard of it. What in the world had gotten into Ned? She didn't have to wait long for an answer.

"Frankly, Father, I'd like a chance to stand on my own two feet. I've never even tried, you know." Ned spoke calmly, clearly, without the slightest hitch in his breath. Right now it seemed it was everyone else's breathing Kate could hear.

While her father-in-law sputtered and her mother-in-law fussed with her lace collar and cameo brooch, Kate was thinking, *Bravo, Ned!*

"Here! Here!" boomed Frederick Sikes with a twitch of his mustache. He clamped a hand on Althea's knee then. "The more the merrier, right, dear?"

The blonde smiled wanly.

"It's a difficult trip, Ned. A dreadful trip," his mother said. "I don't believe you're up to it. And, my gracious, what about the baby?"

Ned sought Kate's eyes momentarily before replying. "I wouldn't expect that to be a problem, Mother. The baby isn't due until June."

Kate fingered the spindles of the cradle, noting the slight tremor in her hands. April, Ned. You know it's

April. Are you doing this to spare me the shame, or have you actually come to believe our oft-repeated lie?

Ned put his hand on her shoulders reassuringly. "Kate's a strong girl. I'm proud to say she's given some of that strength to me."

"Good for you, Ned," piped the colonel.

"A veritable tiger, aren't you, big brother?" Althea's smile was cruel. "My, my!"

"Well," Ned said, "it won't be until spring. And we haven't reached a firm decision yet. Have we, Kate?"

"No," Kate murmured. But the sudden firmness in her husband's tone belied his words. They were indeed headed for New Mexico come spring. It was the last place on earth Kate wanted to go.

On tiptoe, Kate placed the last of Hortense's crystal water goblets on the top shelf of the breakfront, then carefully closed its doors and turned the small brass key. Funny, she thought, a year ago she would have walked through fire just to stand for a single moment in such an elegant dining room, just to glimpse the fine crystal and gilt-edged china, the starched, snow-white linens and the delicate spoons. A year ago she didn't know the trappings of respectability were just that—trappings. A trap. And she was caught in it now as surely as she breathed.

With a sigh, she turned toward the dark staircase. Everyone had retired for the night. Ned had gone up right after dinner. His day-long display of bravado seemed to have worn him out. Little wonder, Kate thought now, for although his spells appeared to be improving, she knew he wasn't any better. If anything, he was worse. He wouldn't admit it though, and hid his bloodstained handkerchiefs, replacing them with new ones from the store. How he thought he'd make the arduous trip to New Mexico was a mystery to Kate. Why he even considered it was beyond her.

He hadn't breathed a word of his intention to her, and Kate had been as shocked as Edmund and Hortense this morning when he mentioned it. More shocked, and certainly more apprehensive. But it wasn't the trip Kate was afraid of. It was the Santa Fe Trail itself. The trail, and the man who nearly owned it by virtue of his legendary exploits.

"Race." She whispered his name as she gripped the banister and lowered herself onto a step.

"My, my. Aren't we up late?" Althea's voice was a lilting taunt as she came down the staircase and perched on the step just above Kate. "Were you talking to yourself, Kate?" She arranged the velveteen drapery of her wrapper over her knees. "I can't imagine you'd want anybody to hear what I just did."

Kate didn't answer in the faint hope that Althea would stop if her fish failed to rise to the bait.

"He was here, you know. Last night. On Christmas Eve," the blonde said.

Kate's heart rose in her throat, and though she tried to sound disinterested, her tight voice betrayed her. "Who?"

Althea's voice, on the other hand, was almost musical. "Race Logan, that's who. That's why Ned was so late for church. I don't suppose he told you."

"No. He didn't."

The blonde lapsed into a smug silence then. A silence Kate was finally forced to break.

"What was he...?"

"Doing here?" her sister-in-law finished for her. "Looking for me." She laughed brightly. "You should have seen the expression on that man's face when I told him I'm Mrs. Sikes now. I truly thought he was going to cry. Those pretty blue-green eyes of his got positively misty. 'You had your chance last summer, Race,' I told him." She sniffed. "Silly man."

Once again Althea fell silent as Kate struggled to remain impassive. She glanced over her shoulder at her sister-in-law now. "I don't suppose he inquired about me?"

"No, he didn't. But then, you know how Ned always tells anyone who'll listen about his bride and his impending fatherhood. Race looked bored to death, I must say. Or relieved it wasn't him. It's a sure thing brides and babies aren't that man's favorite subjects."

Kate attempted a lightness she didn't feel. "No. I don't suppose they are. How long will he be staying in town?"

"Oh, he's not. He turned right around and headed back to New Mexico as soon as he found out about Frederick and me." Althea studied a cuticle. "Flattering, really, don't you think? Has anybody ever traveled that far just to court you, Kate?"

Kate could only shake her head. He was here. Race had been in Leavenworth City. Whether or not his reason had been to court Althea, Kate had no idea. It really didn't make any difference. All that mattered was that Race had been here and now he was gone, and in between he had made no effort to see her.

As if last summer had never happened. As if it had meant nothing to him. As if he truly had been just a summer wind, blowing through her life.

Althea yawned now and stretched her arms over her head. "Oh, my. I'm just about done in after all today's festivities." She stood, then lingered on the stair. "Are you coming, Kate?"

"What?"

"I asked if you're coming up to bed? I'm sure Ned's waiting for you."

"I'll be along in a while," Kate said.

"Don't take a chill." Althea rubbed her hands over her upper arms. "It's drafty on these stairs." She turned then and began to mount the stairs. Then the blonde halted. "Oh, and Kate," she whispered conspiratorially, "I'm counting on your discretion. I wouldn't want Frederick to worry for a single moment about an old saddle tramp who had entertained some misguided notions abut my affection for him. You understand, don't you?"

As Kate nodded listlessly, Althea returned to the room she shared with the colonel.

Kate remained where she was, leaning her face into the turned-oak balusters, looking through them as if they were the bars of a cell. If she had felt trapped before, she felt imprisoned now, and she realized that it had been the hope of Race's return that had allowed her to exist here in the Cassidy house. A kind of wishful thinking she had never even truly acknowledged.

Perhaps the wish had been buried so deep she couldn't even express it to herself.

What would she have done, she wondered, if the wind had blown back into her life? If the wind had touched her again, had called "Come with me"?

Maybe it was for the best, she thought, that she wasn't given that chance. She'd never know now what she might have done if the wind had kissed her and whispered "Come."

Later that night as she was lying quietly by Ned's side in their dark bedroom—Ned in his flannel nightshirt and Kate in a high-necked dimity—he reached for her hand. In hushed tones, he began telling her how she had changed his life, how she had fortified his spirit, how she and her child had filled his heart with love. He told her once more how important it was to him to try to be a man, a man who stood on his own two feet, not just for her sake, but for his own. This was what he had always wanted. And Kate had given him the courage to try.

He gripped her hand more tightly. "It's best we go, Kate. This way no one will ever suspect . . . well . . . the child will be truly mine then."

And, all the while he spoke, tears slid from Kate's eyes onto the pillowcase. After all Ned Cassidy had done for her, she had no right to deny him his dream. No right to deny him the legitimacy he wanted for her child. Their child.

"We'll go, Ned. If that's what you want. As long as you feel up to it."

"Frederick plans to get underway as soon as the weather warms," Ned said, his voice tinged with happy anticipation. "The end of March, I suspect. Just think, Kate. Our baby will be born in New Mexico Territory. What an adventure!"

No, Ned, she thought. Race Logan's baby will likely be born in a wagon somewhere out on the plains. And I'm afraid. Of giving birth. Of dying. Of living. Of the wind that keeps chilling my heart and burning holes in my soul.

"What an adventure," she echoed softly.

Chapter Nine

Isaac Goodman, with his dark skin, his barrel chest and his rolling gait, resembled a great bear as he walked into the dining room of the La Fonda del Sol. The inn was favored mostly by Mexican traders. Ordinarily it was loud and busy, but this morning it was quiet. Looking neither left nor right, Isaac proceeded straight toward the table where Race was staring into the depths of a cup of coffee. Then the big black bear of a man picked up a chair, turned it with a flick of his wrist, straddled it and sat.

"Snow's just about melted, Horace."

Race ignored him as he gestured to the heavyset woman who was folding napkins at a rear table. *"Más café, Corazon, por favor."*

Isaac drummed his fingers on the table while the woman poured fresh coffee into two cups. He took a loud sip of his then set the cup back down. "I said—"

"I heard what you said, Isaac. Why don't you quit pussyfooting around and come right out with it?"

The older man's crooked eyebrows registered mild surprise. "Pussyfooting, huh? And here I thought I was being polite by hanging back and not saying anything, by just biding my time and waiting for you to get over whatever it is that ails you." He scratched his head. "Pussyfooting! Huh! Imagine doing something like that and not even realizing it."

Race couldn't keep his mouth from sliding into a grin. "All right, old man. Get to the point."

"The point is, Horace, there don't appear to be a point."

"Meaning?"

"Well, for starters, you bought yourself a big old house and you ain't but slept in it more'n two or three nights. Now I'm not claiming I'm not enjoying all that fine furniture and sliver and linen aplenty while you're still camped in that little room upstairs, but I doubt that was your intention. Making ol' Isaac happy."

"It's an investment," muttered Race.

"Damn shame to invest in an old man's pleasure when you got none of your own."

"Are you through?"

"No, I ain't, Horace. I'm just getting started as a matter of fact. Them dozen new wagons you had built are waiting in Leavenworth. There's still a war going on, in case you've forgotten, and the way I figure, if you don't pick those vehicles up soon the army's going to be confiscating them for their own purposes. You put up your house as collateral for them wagons, and I don't hear you making any plans to go get them."

"Weather's been bad."

"It ain't bad now."

Unable to dispute that fact, Race merely glared. "Anything else on your mind, Isaac?"

"Yup," the older man said. "Wine and women. Near as I can tell, too much of the former and not enough of the latter. Ever since you got back from Kansas. Now it don't take a Gypsy mind reader to know that little gal back there hurt you real bad. The way I see it is you either got to talk about it or you got to just let it go and get on with things."

Race took a sip of coffee. "All right."

Isaac blinked. "All right what?"

"I'll let it go." He extended his leg to dig into his pocket for a coin, which he slapped on the table. "You ready to go pick up those wagons at Fort Leavenworth, old man?"

"I been ready, Horace." Isaac rose, flipped his chair around and slid it back neatly under the table. He stood there a moment longer. "You ever going to tell me about it? About what happened at Christmas?"

Race stood up. "Probably not," he said.

Isaac nodded. "Well, I'll just save my breath asking about it then. I do have ears though, Horace. Just in case you ever need 'em."

What he needed, Race thought later after he left Isaac in order to pack his gear, was a solid kick in the rear end to get him going again. That, or a punch to the head that would erase his memory. Hard as he tried, he couldn't get Kate out of his head. Out of his damn heart.

What he needed was a roll in the hay with a buxom, lusty girl. But every time he even looked at one of the dark, sloe-eyed *señoritas* of Santa Fe, he would catch himself comparing her to Kate with her delicate features, her big green eyes, her pretty mouth. And then whatever notions his body had entertained were blotted out by his head. That fact alone made him mean as a rattlesnake and about as much fun as ants at a picnic.

He slammed his shaving brush into his saddlebag, wondering why he even bothered to scrape his whiskers off anymore since he sure wasn't doing his share of damage to delicate female skin.

What a sorry specimen you are, Race Logan, he told himself. If he could just work up a healthy anger or a fine case of hate to fill up all the emptiness inside. The anger he did feel, however, was directed at himself for being such a fool. After all, she had flat out told him she wanted respectability more than she wanted him. Why hadn't he believed her? he wondered. For the same reason he hadn't listened when she tried to tell him she was a virgin. He had been just too damn besotted with emotion.

As he buckled his gun belt, he thought about killing the moon-faced storekeeper. It wasn't the first time murder had loomed like a black cloud in his head. The sad truth was he thought about it so often it had begun to unsettle him, to shake him to his core. If he had stayed in Cassidy's store one moment longer on Christmas Eve, he might have done it then. He wasn't a violent man. Not that way, anyway. He wished to hell he were! He wished he were the kind of man who could take what he wanted with no qualms, no mercy for anyone who got in his way. He wished Kate had married a no-good son of a bitch who deserved a bullet in his heart, instead of a sweet, weak, doting son of a bitch. A respectable bastard if ever there was one.

He picked up his saddlebags and draped them over his shoulder. Let it go, he told himself. Go pick up the wagons and get back the deed to the house you bought for her. Then sell the damn place. Give it away, along with all the fine china, the silver, the linens and laces, everything a love-struck heart had meant to offer her.

"Why would she wait on a saddle tramp when she could sink her claws in the son of the richest man in town?" Wasn't that what the blond hellcat had said? She should have added, "And climb in his bed with the speed and determination of a woman who meant to produce a tie to bind irrevocably—a Cassidy heir." Damn her! He hoped that pasty-faced bastard kept her barefoot and pregnant for the next twenty years. Wore her down and wasted her on a dozen or more pale, pasty-faced brats. He wished...aw, hell! He just wished he could get over her.

"Let me go," he whispered in the general direction of Kansas. "Katie, for God's sake, let me go."

Kate swayed with the rhythm of the wagon. After ten days on the trail, she swayed even when she climbed down and stood on solid ground. It was as if the plains were an enormous sea and she were a sailor who had grown so accustomed to the billows and swells that her legs no longer responded to terra firma.

She had been driving the wagon since the second day. Ned, poor Ned, had proven to be a wretched sailor. All the jostling made him ill. Deathly ill. His coloring had turned gray and his mood had gone from ebullient to despondent.

He had spent the months after Christmas making plans to open his own Cassidy Mercantile in Loma Parda, a village near Fort Union. He had ordered enough merchandise, in Kate's opinion anyway, to stock a city-size emporium. And he had worked, happily and eagerly, day and night, organizing the three wagons that would carry their goods southwest. Her husband had seemed almost aglow with excitement. His health even appeared to improve. But not now. Right now Ned lay flat on his back inside the wagon.

Althea, too, was worse for the wear and tear of the rugged Santa Fe Trail. She spent whole days inside her own wagon, refusing to come out even for meals. Her existence was marked only by the coming and going of a blue speckle-ware chamber pot and an occasional dramatic moan from the dim depths of the wagon.

Kate, however, was fine. More than fine. Unlike Ned, she found the rocking motion of the wagon soothing. She adored the broad sweep of plains and the enormous canopy of the sky. She loved to rise with the sun, knowing that by night the scenery would be different and there would be more miles behind them, fewer miles ahead.

She was glad to be leaving Kansas and the elder Cassidys behind. Even glad to be heading down the Santa Fe Trail. In the months since Christmas, she had made a kind of peace with her heart and her soul, and had come to accept her lot as Ned's wife and helpmeet. It was clear Race Logan didn't want her, had never loved her, would never whisper, "Come." And

Kate had come to terms with that. She had been a foolish girl, but she had no intention of being a foolish woman. Kate even thought she had grown strong and sensible enough to encounter him, as she undoubtedly would on the trail or at the fort, and actually be able to look into his eyes without feeling her heart wither inside her. She wasn't looking forward to it, but endure it she would.

The child growing within her—*her* child, not Race Logan's—had made the difference. As Kate became more and more aware of its precious life, she vowed to do everything in her power to protect it. The best way to do that, she knew, was Ned, and his name and everything that went with it.

And the baby, thank God, was cooperating. The baby, in fact, was late. The nine-month mark was April fourth and they were now five days beyond it. Heavy and cumbersome as she felt, and much as she wanted her former comfortable body back, Kate prayed for two more weeks.

But when their small party of wagons and soldiers reached the crossing of the Canadian River, a mere four days from their destination at Fort Union, two mishaps occurred almost simultaneously. The axle of the Cassidys' wagon broke, and so did Kate's water.

She was standing with an ashen-faced Ned beside the broken-down wagon. They were watching the soldiers unhitch the mules when Kate felt the warm gush beneath her skirt. There was no pain, but she knew there would be. The beginning of the end was near.

Before she could inform Ned, however, Frederick Sikes approached them.

"Hell of a note, Ned," the colonel said, shaking his head. "We don't have a spare axle. Used our last one back at Lower Spring."

"What are we going to do?" Ned asked bleakly. Kate noticed that his breathing, which had improved so over the past few months, sounded raspy and shallow, almost as bad as it had been last summer.

Frederick tapped his riding crop in the palm of his hand. "Well, we're only four days out of Fort Union. We'll put you and the Missus in with Althea for the remainder of the trip." His mustache twitched, as well as a muscle in his jaw, as if anticipating his wife's reaction to sharing her already-cramped quarters in the wagon. "I can send a detail back to fix this confounded thing in a week or so, I suppose."

"No," Ned said.

Kate and Frederick both regarded him as if he had just spoken in a foreign tongue. Kate squirmed in her soggy underclothes.

Pale and ill as he was, Ned stiffened his shoulders. "I'm not leaving this wagon to be stripped by Indians or scavengers."

The colonel's face darkened. "Look here, Ned..."

But Ned shook his head vehemently. "No, Frederick. Absolutely not. The goods inside this wagon represent a third of my investment and I will not lose them."

Colonel Sikes, obviously not accustomed to contrary points of view, was stonily silent a moment, his lips taut beneath his bushy mustache. "Do you have a better solution?" he finally asked. "I'm due to take over for the quartermaster at the fort in four days, Ned. I don't have time to waste."

"I'll stay," Ned replied. "You take Kate with you."

She wanted to hit him. Of all the times for Ned to be stubborn. To exhibit a backbone of steel. To insist on doing something he wasn't capable of doing in his condition. "Ned," she pleaded.

The look he shot her was hard as flint. "I won't argue about this, Kate."

No, she could see that. Kate sucked in her lower lip as she became increasingly aware of the sodden cotton of her drawers against her thighs. She couldn't go with Frederick and be responsible for delaying his arrival at Fort Union. But, even if the colonel had all the time in the world to get to his new command, she couldn't leave Ned. And somehow she sensed he didn't want her to. In fact, when she announced her decision to stay, Kate heard him sigh, not with irritation, but with gratitude and relief.

The colonel, on the other hand, bit off a curse and looked at her as if she had just taken leave of her senses. "You can't be serious," he exclaimed. "In your condition?"

If you only knew, Kate thought glumly as she forced a brave smile. "I'll be better off staying put for a few days, Frederick. Really."

He shook his head as if he were about to countermand all of their decisions. But Althea's blond, disheveled head appeared from the rear of her wagon just then.

"Why have we stopped, Frederick?" she snapped. "We'll never get off this godforsaken trail if we don't keep moving." She raked all three of them with her glare before disappearing once more inside the wagon.

That seemed to cap it for Colonel Sikes. "All right," he said briskly. "I'll see that you have provisions for a week. And I'll send a patrol back as soon as we arrive at the fort."

"Thank you, Frederick," Ned said.

"I don't suppose you even know how to use a gun, do you? How about you, Kate?" the colonel asked.

Lord! She'd shot a few possums and rabbits with her brother, but Frederick was talking about shooting people. She nodded hesitantly.

"Well, we'll leave a rifle and some ammunition. Not that I expect any problems. We haven't seen any sign of Indians. Still..." His voice trailed off.

Still, Kate thought. She wondered how often Apaches or Kiowas send advance notice of an attack. Panic overcame her for a moment. She had heard terrible tales of Indians killing adults and sparing children only to make them slaves. Ned touched her arm then, and when she felt him trembling, her own fright disappeared. She could do this, Kate told herself. She had to do it. And Frederick was undoubtedly right. There was no reason to think there was any danger.

Later, as Kate and Ned stood beside their broken wagon and watched the last canvas arch disappear over the rim of the hill, Kate threaded her arm through her husband's. "We'll be fine, Ned," she said again. "I believe I'll go lie down for a little while now."

Staring off at the spot where the wagon had disappeared, he didn't seem to hear her. It was just as well,

Kate thought. He'd hear her soon enough when the baby started coming.

Race kept his eyes on the column of dust rising to the north. "What do you think?" he asked Isaac, whose Morgan trotted shoulder to shoulder with Race's big stallion.

"Wagons," the black man said. He was squinting in the same direction and his lips were pursed thoughtfully. "Maybe half a dozen."

Race touched the Colt on his hip. "I hope you're right. I'm in no mood to meet any Kiowas or Comanches today."

"Your mood's about as black as my face, Horace." Isaac grinned at his partner. "Maybe what you need is a quick tangle with a few redskins to cheer you up."

But the glare his comment provoked cautioned Isaac to hold his tongue. Both men rode in stony silence for the next five miles, closing the distance between themselves and the menacing cloud of dust.

When it became clear that it was indeed a slow-moving train of wagons, Isaac whooped. "What'd I tell you? Half a dozen damn wagons. How do I do it?"

"You're a pure miracle, Isaac," Race said dryly. His gaze narrowed on the column of soldiers who rode beside the canvas-covered vehicles. He recognized the colonel immediately. Why they were posting Sikes to Fort Union was beyond him. The man had no experience with Indians other than one desultory skirmish in western Kansas. Of course, nothing the U.S. Army did should have surprised him, Race thought, having bashed his own head for years against the solid walls of paperwork the army put in his way before he could haul so much as a penny nail from Kansas to New Mexico Territory. And now the army was probably going to try to wrangle his new wagons away from him, or take his house if he didn't cooperate. He had about as much use for the army as he had for the railroad trains that were inching west, threatening his business.

He smiled to himself now, thinking that since his marriage to that Cassidy female, Colonel Sikes had probably honed his fighting skills considerably. Race was still smiling as they drew abreast of the column.

"Welcome to New Mexico, Colonel," he said, touching a finger to the brim of his hat.

"Logan, isn't it?" Frederick Sikes asked, signaling his men to halt behind him.

"That's right. And this is my partner, Isaac Goodman."

Before the colonel could acknowledge the introduction, Althea poked her head out the front of the lead wagon and shrilled, "Now why are we stopping, Frederick?" As soon as the words had left her mouth, she saw the reason. Race Logan. Her hands flitted to her limp curls in an attempt to enliven them.

"My wife," the colonel said, gesturing over his shoulder.

Poor sap, Race thought, touching his hat again in Althea's direction. "A pleasure, Mrs. Sikes," he drawled, watching her wrestle her hoops and petticoats through the canvas arch of the wagon and then down to the ground. His horse took a nervous step backward as the woman approached.

"Well, now, Mr. Logan. Don't tell me you're on your way back to Kansas again," Althea crooned.

Race merely nodded. He could tell from the twist of her smile and the white glint of her teeth that the blonde was about to bite into him, but before she could say anything her husband spoke.

"Good thing you happened along, Logan. We had to leave a wagon behind yesterday. Confounded axle broke and we're short on replacements. I'd appreciate it if you'd check on it when you reach the Canadian crossing."

"I'd be happy to, Colonel."

"Any folks with it?" Isaac inquired.

Althea opened her mouth once more, but her husband cut her off. "As a matter of fact, there are," the colonel said. "My brother-in-law and his wife. He's not a well man and her condition is rather, well, delicate. Naturally I'm concerned with the situation."

It took a long moment for the relationship to register on Race. But when it finally dawned on him that Sikes's brother-in-law was Ned Cassidy, Race exploded. "What the hell were you thinking to leave them behind? Man, that's prime Kiowa hunting ground."

Frederick Sikes huffed and sat straighter in his saddle. "We saw no signs of Indians, I assure you." Then his posture sagged a notch as he added, "Besides, the idiot refused to leave his wagon, and his wife refused to leave him."

Race had a hard time picturing Ned Cassidy standing up to the ramrod colonel. Kate, if his memory served him right, would walk up one side of Sikes and down the other. And of course she had remained behind with her weakling husband. It was just like her, dammit. He remembered the way she stuck by her drunk of a father.

"Mr. Logan is well acquainted with them, Frederick," said Althea, now with a malicious glint in her pale eyes. "Kate in particular. Wait till you see her, Logan." The blonde inflated her cheeks with air and extended her arms over an invisible belly. "She's quite something—if you're partial to elephants."

Race could feel Isaac's dark, scorching eyes. He glanced sideways, ready to burn the man with his own eyes, but all he saw on his old friend's face was warmth and sympathy. Or was it pity? Hell! That's just what he needed now, he thought—his woman big as a house with another man's child and Isaac pitying him.

In spite of his aggravation, however, Race's heart pumped harder. Kate was close. He wondered why he hadn't been able to feel her very nearness in the air. He shifted in his saddle toward the colonel. "The Cassidy wagon's at the Canadian crossing, you said?"

Sikes nodded. "That's right. Tell them we'll have a new axle for them within a week, will you? And buck up their spirits if you can, Logan. My brother-in-law is rather... um..."

"Weak," Althea volunteered.

No thanks to you, lady, Race thought as he tipped his hat once again in her direction, then said to her husband, "We'll be on our way then, Colonel."

Sikes saluted him. "Have a safe journey."

Althea caught the cheek piece of his horse's bridle before Race could turn the animal away. Her voice was a menacing hiss, meant for Race's ears only. "Stay away from her, Logan. Do you hear me? If you so much as look sideways at my brother's wife, I'll see that you're ruined in this part of the country. I can do it, too. Don't think I can't."

He didn't doubt it for a minute. But he'd be damned if he'd give this hissing, sharp-clawed female so much as a clue about his intentions toward Kate. Race leaned down as if he were going to kiss Althea Sikes. His voice was rich and deep—the full-throated purr of a mountain lion. "You won't ruin me, cat. Who would you have to play with then?"

When she blinked, he jerked the bridle out of her grasp and urged his stallion away at a brisk clip.

"What was that all about?" Frederick Sikes asked his wife.

"Nothing," snarled Althea as she stared at the departing riders. "I asked Logan to give my regards to Kate."

They had ridden hard for six hours. The sun was already behind the ridge of the distant peaks of the Sangre de Cristo range, and a cold moon had risen in the east.

Isaac hadn't asked about Kate, and Race wasn't about to volunteer any information that would bring that pitiful expression back to his friend's face. Bad enough, Race thought, to be the victim of his own self-pity. Bad enough to feel like a fish with a hook snagged in his gut. That little girl had really done a job on him with her apples, her bare feet and her big-eyed innocence.

It had been hard enough to handle his feelings knowing she was back in Kansas, living as the respectable Mrs. Cassidy. But now she was here in New Mexico Territory. About the last thing he wanted to see right now was Kate with her belly all puffed out with a damn respectable Cassidy baby. What he ought to be doing, he thought, was turning the stallion's head east to avoid the crossing where the wagon had broken down, where Kate, loyal Kate, had stayed behind with her helpless mate.

What he ought to do, Race acknowledged bleakly, was have his head examined. He already knew what the hell was wrong with his heart.

"I'm riding through, Isaac," he said. "If you want to stop, go ahead. You can catch up with me at the Canadian tomorrow."

The black man sighed. "I was never one to postpone trouble, Horace. If you don't mind, I'll just keep plugging along with you."

"You feel it, too, huh?" For the past few hours, in addition to the jumble of thoughts inside his head, Race's skin had been crawling with apprehension. "What do you think it is? Kiowas?"

"Maybe." Isaac shrugged his massive shoulders. "Trouble, anyway."

Race nodded in solemn agreement. "Big trouble." More than you know, old friend.

Chapter Ten

By dawn, both their horses were blown as Race and Isaac guided them across the shelf of dull red sandstone that banked the Canadian River. There was no stopping though. Not now. Ahead they could see the wagon—scorched, its canvas top blowing in burnt scraps in the morning breeze.

Isaac cursed through clenched teeth. Race couldn't even speak. His mouth had gone dry as dust. His heart was surging with fear as he pushed his mount the last few hundred yards, and he swung to the ground before the huge animal had come to a stop, and then Race dropped to his knees beside the charred remains of Ned Cassidy.

"God in heaven," he breathed.

Isaac tugged an arrow out of the dirt. "Kiowas."

Then when the lusty cry of a baby came from beneath the fire-blackened wagon, Race was on his feet immediately. He saw Kate then, by a rear wheel, and he was beside her in an instant. Her face was pale as death, framed by damp, matted hair. Her lovely mouth was thin, quivering with fear. In the shadows beneath the wagon, her eyes looked haunted and wild.

Kate fought the blackness that kept threatening to claim her. For hours it had been pushing at the edges of her brain, diminishing her sight, playing havoc with her mind. She had lost all reckoning of time, all ability to distinguish what was real from what was not. Dear God, she couldn't awake from this nightmare, couldn't push the shadows away.

"Kate." The voice she heard now was broken, choked with tears. A voice made of mist and darkness. Warm and gentle fingertips explored her face. Strong arms were drawing her close. They felt so real.

"Katie, love. Sweet Jesus! You're alive. You're safe."

She gave in to the shadows then. She surrendered to them almost gratefully, closing her eyes and allowing the darkness to pour over her like a warm tide.

Isaac slid beneath the wagon now. "She all right?"

"I don't know. I think she's passed out."

"Probably for the best," the black man said, "considering what she must've heard and seen. Damn lucky she had that baby when she did. Kept them savages from touching her. Childbirth's powerful magic to their way of thinking."

The baby in Kate's arms gave another little squawk.

Isaac slithered back. "Let's get her out into the light and see what needs doin'."

Rays of yellow sunshine cut through the smoke that was still drifting from the wagon. As gently as he could, Race pulled Kate out into the light.

His mouth tautened to a hard line as he surveyed her bloody cotton gown. "My God," he breathed, casting a helpless glance at Isaac.

"First things first." Isaac reached for the hem of Kate's gown and tore off a long strip. Then he ripped it in half lengthwise and tied the strips several inches apart on the bloody cord. He pulled his knife from the sheath at his hip.

"Now hold on just a damn minute," Race said, clamping his hand on Isaac's arm. "Do you know what you're doing, old man? I won't let you cut her, if that's what you're thinking."

The black man eased back on his heels. "I never did tell you that my mama was a midwife, did I? Lord, I musta seen close to a hundred babies born by the time I was seven years old. Head first. Feet first. Every which way." Isaac grinned. "I guess I have some small notion about what to do, Horace."

With a flick of his knife, Isaac severed the cord between the two knots. He slipped the baby from Kate's lax arms.

Isaac peered down at the well-formed, squalling girl with the full head of dark hair. He knew a Logan when he saw one, Isaac thought, but he supposed he'd best keep his mouth shut and let things work out by themselves. "Look at this fine baby girl," he murmured. "Here." He passed the baby to Race. "You take her over to the river and clean her up some while I see to Miz Kate."

Race looked at the squirming, blood-crusted baby. He looked back at Isaac.

"Well, go on. You've seen females in their birthday suits before, Horace. Just don't drop her, you hear?"

He stood up gingerly, afraid of just that. Dropping the slippery little critter. Holding her too tight and crushing her little kitten bones. He walked to the river as if he were carrying an egg on a teaspoon, then folded his legs beneath him and sat on the sandstone bank, gently cradling the baby in his arm as he smoothed water over her. Soon Race was soaking wet, but the child was clean and apparently content to lie quietly against him.

"You're something, little one," he said softly as his broad thumb grazed the side of her tiny skull. She turned her face toward the touch, her small rosebud of a mouth all pursed. "You're looking for your mama, aren't you?"

His own mouth hardened then. "Don't bother looking for you daddy," he said gruffly. "The damn fool's dead. If he weren't, I believe I'd put a bullet in that sapless heart of his for dragging you and your mama out here."

"A fine thing, Horace Logan, Jr., talking murder in that tiny little ear." Isaac squatted down beside him now, leaning forward to rinse his hands and ropy forearms in the water. He grinned at the baby. "Pretty little thing, ain't she? Just like her mama."

"Darker," Race said.

Isaac nodded. He glanced sideways to see if the fact that the baby had his coloring, Logan coloring, seemed to register on Race. But all Isaac saw was sadness etched on his friend's face. Maybe he didn't want to know, he thought. Maybe it hurt less on account of his lady went and married somebody else. He shook the water from his hands. "I done buried what was left of her husband. Well, you want to take the first watch or shall I?"

"You go ahead and get some sleep. Where's Kate?"

"Back under the wagon. Asleep. She ain't bleeding now. She'll be fine. Her body, leastways."

Race looked down at the baby in his arms. "No thanks to that respectable son of a bitch she married."

"Seems to me you're wastin' a lot of breath on a dead man, Horace."

"I guess you're right." Race sighed as he smoothed his big hand over the baby's fragile skull. "Anyway, she's mine now. They're both mine."

Isaac yawned wearily as he turned back toward the burnt wagon. "Maybe, Horace," he muttered. "Maybe not."

For two days Kate refused to come out from beneath the wagon. She cried most of the time, and when she wasn't crying she stared at nothing with wide, burning eyes. At Isaac's urging and with his help, she held the baby to her breast. Though Kate remained listless, almost oblivious, the child nursed vigorously.

Race had coaxed her, pleaded with her, begged her to come out, to let him help her. All to no avail. He wasn't sure she even knew him. He was sure, however, that forty-eight hours was long enough for his Kate to remain in her private hell. And he was also fairly sure that his own time was running out. It hadn't mattered much before that he might lose his house in Santa Fe if the army confiscated his new wagons.

But that had been when Kate was lost to him. She was found now. She was his. Race meant to provide her with every bit of respectability that weak-kneed Cassidy had. Every bit and more. If he lost his house, though, as well as the wagons, it would take him years to recoup his losses. He still had the cash he'd held back to lavish her with carriages and silks. He could still provide an adequate roof over her head. But not the fancy roof he already possessed. The elegant home he intended for her in the first place.

He tossed the dregs of his morning coffee onto the ground, muttering a curse as he stood. "How long do you expect it'll be before Colonel Sikes sends that patrol, Isaac?"

"I don't imagine we'll be seeing 'em for another six days. You getting restless, Horace?"

"I'm thinking I'm about to lose my mind waiting for Kate to come to her senses. And I'm thinking that while I'm sitting here doing nobody any good, some jackass up in Leavenworth is getting ready to commandeer my wagons and cause me no end of difficulty."

Isaac angled his head, shading his eyes from the bright morning sun. "You think that big house will mean a lick to Miz Kate after what she's been through?"

"She'll get over this," Race said gruffly. "When she's back on her feet and thinking clearly, she's going to want what she wanted before. And I intend to see that she has it."

"Just how do you plan to go about it?" Isaac asked.

Race chewed on his lower lip a moment, staring down into the low-burning campfire. "I'm going to take off for Leavenworth. I can get there in a week if I push it. Should take me another week to hire a crew and take on freight. I figure I can be back at Fort Union in five weeks, maybe six at most. Then I'll take Kate and the baby to Santa Fe."

"You got it all figured out, huh, Horace?"

His partner's barbed tone brought a scowl to Race's face. "Yeah, I do, Isaac. Those Indians won't be back, and I figure you can take better care of Kate and the little one right now than I can, considering your midwife experiences and all. You can't go get those wagons alone, that's for sure. Your skin color, pretty as it is, doesn't command a whole hell of a lot of respect up at Fort Leavenworth, old friend."

Isaac merely nodded.

"What do you think? It's not such a harebrained plan after all, is it?"

"No, Horace, it ain't. Only thing is it's *your* plan."

"So?"

The black man sighed. "So, Miz Kate just might have a couple of her own."

Race dismissed his partner's caution with a brusque wave of his hand. "She doesn't have to plan anything. I'm going to take care of her from here on out." He scowled again when Isaac quirked an eyebrow. "What? Don't you think I'm capable of that? Of doing right by her?"

"I didn't say that, now, did I?"

"Well, what then?"

Isaac shifted on his haunches and crossed his arms over his chest. "You're good at what you do, Horace. The best, probably. You make decisions quick. You're a fine leader. Trouble is, you've been leading so long you don't know diddly-squat about following."

"What the hell's that got to do with anything we've been discussing?"

"Miz Kate ain't no teamster who just signed on to one of your crews. That lady just may have a whole different notion of what she wants to do once she's feeling better. It might not be a bad idea for you to listen to her before you do all this planning of yours."

Race glared in the direction of the wagon then. "When she's ready to talk, Isaac, I'll be only too happy to listen." He turned then and stalked toward the riverbank.

Watching him, Isaac shook his head and muttered to himself, "What you say, Horace, and what you do usually lie a good ten or fifteen miles apart."

Awareness returned to Kate slowly, like the burning off of a morning mist beneath the resolute beams of the sun. There was no great rush of anguish. Her memory, it seemed, had gone from impenetrable fog to a dull and misty gray and then finally to a stark and undeniable clarity. Ned was gone. But she was alive. Her baby was alive. Right now those simple facts of life and death were all that she could deal with.

Life! She had survived. Looking down at her tattered, bloodstained gown, she suddenly wanted nothing more than to put on clean clothes, to exchange this bloody shroud for a fresh one, a symbol of life. She scooted out from beneath the wagon then. A cool breeze touched her cheeks, and Kate turned her face up to the golden sun and the brilliant blue that surrounded it. She could almost smell the sunshine, almost taste the sky. She was alive. Not too far from where she stood, the sun was turning the Canadian River to quicksilver. Taking a deep, lung-filling breath, Kate walked toward the bank.

Isaac's hand caught Race's arm. "Let her be, Horace."

He'd been sitting by the campfire, talking wagons and weather with Isaac, when Kate appeared from her sanctuary under the wagon. Race's heart had halted momentarily, then it had surged up into his throat. Despite the bedraggled dress and the tangles in her hair, Race thought he'd never seen a more lovely creature in his life. He had to remind himself to breathe as he watched her. Her green eyes had some luster back. A smile even touched her lips. When she headed toward the river, he started to rise and follow. Then Isaac clamped a restraining hand on him.

"Let her be," Isaac said again.

Race threw his partner a black glance, then returned his gaze to Kate, who had waded ankle deep in the river and was just standing there now, staring off at the horizon, gazing at nothing as if it were something. From that distance, the white cotton gown reminded him of the dress she'd worn when he first laid eyes on her. And her stance—stiff backed and proud—was the way she had stood in the town square on the Fourth of July less than a year ago. It seemed more like a hundred years. It felt as if he'd loved her a century or more.

He watched as she dipped the hem of her gown in the water and began to rub at the stains. She lifted her hands and began fumbling with the buttons down the front. Then her shoulders sagged and her knees seemed to buckle beneath her and she sank down in the water.

It would have taken more hands than Isaac had to restrain him then. Race covered the distance between the campfire and the riverbank in an instant, then he charged through the shallows and, with one swift motion, scooped Kate up into his arms and carried her to the riverbank. He sat on the warm sandstone, a soaking-wet Kate cradled on his lap, rocking her while she sobbed, pressing his lips to her damp, matted hair.

The harder she fought his comfort, the harder she cried. Ned was dead. She was alive. She was alive, and Race Logan was holding her the way she'd always longed for. His warm mouth moved against her temple. His strong hand caressed her arm. His heart was drumming just beneath her cheek.

Kate shuddered as she drew in a deep breath—a breath fragrant with buckskin and wood smoke, with animal, both horse and man, with life.

"Ned..." she began, then the tears overwhelmed her once more.

"Shh. It's all right, Kate. Don't talk." Race pressed his lips to her hair. "Everything's going to be fine. You'll see."

It took her a while to find her voice again. "When the Indians came, Ned was down here, at the river. He was getting me water. 'I'm dying of thirst,' I said to him." Kate sniffed. "He squeezed my hand for encouragement, then gave me a tiny little smile and said he'd be right back."

Race stroked her matted hair. "Shh. Hush, Kate. Don't talk about it now."

She sighed a long, wet sigh. "I felt the Indians before I ever saw or heard them. The ground shook beneath me. At first I thought it was an earthquake. All that rumbling. Judgment Day, I remember thinking. The end of the world. Then I heard their whoops and shouts. I don't know why, but Ned didn't seem to hear. He was bending down, filling a canteen with water. His back was toward me. How could he not have heard them, Race?"

Race only shook his head as he continued to smooth his hand over her hair.

"I called to him, but I'd already been screaming and yelling so much with the baby coming that he must have thought it was only more of the same. Then everything was dust and hooves. I couldn't see anything else from where I was lying under the wagon." Kate filled her lungs again. "Frederick left us a rifle, but I didn't dare use it for fear of hitting Ned."

"It's all over, Kate," Race murmured. "Don't talk about it anymore."

"I need to," she insisted. "I need to remember."

And then as Kate tearfully described Ned's efforts to save her, Race remembered Isaac's words about how he needed to listen. So he tried. He sat there quietly if not patiently, stroking her red-gold hair and looking into her spring green eyes, listening to the heroic, though doomed exploits of the respectable Mr. Ned Cassidy, the man who had dragged Kate out here and so successfully put her precious life in jeopardy. He felt rage mounting in him with every word Kate uttered.

He wasn't a man well practiced in swallowing his anger or in keeping his opinions to himself. But, hell, Race thought, he wasn't too old to change. He could learn—to listen, to comfort his Kate, to answer all her needs. But he couldn't take much more of this particular conversation. Just the name Cassidy made bile rise in his gorge. He could barely keep his hands from tightening into fists right now as he touched Kate's hair and smoothed away her tears.

In the same surge of emotion, he wanted to thank God for her life and curse Him for ever having allowed her to marry Ned Cassidy, to make her bed with him, to give birth to Cassidy's child. He didn't dare speak—even to tell Kate how much he loved her—for fear of giving vent to that anger.

If nothing else, it convinced Race that he had made a sound decision about proceeding on to Kansas. The comfort he could give to Kate was boundless. But for Ned Cassidy's widow there was nothing but anger and a jealous rage.

She needed to grieve. That was obvious. But he didn't have to hear it. He couldn't hear it without exploding. By the time he returned from Leavenworth, though, in five or six weeks, Kate would have her grieving behind her. She'd be done with looking back by then, and be ready, even eager perhaps, to look toward the future. And, by heaven, that's what Race intended to be. Her future. Hers, and her child's.

Kate wept for a long time. She was still crying when Race finally carried her back to the wagon. She stopped, however, when he brought the baby to her.

He knelt beside her, the small squalling bundle in his arms. "Isaac said it's time for the little one's breakfast, Katie," he said softly, nudging the baby into her arms.

Her gaze moved from the man to the child. The baby's dark cap of hair was the same rich color as her father's. Already her eyes held the same blue-green jeweled promise of Race's. Couldn't he see that? she wondered. How could he not notice that this small being was his perfect image already? Or had he noticed, then chosen not to acknowledge it?

Trembling from her strength-sapping tears, Kate fumbled unsuccessfully with the small buttons on the front of her gown as the baby began to howl and kick its little legs. "I don't seem to be able to manage this," she moaned, plucking at the buttons now as if to tear them off.

Without a word, Race's big hands eased hers aside and began, slowly, methodically, unfastening her bodice. "There," he whispered as he slid the final button through, then turned his head while Kate lifted the baby to her breast and draped a veil of red-gold hair over the suckling child.

Silently Kate studied his profile as he gazed off toward the river. She remembered again her surprise on that summer night that such a big man could be so gentle. Feelings welled up in her throat, threatening to choke her. Feelings for Race. Emotions she dared not allow to overcome her now. It wasn't right with Ned just dead. It wasn't right to let her grief be diminished or defiled.

Kate swallowed hard. "Thank you for helping me, Race," she said, attempting to sound in control of herself. "You're looking well. How've you been?"

He turned back, taking in the sight of his Kate and the babe tugging greedily at her breast. His heart lurched against his ribs at the loveliness of the scene before him. He wanted to encircle them—Kate and her baby—in his arms to make himself a part of their intimacy. It was too soon, he told himself. "Let her be," Isaac had cautioned. So Race forced a smile, the most carefree he could manage under the circumstances.

"I've been fine, Kate. Working hard like always." It wasn't true, he thought. He'd been drinking and dozing and doing whatever he could to get her out of his head. And he'd tell her precisely that, Race vowed, as soon as the proper time came.

Kate nodded, answering his smile with one she somehow summoned from the bleakness inside her. "Your friend, Isaac, has been kind to me, too. I'm very appreciative."

Race shifted on his haunches. "He'll take good care of you and the baby both while I'm gone."

"You're leaving." It wasn't a question. And it surprised Kate that there was no surprise in her tone. Only dull acceptance. Of course, the wind was blowing on.

"I hate to," Race said quietly, "but there's business in Leavenworth that won't keep."

"I see." Kate's heart felt like a tight fist in her chest. Closed. Defensive. She wanted to cry out, "Why must you leave me again? Why didn't you come back for me?" Instead she bent her head over the baby's, hiding her sorrow, trying to sound matter-of-fact as she said, "Well, then. Have a safe trip, Race."

He leaned toward her and touched his lips to the crown of her head rather than speak his heart. There would be time for all that. A better time and a far better place. Once her grieving was done. Once he had Kate and her baby safe in the big house in Santa Fe. Once their future could begin. "Goodbye, Katie," he whispered.

Race had been gone three days—three long, dry-eyed days and three endless, tear-filled nights. Isaac had pulled off part of the wagon's tailgate and fashioned a grave marker for Ned. He had also rescued the cradle from the scorched wagon. Kate settled the drowsy, well-fed baby on a soft pile of linens there.

"She's growing, Isaac," she whispered to the man who was stretched out beside the campfire. "Can you tell?" Kate asked. "I swear she's two inches longer already. Heavier, too."

"She's a healthy little girl, Miz Kate. You done real good."

With the baby quietly asleep, at least for the next few hours, Kate did up the top three buttons of her bodice and sat beside the big man whom she now considered a trusted friend. "I couldn't have done it without you, Isaac. Race, too," she added almost grudgingly. "If the two of you hadn't come along when you did, I surely would have died."

Isaac shook his head. "Not you, Miz Kate. You would have done just fine. You thought of a name for that little one yet? She's got to have her a name."

Kate tucked her legs beneath her and arranged her skirt over the rough ground. She glanced in the direction of her husband's grave marker. "I'm going to call her Edwina in memory of my husband. Edwina Cassidy." She sighed. "Seems like such a big name for such a tiny thing. I believe I'll call her Nedda."

"Won't always be tiny," Isaac said. "That child's gonna be tall like her daddy. Already got his blue eyes."

"Ned had fine blue eyes," she said cautiously, poking at the fire with a stick.

"Yes, ma'am. But not that particular blue."

Across the campfire, Kate's gaze locked on his. She had already cataloged all of her daughter's tendencies to take after her father, from the color and texture of her hair to the jeweled tint of her eyes. "Is it that obvious, Isaac?" she asked him quietly.

The old man shrugged. "I expect people see what they want to see."

"Did Race notice the resemblance, do you suppose?"

Again he shrugged.

"Guilty conscience," Kate muttered.

"Horace didn't take too kindly to your husband, Miz Kate, but he does have a healthy respect for the institution of matrimony."

"Obviously not enough to participate in it himself," she sniped.

Isaac chuckled but offered no more in the way of explanation. The man could be infuriating, Kate thought. He closed up tight as a clam whenever their conversations turned, as they frequently did, to the subject of Race Logan. He wouldn't tell her much of anything. Every question earned the same reply. "Ain't my place to say, Miz Kate."

She stared into the fire now, not knowing why she even bothered to press Isaac for answers. Race didn't need reasons for doing what he did. When had the wind ever needed a reason for blowing away?

Chapter Eleven

"I want my goddamn wagons." Race slammed his hand, hard and flat, on the desk top.

The force of the blow shifted a neat stack of papers and sent General Elvah Sturgis's antelope-horn pen flying from its brass holder. The gray-haired officer realigned the papers, then picked up the pen and pointed its metal nib at Race. "I told you, Logan, they're gone."

Race leaned on both hands now, casting his shadow over the desk, looking down the pen as if it were the barrel of a gun. "Just where do you get off confiscating private property, Sturgis?"

"There's a war going on. Or hadn't you noticed?"

"Oh, I noticed, General." Race's mouth twisted in a deceptive grin. "Seems like I was in this very office in '61, trying to sign up. Seems to me you told me then I was doing my country an invaluable service by keeping my wagons moving southwest. Or did I just dream that up?"

The general poked the blunt end of the pen through the thick and fashionable muttonchop on his cheek, then proceeded to scratch. "Dammit, Logan," he muttered, "there was nothing I could do. Grant's trying to take Vicksburg and he needs all the supplies he can get. We packed your wagons and sent them down the river by flatboat two weeks ago."

Still looming over the desk like a storm cloud, Race let his head sag a bit as he breathed out an oath. "You sent my house down the river with them."

General Sturgis returned the pen to its holder, then folded his hands on the desk top. "I didn't know you had a house, Logan. I always thought you, er, made use of hotel facilities when you weren't on the trail."

Race just shook his head disgustedly. Images of Kate in her ragged, bloodstained gown flickered through his head. He had ridden all the way up here dreaming of dressing her in silks and fancy laces. He'd had visions of raising that baby girl with a silver spoon in her mouth. Goodbye to all that. The U.S. Army had sent his fancy and respectable future down the river, too.

"There is the possibility of getting them back," the general offered almost sheepishly. "Once Grant takes Vicksburg, he'll be moving again and I'd be surprised if he took those heavy vehicles with him. In all probability, Logan, he'll be leaving them behind. You could always get them yourself."

"Yeah, I could do that, General. Shouldn't be too hard moving six big wagons all by myself. Better yet, I can hire me a crew of butternuts in Mississippi. I'm sure those boys are all just dying to desert their country and their cause. Maybe they can bring their rebel mules along with 'em." Race lowered himself heavily into the chair he had bounded out of only moments before in order to pound on the desk.

"I regret the inconvenience," the general said, only to be cut off by Race's saber-sharp glare.

"Inconvenience," Race muttered. Damn. He couldn't just sit here feeling sorry for himself. He'd have to figure something out.

As Race shifted his feet in order to rise, the general lifted a hand to stop him. "I can let you have five men," he said quietly.

Race leaned back in his chair. "I'm listening."

"They're not experienced teamsters, but I'm sure they'd get the job done for you."

Lifting a suspicious eyebrow now, Race said, "That's mighty generous of you, General. Mind if I ask what's the catch?"

"No catch, Logan. I told you I regretted the inconvenience. I'm merely offering to assist you as best I can."

There was, of course, a catch. There always was with the army. Race told himself he should have known better as he watched the beefy sergeant escort the five prisoners from the brig. Boys, all of them. Pups. And troublemakers, too. With his generosity, Elvah Sturgis was ridding himself of a perpetual burr under his own army-issue saddle. Race would have to ride these ne'er-do-wells like an Irish master sergeant just to keep them in line. Hell, by the time he got his wagons back, they'd probably be decent soldiers.

The big sergeant was grinning like a cream-fed cat as he introduced Privates Doherty, Jones, Jenks,

Montgomery and Creel. To Race, they all looked like gangly farm boys, green as springtime and raw as blisters. Each one of them was about half Race's size, not to mention half his age.

"Good luck, Logan," the sergeant said, and smirked.

Private Creel, his forage cap at a cocky angle, stepped forward. "Listen here, mister. We signed up to fight rebs, not to drive any damn wagons."

Race took in the boy's hot glare, his hard jaw and the sprinkling of whiskers there. He sighed inwardly, then reached out and grabbed the boy's entire shirt-front in a single fist, drawing Private Creel forward and upward until his heels left the ground and his nose was just inches away from Race's own.

"I didn't sign up for *anything*, sonny, which means I don't have to bother with the brig or a hearing or even a court martial. You step out of line just once—just half an inch—and I'll put a bullet in your heart. You got that?"

Private Creel swallowed hard and loud.

Private Jenks inched forward. "Hey, mister, you can't—"

Race grabbed the protester by his shirtfront and hauled him up against his chest, as well. "My hearing's not as good as my aim, boy. What was that you just said?"

"N-nothing, sir," stuttered Jenks.

Race cocked his head. "Pardon?"

"I said I like driving wagons, sir."

After he dropped the stunned Jenks, Race returned the full brunt of his glare to Creel. "How about you, sonny?"

"Me, too." The boy gulped. "I like driving wagons real well."

"Good," Race grunted. "Then I don't have to shoot you." He opened his fist and let the young soldier fall to the ground.

Race leveled his gaze on the sergeant then. "I plan to leave on the first steamer out of here tomorrow, Sergeant. See that these men are waiting at the levee."

"Yes, sir." The sergeant saluted crisply.

Quickly, before they could see the suppressed grin that was itching his lips, Race walked away. It just might work, he thought. Just maybe.

He wished Isaac were with him—for companionship, and to take some of the harsh burden of leadership from him. A useless wish. Isaac couldn't go back South. There was probably still a price on his grizzled head nearly forty years after he'd run away from Starling Plantation. Anyway, Race was glad his partner was with Kate. He didn't worry for a moment about the black man's loyalty to him, or by extension, to Kate and her baby. Isaac knew just what they meant to him.

As he left the fort and headed toward the levee, ready to book passage for six, Race grumbled to himself. Hell, now he had to wait for Grant to take Vicksburg before he could take Kate. This war was definitely getting in his way.

* * *

Frederick had been true to his word. Help had arrived four days after Race's departure, and Kate, along with Isaac and the baby, were escorted to Fort Union. It wasn't at all what Kate had expected. Rather than a fortress, it resembled a city of tents as construction of the new fort got underway. They were greeted by the sound of hammers and saws rather than bugles and canon.

Althea, as it turned out, had spent one night in Frederick's tent, then informed him he would have to find accommodations for her elsewhere.

"You'll stay with her for now in Loma Parda," the colonel had immediately decided upon Kate's arrival. "Damn shame about Ned, Kate," he had told her. "There was no way to know, you understand. I never would have allowed you to stay behind if I had had any suspicions... Well, we must carry on. You have the child, after all. The Cassidy name will go on. That's important."

So Kate and little Nedda had been installed in a tiny back bedroom of her sister-in-law's temporary quarters in the little village a few miles south of the fort. Althea had taken one look at her new dark-haired niece, then had sniffed, "Well, I guess that answers that, doesn't it?"

Kate kept waiting for the other shoe to fall. She was certain it would. Surely Althea would do whatever she could to rid herself of Kate the Gate and her un-Cassidy child. Day after day, week after week, it amazed her that the blonde remained silent on the subject. Not pleasant by any stretch of the imagination, but blessedly silent.

Kate had just tucked Nedda back into her cradle after feeding her when Althea whisked into the little room. The blonde waved several papers under Kate's nose.

"I've just had a response from Mother and Father, Kate. I wired them right after your arrival to let them know about poor, dear Ned."

Plopping down onto Kate's narrow bed, Althea fluffed out the folds of her skirt. She fanned herself with the telegrams then. "My, I hadn't realized it was so warm at the back of the house. You really ought to open a window, Kate."

Staring at the fluttering papers, Kate simply muttered, "Too many bugs." She felt a bit like a bug herself, waiting to be squashed. That other shoe was about to come down on her. Surely Althea had told Edmund and Hortense Cassidy the truth about their grandchild, and they had wired their polite but cold dismissal. With a few words, little Nedda would go from a Cassidy to a nobody. Worse. A bastard. Even Kate the Gate had had a father. She could hardly breathe now as she watched her sister-in-law open one of the telegrams.

"Mother and Father are distressed, as you might suppose." She frowned as she studied the thin paper. "They talk about having Ned's body sent back to Kansas. I'm afraid they failed to comprehend just what happened to the poor man." She sighed now. "Well, I'll write them a long letter and clear that all up. They ask me to give you their sympathy, Kate."

Althea stood up then and walked to the cradle. "They asked me to place an angel's kiss on their darling granddaughter's forehead." Her lips curled slightly as she looked to Kate for permission. "May I?"

Kate nodded warily, holding her breath as she watched Althea bend over the cradle and purse her lips just above Nedda's forehead. It wasn't really a kiss, Kate noticed, but rather a wet little noise. Kate let out her breath, relieved the woman hadn't spit in her baby's face.

Althea straightened up and adjusted her blond curls. "They'll never see her, you know," she said.

Kate blinked. "What?"

"My parents. Mother won't travel—ever. Father's much too preoccupied with his businesses. If you don't return to Kansas, Kate, they'll never find out this child isn't Ned's."

It was Kate now who sat on the bed, afraid her trembling knees would not support her a moment longer. She wasn't sure how to respond—whether to bluff and bluster or to confess.

Althea waved a hand. "Don't be such a goose, Kate. And you can stop looking at me as if I were a witch. You didn't think I'd tell them, did you?"

"Well, I..."

With a snap, the blonde reopened one of the papers in her hand. She squinted as she began to read. "Ned left very little, but what there is will be forwarded to his widow. We are in the process of setting up a trust for little Edwina's benefit. Since we don't know if Kate is capable of handling these rather substantial sums, we intend to make you the trustee for your precious niece, Althea, dear. I know you will not object." Althea raised her pale blue eyes from the page. She smiled at Kate.

"Your daughter's a rich little girl. Of course all the money's got to pass through my hands first. It's a great deal of work—" she sighed "—administering a trust. So many figures and sums. So much paperwork. Naturally I'll expect to be compensated for my efforts."

Kate understood. Clearly. She really should have anticipated this, she told herself. Althea never did anything that wasn't in her own best interest. There was nothing to be gained from turning her niece out in the cold. Better to keep her close and warm...and rich. As the situation dawned on her, Kate wasn't sure whether she felt anger or blessed relief. Nedda was safe. The Cassidy name, the Cassidy shield, remained to protect her. But Althea's thumb was on that shield now. Kate didn't know which was more dangerous—having her sister-in-law as her enemy or her protectress.

"I'm sure you'll be adequately compensated, Althea," Kate said. "Generously, no doubt."

Althea's smile had all the brilliance, if not the warmth, of an icicle. "Well, now that all those details are settled, I'll leave you with my precious little niece." She started for the door, then halted. "Oh, I nearly forgot. It's a telegraph for you from Race Logan. I'm afraid I opened it by mistake. It appears he's left you in the lurch once more." She held the paper out toward Kate.

"Just leave it on the dresser, please." Kate thought her legs probably wouldn't have supported her the five or six steps necessary to take it from Althea's grasp. And she didn't want the blonde to see how badly her hands had begun to shake. It was all she could do to keep her voice at a calm and even level. "I'll read it later."

"Not much to read," Althea sniffed as she tossed the telegram onto the dresser top, then left the room in a rustle of silk.

For a long time Kate sat on the bed, gazing at the soft, dark hair of her sleeping daughter. Race's daughter. She had tried to put that out of her mind these past few weeks. After Race had ridden away, Kate had tried so hard to keep him out of her thoughts. She wasn't always successful, though. Like the wind, he kept blowing through the cracks in her defenses.

As always, her thoughts were a muddled mix of anger and pain and disappointment. She'd been a fool to believe him last summer. Then she'd been a bigger fool out there on the trail, thinking that she and the baby truly meant something to him. But she knew better than that. When people loved, they didn't keep running away.

With a sigh, she walked to the dresser and opened the telegraph message. "On my way to Mississippi," she read aloud. "Tell Isaac I'm chasing...'" Kate couldn't make out the words that followed. It looked as if ink had been spilled on them. It didn't matter much, she thought as she wadded the paper up in her fist. Race Logan could be chasing his tail for all she cared. She was done chasing rainbows and trying to catch the wind.

She was going to stay right where she was. If the news Althea had given her was true, there would be a small legacy coming soon. That, plus the merchandise in the two wagons that had made it safely to the fort, would allow her to carry on with Ned's plan to open a mercantile here in New Mexico.

Kate tiptoed around the cradle and looked through the dusty window glass. Loma Parda wasn't much of a town. There was an adobe church at one end of the street. At the opposite end was a blacksmith's shop and livery. In between there were as many dance halls as houses and small commercial enterprises. Soldiers from Fort Union, straying to town for entertainment, accounted for most of the population.

"This place could use a good little mercantile, Nedda," Kate whispered to her sleeping child. "We're going to push our roots deep in this dusty, sleepy little town, you and I. We're going to be shopkeepers, little girl. Solid, respectable shopkeepers."

Chapter Twelve

The rebels in Vicksburg surrendered on the Fourth of July, 1863. Race had taken that as a sign from the Almighty Himself that things were going to work out fine. But just to insure that success, he had made certain his wagons were as far as possible from the troops preparing to advance east across Mississippi and north to Tennessee. In fact, he and his boys had hidden all six vehicles in a grove of live oaks just north of town.

His boys! After ten weeks—the long weeks while they waited out the siege of the Mississippi town—he'd come to regard the five gangly young privates with something close to warmth. They'd bucked his authority at first at every turn, but now they were all "yes, sir" and "no, sir," ready and willing, if not downright eager, to follow his every command.

Right now they were busy hitching the woebegone mules Race had purchased from a local farmer—a dozen of the scrawniest, most flea-bitten beasts Race had ever seen. At two to a wagon, it was going to be slow going back to Missouri. That was all right. At least he'd be heading in the right direction. Back to his Kate.

"We're just about done here, sir," Private Creel shouted to him now.

Race signaled him with a thumbs-up, then swore as he slapped a mosquito on his neck. Damn, but he'd be glad to leave the Confederate States of America behind. He didn't know which he hated worse—the strength-sapping heat or the bloodsucking bugs.

He did know, though, that once he got back to New Mexico he was ready to give up the trail. He'd hire somebody—young Creel had expressed an interest—to make those long, long hauls, while he settled down and became good, respectable husband material for Kate. Good father material, too.

That had bothered him some—wondering if he could be a decent father to Ned Cassidy's child. What if she grew into the Cassidy mold and turned out to be a pale, moon-faced weakling like her sire? It was possible. Very likely, in fact. Then Race would be staring every day at his predecessor, at the man Kate had chosen in his stead. He wasn't looking forward to that, to having his guts twisted every day of every year, but he had decided it was a fate he couldn't avoid. Not if he wanted to spend the rest of his life with Kate. And that was exactly what he wanted.

They pushed the wagons north from Vicksburg, staying fairly close to the railroad tracks that led to Memphis, trying to avoid rebel patrols and towns and farms. "No sense letting a rebel farmer with a shotgun get his little piece of glory for his country," Race had said. The sorry mules couldn't do much more than three or four miles without a rest. At fifteen or twenty miles a day, Race figured he'd be lucky to get back to New Mexico by October.

On their third night out of Vicksburg they made camp near a village named Elizabeth. His boys had been complaining all day about having to make do with the beef jerky and hardtack the army had given them, so, intending to surprise them with rabbit or possum stew, Race slipped off into the woods while they were unhitching the wagons.

He didn't have a rifle, but he figured if he sat quietly enough for long enough, some four-footed critter would walk within range of his Colt. He watched the shadows deepen while he counted sparrows and thrushes and slow box turtles, listened to his stomach growl, and heartily wished a bison would magically appear from behind the trunk of a nearby oak, or—less magically—a cow.

Race thought about Kate, too. Funny—he didn't even know if she could cook. She could pick apples, though. He knew that for a fact. He smiled to himself, figuring he'd be happy to eat just apples for the rest of his life if he had to. It didn't make all that much difference if she knew her way around a kitchen or knew which end of a spoon to use. He intended to provide her with enough servants to make all that unnecessary. If she wanted to stay in bed all day and eat bonbons, that was fine with him. As long as he could stay in bed with her.

He sighed at the russet beams of the sunset that were filtering through the leaves. Not long and it would be too dark to see anything smaller than a bison. He could have sat there all night, alone with his dreams. Trouble was those pleasant dreams took a hard toll on his body. He hadn't been with a woman since that blazing Fourth of July. The sigh he uttered now was edged with frustration. Just one more reason to get home soon.

Strolling back toward the wagons, Race wasn't looking forward to another tooth-cracking meal himself. Maybe tomorrow he'd visit that little town, pass himself off as a reb and buy a couple chickens. Maybe a little white lightning to celebrate their progress north. Maybe...

The sound of rifles brought him to a standstill. Judging from the direction of the shots, he knew immediately his boys were in trouble. Colt in hand, Race moved quickly and soundlessly through the trees until he could see the wagons in the gathering dark. The wagons, though, were the last thing on his mind as he saw four of his boys lying bloody and lifeless on the ground. Only one—Private Creel—remained on his feet. A dozen rebel guns were pointed at the boy's head, which was bowed in surrender. His thin shoulders were shaking. He looked as if he were about to collapse. And this was after just a few minutes of captivity. The gangly farm boy would last about as long as a raindrop on a hot griddle in one of their lousy reb prisons.

He should never have left them alone, Race thought. What could he do? He had the advantage of surprise now, as well as the cover of the dark woods. He could pick off three or four of those butternuts before they ever knew what hit them. Only problem was that would leave eight or nine, all of whom would shoot at the first available target—Creel. By trying to rescue him, Race would be signing the boy's death warrant instead.

Race shoved his gun back into his holster. His jaw tightened. He wanted to strangle his instincts, drown all his natural impulses. He wanted—God help him—to slip quietly away through the trees, to pretend he wasn't responsible for Creel's safety, to slink home to Kate. The last time he'd tried to pull a boy to safety, he'd gotten his leg broken.

The hell of it was this was going to take him even farther away from New Mexico. Farther away from his dreams. And—dammit all—he'd be saying adios to his wagons again, probably for good this time.

Race muttered an oath in the darkness. Then he called out to the rebs and strode into the clearing with his hands in the air.

Kate lifted a hand to shade her eyes from the intense August sun that was beating down over Loma Parda. She squinted toward the front of the mercantile—Cassidy's Mercantile—where Isaac was about to nail the sign above the front door.

"A little to the left," Kate called to him.

The black man glared over his shoulder. With nails clenched in his teeth, he muttered, "You just told me to move it right."

"Well, I'm sorry, Isaac. You moved it too far. Just a little . . . there. That's perfect. Nail away."

As the hammer rang out, Kate watched with pride and satisfaction and only a small amount of trepidation. All of the two-thousand-dollar legacy she had received from Ned's will was now in this two-story stone building she had bought from the McMartin brothers. The two Canadians had grown wealthy selling bare necessities to the local population. When they announced in late June that they were moving to California, on to greener pastures, Kate was quick to make them an offer for their building and whatever stock remained.

The wily McMartins had accepted her cash, then had disappeared overnight along with their shelves and barrels and fixtures. They had taken the window glass, too, as well as the brass knob on the front door.

Thank heaven for Isaac. Kate didn't know what she would have done without the huge bear of a man. He had built new shelves for her immediately—better than the old ones—then, when he made a trip to Kansas, he'd brought back glass and fixtures, as well as the hand-painted sign he was now in the process of hanging.

He backed down the ladder and joined her out in the street, admiring his handiwork. "Looks like you're in business for real now, Miz Kate."

She smiled. "It does indeed, Isaac." She placed a hand on his huge arm. "And I couldn't have done it without you. You know that, don't you? You've been such a good friend to me."

"Well, now, you needed me. 'Sides, Horace would skin me alive if I didn't help you."

Kate's mouth thinned and her brow furrowed before she replied. "I know you think you're doing this for Race, Isaac, and I truly appreciate it. But it's also about time you realized he's not coming back.'' She paused as the creases in her forehead deepened. ''Not to me, anyway.''

It was a discussion they had had numerous times during the past several months. Isaac kept insisting that Race would be back—next week, next month. ''Just as soon as he gets them wagons.'' Kate wanted so to believe him. After all, Isaac had known Race far longer and far better than she. But no matter what the old man claimed, Kate sensed, deep in her heart, that even if Race returned, he wouldn't be staying.

Now, as always, Isaac concluded their discussion. ''You mark my words, Miz Kate. Maybe I can't say when, but I can say for God Almighty certain that Horace will be back.''

Later, after Kate had counted the proceeds from her first day of business and had locked the money in a metal box and stashed it under the floorboards, she mounted the stairs to the living quarters she had fixed up for herself and Nedda in the two small rooms above the mercantile.

Fernanda, the Mexican widow Kate had hired to watch little Nedda during the day, was humming a quiet tune as she rocked the baby's cradle. ''The *niña* is sleeping,'' she whispered when Kate entered the room.

''Good.'' Kate sighed as she slipped off her shoes, then sat to rub her tired feet. ''You wouldn't think just standing around all day could be so exhausting.''

''You won't have to do it long, *señora.*''

Kate raised an eyebrow, about the only part of her body that wasn't aching at the moment. "Why ever not?"

"You are a young woman. A pretty woman. I have seen how the young officers look at you. It won't be long before one of them is asking for your hand in marriage." The woman gazed down at the baby in the cradle. "This sweet *niña*. She will be happy to have a father. And you. You are too pretty and much too young not to have a man to share your bed."

Kate rolled her eyes. "I'm not interested in that, Fernanda," she said.

The woman studied the sleeping child as she spoke, folding back a corner of her flannel coverlet. "You will be, *señora*. Señor Cassidy must have been a very handsome man. I see him here. Dark, no? And strong? Eyes like the *turquesas* they mine to the south." Fernanda grinned as she lifted her gaze to Kate. "He must have been *mucho hombre,* no?"

"N-no," Kate stammered, feeling the rush of color in her face at the same time as tears pricked her eyes. "I mean, yes. He was a well-respected man. A fine man."

Fernanda clucked her tongue and shook her head. "*Gringa,*" she muttered more to herself than to Kate as she rose and walked toward the door. "I wish you pleasant dreams in that little bed of yours tonight, *señora.*" She laughed softly. "*Beunas noches,* Señora Cassidy."

Fernanda's laughter seemed to linger in the room after she was gone—like a chord of music, like the remnants of a gentle breeze. Kate shivered as if fingertips had just drifted over her skin, over her breasts, along her thighs. And whose fingertips they were she knew all too well. Only one man had ever touched her that way. No one but Race had ever made her shiver one moment and then induced her to burn the next. No one had ever moved over her like river and fire, like a wind blowing ice and flames at once.

Kate closed her eyes, wrapping her arms tightly about herself. She had vowed not to remember. She had tried so hard to douse even the smallest flickers of memory, afraid they would spark a conflagration. Like this. Like now. She was on fire. And all she had to put out the flames were the tears that were suddenly streaming down her cheeks.

There was the swish of silk on the stairway outside the door then. "Kate, you really ought to lock the..." Althea paused in the doorway. "Well, whatever's the matter? Did that old crone say something to upset you? I just passed her downstairs and she was cackling like a witch. I told you not to employ one of those people to watch out for Nedda, didn't I?"

Kate used the back of her hand to scrub the hot tears from her cheeks. "Fernanda didn't do anything, Althea. It was nothing. I'm just tired."

The blonde flounced into the room. "I'm not surprised. I said it would never work, didn't I? All this mercantile foolishness. Are you ready to give it up now and start conducting yourself properly?"

"Properly?" Kate asked with a touch of indignance as she wiped her wet hands on her skirt. "All I'm doing is trying to make a living for myself and my child. I don't see anything improper..."

Althea sniffed. She strode across the room toward the crib, glared down at the baby, then turned her ice blue gaze on Kate. "I think you ought to remarry."

First Fernanda, now Althea! In her exasperation, a little bubble of laughter broke from Kate's throat.

"It isn't funny," Althea snapped.

Kate forced her mouth into a sober line. "No, I know it isn't. It's just plain silly. I have no intention of getting married again, Althea." Kate swiped away the last tear that clung to her eyelashes. "Anyway, I've only been widowed four months. You of all people must know the proper amount of time hasn't passed for..."

"Mourning?" the blonde shot back. "Grieving for your dear, departed husband? Don't make me laugh. I know what you're doing, Kate. And I won't stand for it."

"Just what is it you imagine I'm doing, Althea, other than trying to get from one day to another?"

"You're waiting for that saddle tramp, Race Logan, to come back and claim both you and your little bastard. I dare you to deny it." Althea's pale face heightened with color. Her sharp features grew sharper still. "Go on. I dare you."

Kate strode to the door. "I want you to leave right this minute, Althea." She grasped the knob when what she really wanted to grasp was a fistful of her sister-in-law's yellow curls.

"Well, at least you can't bring yourself to lie. I suppose that's commendable." She gave a last, quick glance into the cradle, then swept toward the door, where she paused. "We'll discuss this again, Kate." A smile frosted her lips. "I'm only looking out for my sweet, defenseless niece's best interests, you know. I'm trying so hard to help you do the right thing. Considering your upbringing and your reputation, Kate, dear, you need all the help you can get."

Her teeth clenched so hard a jolt of pain shot through Kate's jaw. If it weren't for Nedda, she would have slammed her fist right into that pale face and its frozen smile. Kate had to remind herself again and again that it was Althea—alone—who stood between her daughter's safe Cassidy world and the living hell of illegitimacy with all its sorry prospects. Kate told herself she could endure any humiliation her sister-in-law chose to inflict as long as Nedda remained safe.

"I appreciate your offer," Kate told her. "Please, just leave now."

Althea turned for the staircase, then paused. "Think about what I said, Kate. About getting married. Marriage does wonders for a woman's reputation. Of course, you already know that."

Chapter Thirteen

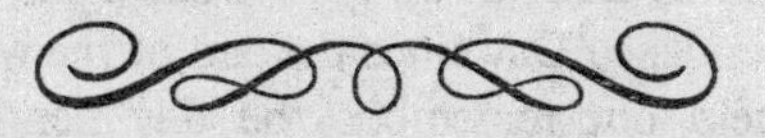

Loma Parda
July 4, 1865

Everybody in town was out on the street that night. Even the dance hall girls had dragged chairs outside and sat with their legs crossed every which way and their faces turned up like flowers in a moonlit garden. And then the black sky over Fort Union exploded in another shower of dazzling light. A chorus of oohs and ahs rose from the crowd.

"Ooh," exclaimed two-year-old Nedda as she bounced with delight on her mother's lap. "Boom," she echoed as the concussion sounded after several seconds.

Kate laughed. "That's the last boom for you tonight, Miss Sticky Face. Fernanda's ready to take you up to bed. Give your Uncle Isaac a kiss good-night."

The little girl's lower lip slid out, then seeing her mother's frown, she planted a loud kiss on the black man's cheek before she followed the Mexican woman inside.

"She's growing up fast, Miz Kate," Isaac said quietly. "That child looks more like her daddy every time I see her."

Kate circled her arms around her knees. They'd been sitting on the steps in front of the mercantile watching the celebration up at the fort for the past half hour. The army had put on quite a show for this, the first Independence Day since the end of the war. Kate couldn't help but remember the day her brother, Charley, had left Leavenworth City, so sure he'd be back after just a few adventurous months. And, despite her best intentions, she couldn't help thinking of another Fourth of July and other, different fireworks when she and Race had made love. That night was something she'd tried hard to forget for the past two years.

Tried and failed miserably, she thought now. How could she forget Race Logan when his face was before her every day in the form of their daughter. "She's probably a lot like her daddy, too," Kate said now. "She's a stubborn little cuss more often than not. Good thing she was so tired tonight or we might have had another War Between the States right here on the front porch."

Isaac was sitting directly behind her in a rocker, and Kate had been listening to the porch boards creak as he pushed the chair back and forth.

"Horace'll set her straight once he gets back. You wait and see."

"Isaac," Kate warned, "don't start."

The creaking stopped as he brought the chair to a halt. "He ain't dead, Miz Kate. I told you what that

General Sturgis told me, about how that boy Horace was with got captured in Mississippi. His name done showed up on a list of prisoners. Creel, it was, best as I can recollect."

"But not Race's name," she countered.

"No. No, it wasn't. But..."

Kate stood, twisting and rubbing her neck to work out the kinks from looking up at the fireworks. She didn't think she could bear discussing Race tonight of all nights. Her memories were painful and vivid. Her heart felt exhausted. "Tell me about your trip north, Isaac," she asked in an attempt to change the subject. "When are you leaving? Tomorrow?"

"Yup. Soon as I get all those good-for-nothings out of their beds and into the wagons. We're carrying hides mostly this trip. Coming back, I'll have supplies for the fort."

"And my merchandise," Kate reminded him.

"Oh, I wouldn't forget that, Miz Kate." He laughed softly. "It'd be nice, though, if you'd start selling the stuff instead of giving it away."

Kate's mouth thinned, as much in disapproval of Isaac's comment as in disgust with herself. She wasn't a good businesswoman. Kate knew that. But she couldn't stand to see people go without when she was sitting on so much. The deprivations of her own girlhood were not all that far in her past. Still, she resented it when Isaac took every opportunity to remind her that, slowly but surely, Cassidy's Mercantile was going broke.

"If you're worried that I won't be able to pay you for those goods, Isaac..."

He reached out, grasped her hand and squeezed it. "I wasn't worried about that. I could say that it don't make no difference one way or the other what happens with this store because when Horace gets back he's going to be wanting to move you away from here." He grinned in the shadow of her glare. "But I won't say that. I'll just ask you if you've got any messages you want me to take back to Leavenworth."

Kate shrugged. "Nothing special. If you happen to see Mr. Cassidy, just tell him his granddaughter's doing fine. If he asks about the tintype of her, tell him I'm still trying to locate somebody to make one."

Isaac raised a quizzical eyebrow. "Like you been *trying* for two years now?"

"Even if I put her in a bonnet, I can't disguise the fact that she's not Ned's child. But she's the Cassidy's pride and joy, Isaac. As long as I don't have to, I'm not going to take that away from them. Stuffy as they are, Edmund and Hortense Cassidy were good to me, and I'd like to spare them another loss. Ned's death just about destroyed them."

"I 'spect they'd be wasting their time hoping for a grandbaby from Miz Sikes. That lady too proud of her fine figure to give it up for young ones."

Isaac wasn't often wrong, but Kate knew he was wrong about that. Her sister-in-law wanted desperately to produce a truly legitimate heir to the Cassidy fortune. If Althea Sikes were to give birth, Kate was sure it wouldn't take her two seconds to inform Edmund and Hortense of Nedda's origins. In the meantime, though, the greedy blonde was content to keep looting her niece's trust.

No sense telling Isaac, though, and getting him all riled up. She was about to change the subject one more time when a voice called from around the corner of the building.

"Kaaa-tie."

A second, more taunting voice came from somewhere across the street. "Kaaa-tie. Whatcha doing tonight, Katie?"

Isaac bounded out of his chair as if it had caught fire. His big black hand was poised near his gun and, even in the dim torchlight, Kate could see the fury on his face.

She threaded her arm through his and tugged him toward the door. "It's nothing, Isaac. They're harmless. Just young, randy soldiers away from home for the first time."

"That ain't no excuse, Miz Kate," the big man said, twisting to get a glimpse of the callers. "It ain't right those stories followed you all the way from Kansas."

Kate practically shoved him inside the mercantile. She forced a laugh as she sat him in a chair. "Gossip travels faster than a locomotive, Isaac, and it doesn't even need rails or steam." All it needed, she thought bitterly, was a pink pouty mouth, a venomous tongue and her sister-in-law's nasty disposition. "It doesn't bother me anymore. Honest."

"Bothers me plenty." He craned his neck toward the front window. "It'll light a fire under Horace, too. You just wait till he gets back, Miz Kate. Them boys'll wish they never heard your name much less caterwauled it in the dark."

"All right, Isaac," she said soothingly. "I'm going to go out back to the kitchen and fix you a nice hot cup of coffee, then I'm going to pour just a tad of whiskey in it to make you forget you ever heard those fools."

The fools were out back, too, though, she discovered as she was putting the water on to boil. Their calls drifted in through the open window like acrid smoke—like mosquitoes looking to draw blood. Kate pulled the shutters closed, but it didn't help.

"Kaa-tie. Come on out and play, Katie."

"Don't be late, Kate the Gate."

She put her hands over her ears at the sound of that horrible name. Ignore it, she told herself, but it was hard not picking up a broom or a skillet and charging out the door. She'd done it before, but it hadn't changed things. In fact, her reaction had only seemed to egg the soldiers on.

Kate heard a few choice words in Spanish, followed by the whoosh of water from an upstairs window and then the wet howls of her tormentors. Fernanda came into the little kitchen a few minutes later, smiling smugly.

"I go home now, *señora.* The *niña* is asleep and everything is quiet. *Los gatos,*" she said disgustedly, "are gone."

"Thank you, Fernanda."

The gray-haired woman put her hand on Kate's shoulder. "*De nada, señora.* Oh, but I wish you would marry so your husband could skin those cats alive."

Kate's hands were trembling when she carried the steaming, whiskey-laced coffee out front to Isaac.

When she failed to see him in the chair where she had left him, Kate walked out onto the porch in front.

"Isaac, what are you doing?" she gasped.

The huge black man was standing there with a dripping corporal in his right hand and a bedraggled young private in his left. He shook them as if they weighed no more than children.

"Now you apologize to this fine lady," he demanded.

"Sorry, ma'am," they said in unison.

Beads of water sprayed from their hair as Isaac shook them again. "And you tell her it won't happen again."

"It won't."

"No, sir. No, ma'am."

Isaac tilted his head in Kate's direction. "It's up to you now, Miz Kate. I can let these scalawags go, or I can take 'em down to the river and hold 'em under for a while."

The pure terror on the boys' faces almost made Kate giggle. "I think they've learned a few manners, Isaac," she said. "Why don't you let them go?"

As soon as he did, the private and the corporal fled on wobbly legs toward one of the dance halls as Isaac called to their backs, "And if I catch either one of you here again, I'll make sure your dancing days are over for good."

Kate did giggle now.

"It ain't funny, Miz Kate." The big man glared at her. "You hadn't ought to put up with trash like that."

Her laughter subsided to a sigh as she linked her arm through his. "It doesn't bother me the way it did when

I was a girl, Isaac. I'm not saying it doesn't hurt now, but not like it did back then. Guess I used to think I deserved the bad reputation somehow. Guess I didn't have a lot of self-respect."

"You got to have that," he said. "Even when I was a slave and folks treated me worse than a dog, I always did believe I was cut out for more, for better." Isaac chuckled softly. "Had to run away to find it, though."

"Well, I'm not running just because some randy soldiers have been misinformed. I like it here." She let her gaze drift toward the little adobe church at the far end of the street. "I like me, Isaac. I've turned into a pretty capable woman who can run a store and raise a daughter. And, in my own most humble opinion, I'm a very respectable lady. I may not be the best businesswoman in the world, and I lose my temper too often to imagine I'll be getting any blue ribbons for motherhood, but, by golly, Isaac, I do have self-respect."

He clasped her arm more tightly to his side. "You done growed up a whole lot these last two years. Horace will be mighty pleased to—"

Kate tore her arm away. "Stop it. Stop ending every conversation we have with Race's name." She gestured helplessly with her hands. "Stop planning a future for us. It's not going to happen, and I just can't keep listening to you going on and on about it."

He started to interrupt her, but Kate had no intention of stopping once she had gotten started. She stood with her hands planted solidly on her hips now, her chin tilted up into his dark face.

"I won't listen to it anymore. I'm tired of having my dreams relegated to the past, Isaac. I want to start dreaming about the future. And, dear Lord, even though I wish he were, Race Logan's not going to be a part of my future." She took one of his huge hands in both of hers now. Tears welled up in her eyes. "I don't want to hurt you, Isaac. You're my dearest friend. And I know you believe with all your heart and soul that Race is alive. I know you truly believe that. But I don't. My heart and soul are telling me he's dead."

The black man simply shook his head.

"Well, I admire your tenacity, Isaac," Kate said, a weary note entering her voice. "But I'm afraid all we've got left of Race is little Nedda and a lot of memories."

She walked into the mercantile then and closed the door as if she were closing it on her past.

Chapter Fourteen

The teamsters' quarters at Fort Union hadn't changed much in the two years he'd been gone, Race thought. The rooms where he and Isaac always stayed were still about the size of a cell in a county jail. The cots still wobbled and creaked and made a man feel like he was going to pitch to the dirt floor any minute. He'd done his share of complaining about this place over the years. Never again, though. After seven months in a rat-infested rebel prison at Belle Isle, and another eight months in that hellhole called Andersonville, he'd never complain about his accommodations again.

Hell! After what he'd been through, this cramped little chamber seemed like the finest suite in the finest hotel in the country. He grinned as he cocked his arms behind his head and crossed one leg over the other, ignoring the creaking protest of the cot beneath him. Lordy, it was good to be home.

Almost home. Home was Kate. He'd been on his way to Loma Parda this afternoon when he'd felt the first cold fingers of the shakes inching along his spine.

He hadn't had an attack of swamp fever for five weeks now and he was hoping maybe the quinine he was taking had finally driven the damn disease out of him.

No such luck. He'd turned back to the fort immediately, figuring it would be better to postpone his homecoming till the fever had run its course. It was one thing to get down on his knees and propose marriage to Kate, he thought bleakly now, but falling flat on his face in the throes of malaria was something else.

He'd been lying in bed, listening to the fireworks, waiting for the shakes to start. They hadn't though. The icy fingers working up his backbone had slowly melted away and he'd nearly wanted to cry with relief. Maybe he was completely well now.... Maybe it was all the praying he had done. Or just the fact that he was close to Kate.

Mindful of the precarious cot, Race turned on his side and clutched the pillow to his chest. He gave a last look at the oil lamp he'd left burning on the bedside table, checking to see if there was enough oil to keep it lit through the night, wondering vaguely how long it would be till he could fall asleep in the dark again, hoping perhaps that when he slept with Kate in his arms he wouldn't wake to panic and terror in total dark. Slowly then, with the pillow for comfort instead of his Kate, he drifted into sleep.

A few hours later, Isaac opened the door to his room cautiously and silently, his hand resting on his gun. He had seen the band of light upon the doorsill and figured that whoever was lying in wait for him wasn't nearly as bright as that warning.

"Well, now," he murmured softly when he saw who was curled up on his cot. "Well, now." The old man doffed his hat and lifted his wet dark eyes to the ceiling. "Thank you, Lord. I surely do thank You."

Isaac unbuckled his gun belt, placed it quietly over the doorknob, then sat, gazing at the man sleeping on his cot, hardly seeing him at first for the tears clouding his eyes. When he did see him clearly, he noticed the changes the last two years had wrought. The wild dark hair was shot through with silver now. The lines in his face were etched deeper. From the slack in Race's clothes, Isaac judged he'd dropped a good bit of meat from his bones. Twenty, maybe thirty pounds.

"You done a hard two years, Horace," he whispered, thinking it was the first time the two of them had been separated since Race was just a little bit of a boy, rushing out and getting lost in the tall prairie grasses. How long ago was that? Isaac rubbed his whiskery jaw, trying to recall. Seemed like Horace wasn't any bigger than little Miss Nedda when his momma had run off. Then, he was barely wet behind the ears when Horace, Sr., had died. That was when young Horace had stopped being a boy.

Isaac liked to think he'd had some part in bringing him to manhood, in making him the strong-willed, hardworking, honest man he became. He'd worried plenty over the years, especially about Horace not having a proper family. It had been just the two of them for so long he was afraid it was getting to be a habit—a lonely old man's fate. He was happy when Horace found Miz Kate and got it in his head to settle down. Lord knew he'd rest a whole lot easier once the two of them were finally married. Of course, judging from the way they had been tripped up by fate—twice now—Isaac wasn't anticipating a smooth glide down the aisle.

His eyes misted over with tears again. For a moment Horace looked like a boy, sleeping so soundly, hugging that pillow the way he used to hug that old toy monkey Isaac had made for him out of cotton batting and a pair of red wool socks. The boyishness disappeared then, replaced by bone weariness. He had the look of a man who'd been to hell and back.

But he was back. That's what was important. He was back. And he had a whole life—a fine, high-spirited woman, a pretty blue-eyed little girl—waiting for him.

Isaac sighed softly. "You gladden my heart, Horace," he whispered as he sat keeping watch over the son he never had, the son he'd almost lost.

"Wake up, you old coot."

Isaac's head jerked up. He rubbed a big knuckle in one eye, then focused on Race and smiled. "If you ain't a sight for my sore old eyes, Horace. How're you feelin', boy?"

Race grinned as he shoved the pillow under his head and crossed his arms over his chest. "Like I was run over by a locomotive. Twice. How've you been, partner?" His voice thickened with emotion. "By God, it's good to see you."

The black man leaned forward and rested his elbows on his knees, rubbing both eyes now as if cinders had suddenly lodged there. He snorted indignantly then. "You got me blubbering. I ain't done that since I was a pup."

Race just lay there grinning while Isaac pulled a bandanna from his back pocket, wiped his eyes and then sonorously blew his nose. "You all done bawling now, old man?"

"Your eyes ain't any too dry, Horace," he said, stuffing the handkerchief back into his pocket. "You look thin, too. You been eating right?"

"Thin! You should have seen me a few months ago. I've been eating like a mule just to put back half the weight I lost." He eyed his partner's middle. "You're spreading over your belt a little more than you were two years ago."

Isaac sucked in his belly. "That's just ol' Mr. Gravity working on me."

"Mr. Gravity and Mr. Mashed Potatoes and Gravy," Race countered. "You still overly partial to cream gravy, Isaac?"

The black man quirked up an eyebrow. "You want to lay there and jaw about vittles all night, Horace, or you want to ask me about Miz Kate?"

Race's broad grin disappeared. "I was kinda working my way up to it, Isaac." That was one way of putting it, he thought, when what he was doing was being a coward and postponing any bad news Isaac might have for him. "Two years is a long time, and Kate's a beautiful girl," he said hesitantly.

"Beautiful woman," Isaac corrected. "Miz Kate done growed up a whole lot while you were gone. And that baby girl of hers is walking now. Walking and starting to talk. Why, just this evening she said..."

"All right, Isaac," Race snapped, not eager to hear details of Ned Cassidy's child, at least not yet. "Just tell me."

"Tell you what, Horace?"

Race rolled his eyes. "Did she wait, dammit?"

"For you?" Isaac's mouth twitched with mirth.

"Yes, for me, for God's sake!"

"Don't know why anybody'd want to wait for such an ill-tempered young cuss when she could have her pick of all the fine officers here at the fort. Don't know why—"

Race interrupted him now not with heated words but with a look hot enough to melt iron.

"Well, of course she waited for you, Horace." He grinned from one ear to the other. "What female in her right mind wouldn't?"

Without realizing it, Race had been holding his breath. He released it now in a long and ragged sigh as his eyes closed briefly. "It would have just about killed me, Isaac, if she hadn't. I don't know if I'd have made it, especially the last year, if I hadn't had Kate to hold on to. You can't imagine..." His voice subsided to a whisper. "I better get to heaven, partner, because I sure can't stand any more hell."

"I'm listening," the old man said softly.

"There was this boy," Race began, "this skinny, dumb, sweet farm boy named Creel. He thought he was going off to glory when he signed up. He thought the girls back home would be fighting to be first in line to kiss him when he got back." His voice broke. "Damn, dumb kid. He thought he'd get back. And I tried like hell, Isaac. I tried like hell."

He closed his eyes tightly, knowing Isaac would wait patiently—forever, if necessary—for the rest of the story. Only Race wasn't sure he'd ever be able to tell it, or for that matter even want to tell it. He wasn't sure if all that pain and stink and hell deserved a telling. It might be better just to bury it inside him. Bury it so deep he might even forget it one day. One day—if he lived a century or two.

From that first evening in Mississippi when Race had walked out of the woods, there had been little hope of escape. The boy had taken sick immediately. Race could have gotten away—Lord, how he'd wanted to—but not without the boy. So he had stayed with him in the rat-infested prison at Belle Isle and later in that hellhole called Andersonville, cajoling him, coaxing him, and finally just plain bullying Creel into staying alive.

Race's health had been good at first, but not even the strongest and the fittest prisoner could escape all the diseases that ravaged the men. But as his own body began to weaken with scurvy and malaria, he managed to maintain a certain strength of will and purpose. If nothing else, it was pride and stubborn endurance. Race had made up his mind to see that young Creel survived. That goal had kept him going.

That and his dreams of Kate. Race relived their Fourth of July again and again, made love to her in his dreams, and held her vividly—her sunstruck red-gold hair, her emerald eyes—in every waking thought. At first. When he'd told Isaac that he couldn't have survived without thinking of Kate, it wasn't exactly the truth. Slowly, as the months passed, Race began to relegate his Kate to a locked portion of his heart. Somehow, as time dragged on and as the nightmare of prison life grew worse, he didn't want his love for her to be touched by what was happening to him. With an effort of will, he closed the door on those memories and dreams. The heaven of Kate and the hell of his circumstances were not meant to be allied in any way.

For all those long months he had kept Private Creel the center of his hellish existence. And then the boy had just closed his eyes one night and died. Without a word. Without so much as a whimper. Race had picked up his thin, cold body, had stumbled to the place by the gate where they stacked the dead like so much cordwood, and then had lain down beside Creel. Turned out it was the perfect escape, even though that hadn't been his intention. He simply hadn't been able to let the boy go. Race wasn't even sure now if he hadn't somehow thought he could wrestle the dead soldier back from the pearly gates.

It was only later—after living like a starving, half-blind animal in the Georgia woods, when the Union troops had practically walked over him while he slept—that Race came to his senses.

He had escaped. He had survived. He was alive. By then it didn't seem to matter much. He was so weak he could barely walk. His ribs stuck out. The scurvy that made him blind at night also made his teeth feel like loose change in his mouth. The troopers had looked at him as if he were a hundred-year-old man. "Poor devil," he'd hear them whisper. They had offered him food—hardtack, jerky, dried fruit—and then had shaken their heads sadly when all he could do was stare stupidly at sustenance he couldn't chew or even keep down.

"Well, hell," Race muttered now, aware of Isaac's patient gaze. "It doesn't do much good to look back. Won't help me get the freight business back in shape. And it for sure won't get my house back for me. I've got a lot of work to do, Isaac."

"Not so much," the older man said.

Race raised a curious eyebrow.

"The business has limped along without you, Horace. I'm taking six wagons north tomorrow as a matter of fact, then coming back with seven."

"Just what are you using for wagons? Those old ones were just about ready to fall apart. If you'll recall, that's how I wound up in Mississippi in the first place."

"Yup. I do recall that. I also brought that fact to the attention of General Sturgis. And I managed to make him feel so bad he had the army build us half a dozen heavy-duty vehicles. I picked 'em up last April."

Race shook his head in amazement. "You wily old bastard. I suppose you managed to talk the bank out of taking back my house, too."

"Nope. Sorry about that, Horace. The bankers took the house, the fancy linens, and all that fine silverware. They took it all, then proceeded to sell it real cheap."

"Hell," Race muttered. "Who bought it?"

"You're lookin' at him." Isaac's face broke into a gleaming grin. "I'm willing to negotiate as soon as you're feeling up to it, boy."

Race laughed. "With you? I've got the distinct feeling I'd be lucky to still have all my teeth after negotiating with you." He lapsed into silence for a moment, then looked at Isaac through a mist of tears. "I love you, you old buzzard. You know that, don't you?"

"I suspected as much, Horace. Still it's nice of you to say so. It surely is. And I'd say the same only I'd start blubbering again."

"Well, don't do that," Race teased. "You want your cot back, Isaac?"

The black man shook his head. "No. Room next door's empty. I'll just catch me a few winks in there." As he stood up to leave, Isaac reached toward the oil lamp. "I'll turn down this wick for you, Horace."

Race lifted a hand to stop him. "Just leave it," he said.

"You sure?"

He nodded.

Isaac nodded, too, as if he understood the need for a shield of light against the dark.

Althea Sikes stood at the open bedroom window looking out at the dark parade ground and the black sky above it. Hard as she tried, she couldn't blot out the sound of her husband's snoring—that wet, ugly noise that filled their bedroom night after night, that sometimes even seemed to rattle the porcelain figures and the cut-glass bottles on her dressing table.

She lifted a hand to finger the velvet drapes and found herself wondering if Race Logan snored, wondering if he grunted like a pig the way Frederick did, if he rolled away from a woman after he'd had her, or if he held her for a while. Race Logan was out there, damn him. He was back. The news of his return had spread through the fort like a flash fire. Everybody was so damn glad.

Ha! Althea hugged her arms about her as she stared harder into the dark. She wasn't glad. She had hoped the scoundrel was six feet under at the very least, or deeper—with his soul burning to a crisp in hellfire.

Everything had been going along so perfectly until today. She had kept Kate's dirty little secret from her parents back in Kansas, and had managed to turn it quite nicely to her own advantage. Nedda's trust provided Althea with the necessities that her tightfisted husband denied her. Frederick, damn him, would have her wearing gingham and eating off tin plates if he'd had his way. "What's this nonsense?" he'd say whenever a package arrived. Everything, Althea insisted—the bolts of satin and lace, the heavy English flatware, the embossed vellum from New York's most expensive stationer, everything—was a gift from her mother.

She could usually even squeeze out a few tears. "What can I do, Frederick? Mama misses me terribly. It would hurt her feelings so if I were to send anything back."

Kate, on the other hand, knew precisely where Althea's acquisitions came from, but either she was too afraid to do anything about it or too dim-witted to care. It was probably the latter, Althea thought, judging from the way Kate ran the shabby little general store. Money didn't seem to matter to her. Probably because she'd never had any. She never would, either. Not if Althea had any say in the matter.

The rhythm of Frederick's snoring picked up, and she twisted her head around to glare at his bulk in the bed. The bed she'd be abandoning just as soon as she conceived a legitimate Cassidy heir. But for all his grunting and groaning and sweating, her husband had proven to be useless on that score.

Her eyes searched the dark parade ground again. A little shiver of breeze came through the window, moving the silk of her nightgown against her skin like the caress of fingertips. He was out there. She should have known he'd come back. Men like Race Logan didn't die. They just kept turning up—like bad pennies—to tease and torment decent women. They treated ladies like whores while they gave their hearts to tramps like Kate the Gate.

Well, fine. Althea didn't want his heart. She didn't even want his body anymore. After three years of Colonel Sikes, her notions of pleasure had been dulled and deadened to the point where she didn't care if a man touched her ever again. But she cared about money and she cared about the fine things she felt she deserved. And she needed her niece—her *Cassidy* niece—to keep the Cassidy money flowing into her hands.

Chapter Fifteen

The wind gusted through the open front windows of the mercantile, spattering rain across the plank floor. Kate rushed to close the shutters, nearly tripping over Nedda, who was sitting cross-legged in the middle of the store, sucking on a peppermint stick.

"Ladrónes!" Fernanda muttered from behind the counter.

Kate rolled her eyes as she latched the wooden shutters against the sudden storm. Just what she needed, she thought. Another reminder about how the McMartin brothers had cheated her by stripping the building of all its fixtures before they left town. Another reminder about what a poor businesswoman she was.

"Thieves," the Mexican woman snarled.

"I heard you the first time, Fernanda." Kate stomped back to the counter, wiping her rain-wet hands on her apron. She didn't bother to disguise her exasperation—at the McMartins or at Fernanda now. "I'll order that window glass just as soon as I can. I told you that."

"*Sí.* You told me two years ago when I first came to work for you. You tell me each time it rains. 'Fernanda, I will order that glass.' *No soy sorda, señora.*" She tilted her head and clapped the palm of her hand to her ear to prove she wasn't deaf.

"Well, I'm not deaf, either," Kate shouted, "and I'm not made out of money."

At the sound of her mother's shrill tone, little Nedda began to cry.

Kate glared at the Mexican woman. "There. Now look what you made me do," she said as she hurried to pick up the squalling child, who proceeded to sob louder when she dropped her peppermint stick onto the floor.

Fernanda merely gazed at the two of them, clucking her tongue.

"What?" Kate spat. "What am I doing wrong now?" She moved the little girl onto her hip to free one hand for gesturing. "Let's see. I need window glass. I know you think I need to have more shelves built. Oh, and bigger, fancier jars for the pickles. What else?" Kate's color was rising with her voice.

The Mexican woman shifted her gaze to the small steel box on the counter in front of her.

"The cash box!" Kate exclaimed, raising her splayed hand toward the ceiling now. "I nearly forgot that. Of course, I need one of those fancy registers, too, don't I? The ones with all the buttons and the bells and the nice little drawers. All right. I'll put that on my list, too." She paused only long enough to increase the heat of her glare and to draw a breath. "Anything else?"

"Sí," Fernanda said.

"Well?" Kate tapped one foot as she jostled the sniffling Nedda on her hip. "Go ahead, Fernanda. Exactly what else do I need?"

"*Un hombre,* Señora Cassidy. You need a man."

Kate's jaw dropped. She cast about wildly in her brain for a reply, but there was none so she just stood there, staring blankly at the woman behind the counter.

As a satisfied grin shaped her mouth, Fernanda crossed her arms. "You see? I am right."

Finding her voice once more, Kate replied, "I don't see anything of the kind."

"You think about it, *señora.*" She nodded toward the shuttered windows at the front of the store and then at the metal cash box. "The glass. The fancy register. You don't need those so much. And I know they cost a lot of money. What you need is a man who will warm your bed at night." She smiled as she rubbed her fingers together. "And that, *señora,* is free."

Free, Kate thought later after Fernanda had taken Nedda upstairs for her nap. Nothing was free. Not for her, anyway. She opened the lid of the cash box, scowling at the coins, the single worn greenback, and the growing stack of IOUs. "Free!" She slammed the lid down on the box. "I need money, dammit, not a man," she muttered.

With the front shutters closed against the wind and the rain, the only light came from the window directly behind the counter. It was too dark for customers, Kate thought, but she hesitated lighting a lamp. Sure, there was plenty of kerosene available, but it wasn't truly hers and she tried hard to be disciplined about the merchandise. It was too easy, taking a peppermint stick from the candy jar for Nedda or unrolling a bolt of gingham and cutting off a few yards. She tried hard not to take what she couldn't afford. It was tempting, too, to pay Fernanda's wages out of the inventory. But if she kept doing that, there wouldn't be anything left to sell much less give away.

Sometimes she thought it had been easier being poor with nothing than poor in the midst of plenty as she was now in the store. Sometimes she found herself laughing like a lunatic thinking she was in such dire financial straits while her daughter—Miss Edwina Cassidy—was a confounded heiress. Kate had toyed with the notion of asking Althea for a loan from Nedda's trust, but then had decided against it. No sense both of them—Aunt Althea and Mama, too—stealing from a little girl.

This rain wasn't helping business any, either, she thought as she turned and stood on tiptoe to look out the window. She wondered if Isaac had decided to put off his trip north until the weather cleared. Probably not. He'd probably just stubbornly insist that this was the day he'd planned to leave and that was what he was going to do. Mule-headed old geezer.

Kate sniffed now as she drew her shoulders up stiffly. Well, maybe after the snit she had thrown last night, Isaac wouldn't be so mule-headed about Race anymore. And maybe after her little snit this afternoon, Fernanda would keep a civil tongue in her head and quit yapping about the *hombre* Kate and her bed were lacking.

She needed window glass, Kate thought, and sturdy shelves and, yes, maybe even a plain cash register. She needed just plain cash. But a man in her bed? That was the very last thing she needed.

Water dripped from the brim of Race's hat and ran in glistening sheets off the rubber poncho he had pulled from his saddlebag. Damn storm had blown up out of nowhere this afternoon. Of course, if he had done what he should have, he'd be in Loma Parda already. But he'd found a thousand excuses to hang around the fort—lingering over coffee with Isaac, checking out his wagons before they rolled, then packing his saddlebags and repacking them when they didn't feel just right.

Mostly because he didn't feel just right. Those cold, bony fingers kept teasing along his spine, never quite gripping him but never quite dissipating either. Finally he'd told himself it was now or never. He could sit around the fort feeling sorry for himself, or he could get on his horse, get to Loma Parda, and get on with his life.

It would have been nice to attribute all of his uneasiness to the malaria that kept on clawing at him or the fact that he'd barely slept the night before after Isaac had left him. But the fact of the matter was that he had a bad case of nerves about seeing Kate again. He'd spent the hours until dawn tossing and turning, with the damn cot collapsing twice under the strain.

Kate—all grown-up according to Isaac. That wasn't how Race pictured her. The image he had carried in his heart these past two years had been of a barefoot girl standing stiff and proud in the center of a mean crowd. A girl in homemade muslin with a basket of stolen apples. A woman-child who had looked at him with the green promise of spring in her eyes and who had needed him as surely as she had needed shoes on her pretty feet.

He tugged back on the reins now, halting his horse in the center of the narrow bridge that spanned the Mora River. Shoes! He'd meant to bring her shoes, a gift, something. Instead he was just hauling his own abused carcass through a storm, riding toward her, rain soaked and empty-handed, without so much as an apple to give her as a token of his love.

Race stared down into the rushing stream. He was still a rich man. Isaac had seen to that. He could still give Kate the fancy house and fine frocks and footwear beyond her wildest dreams. Hell, he didn't even know if she wanted them anymore. She had changed. That's what Isaac said. But how? How had she changed?

He knew how he had changed, Race thought dismally now. When he'd met Kate that high-flying Fourth of July, he'd been two hundred twenty pounds of hard and cocksure muscle, the swaggering master of the Santa Fe Trail, the legendary killer of Indians and breaker of female hearts.

Reaching inside his poncho, he extracted a cigar and a match from the pocket of his shirt, thinking a smoke, like a quick shot of whiskey, might help brace up his nerves and put a touch of swagger back in his outlook. But his hands were shaking so badly he could barely connect the flame to the end of the cheroot and finally, when he inhaled the smoke, it seared his lungs and set him to coughing.

His horse twisted his big head back and gave Race a one-eyed glare, as if to say "What a sorry specimen you are."

"Yeah, well, I won't be her first," Race grunted as he pitched the cigar into the rain-swollen stream and gave the animal a quick kick in the ribs to move him forward. "If she'll have me," he added under his breath. Hell, he didn't even want a damn horse to know how scared he was.

It came as somewhat of a relief to see that the town hadn't changed much in the two years he'd been gone. It was still a ragged little village where the dance halls and saloons outnumbered the respectable establishments three to one. The big block-lettered sign on the two-story stone building caught his eye. Cassidy's Mercantile.

With a muted curse, he dismounted and led his horse to the hitching rail in front of the store. He stepped from the muddy street onto the wooden planking, then proceeded to scrape his boots. Finally, when there wasn't a trace of mud left, he simply stood there trying to let his ragged breath level out, to tamp down the panic that was rising in his chest, to relax the muscles that were cramping up in his shoulders.

The wind shifted suddenly, whipping his poncho against his knees. Race didn't know anymore if it was rain or sweat pouring off his face. But he knew one thing for sure—even a damn dog had sense enough to get in out of the rain.

Fingers trembling, teeth clenched, Race reached to open the door.

She was poised on a ladder, and in the gray wash of light from the open window, he saw her red-gold hair dancing like wind-kissed fire around her shoulders, saw her tiny feet peeking out from her skirt, and watched—mesmerized—as she reached through the window into the slashing rain. Her belled sleeves caught in the wind and made him think of angel's wings.

And heaven. He was home. "Katie."

She didn't move for a moment, just hung there as if in midair, with the light shining on her and the rain kissing her and the wind whipping her hair. And then she pulled the shutters closed.

Darkness rushed at him like a great black wave. For a second, with his vision so quickly snuffed out, Race couldn't even breathe. Desperately, like a drowning man, he reached out to steady himself, but there was nothing to hold on to but air. He could hear the clip of Kate's feet coming down the ladder, hear her startled little cries and the quick rustling of her skirts as she came toward him. But, no matter how hard he tried, he couldn't see her. Race opened his eyes wider. Then, as he strained to see, as he channeled all of his strength and will into that effort, the shakes hit him full force—like a sudden cannonball—bringing him instantly and heavily to his knees.

* * *

A little after three o'clock in the morning, Fernanda stood in the doorway to Kate's bedroom, her eyes red from lack of sleep, and her face a display of exhaustion. "The *niña* has gone back to sleep. I gave her a sip of water."

Kate glanced up as she continued to count the strong, steady beats in Race's wrist. "Why don't you go on home?" she whispered. "I think the worst is over."

The Mexican woman shrugged. It seemed as if she were too weary to remove herself from the threshold.

Kate let go of Race's wrist, used her own to brush her hair back from her forehead, then offered the woman a small, lopsided smile. "This is all your fault, Fernanda. You realize that, don't you?"

"Me?"

"You," Kate insisted. "Aren't you the one who kept telling me I needed a man in my bed?"

"Sí." She chuckled as she cast an exasperated glance toward the ceiling. "I prayed for that for you. For a man to warm your bed. I am afraid the good Lord misunderstood me."

Kate laughed. "Well, I'd be grateful if you wouldn't pray for me anymore. Lord only knows what might happen next."

Fernanda's expression became solemn. "I pray. I pray for you and for this man. For little Nedda, too. She will be so happy to have her papa here with her."

"I doubt he'll be staying," Kate said sharply. "And you're not to tell Nedda anything, Fernanda. Not one word. Do you hear me? And not one word to him."

She tilted her head toward Race. "He...he doesn't know."

"He will," Fernanda said softly. "And the *niña,* too. She will look at him as if she were looking in a mirror."

And shatter, Kate thought, when he leaves her. She watched quietly then as Fernanda picked up the pile of wet clothes they had taken off Race earlier.

"The rain has stopped, *señora.* I will hang these out back on my way home."

"Thank you, Fernanda."

Kate listened to the woman's heavy tread as she descended the stairs. She heard the front door close. And then all she heard was Race's labored breathing and the slight rattle of the iron headboard against the wall as he continued to shake.

With the covers drawn up to his chin she could hardly see him, but she had seen enough earlier to know that he had been very ill. He was still a big man, but she remembered when he was a giant, hard carved and bronzed from long days in the sun and the wind. Bigger, indeed, than life. Or maybe, she thought now, that was just a young girl's giddy recollection of a man who had blown through her life one hot summer night.

No. Race Logan was and always would be bigger than life. This afternoon, when she had turned and seen him standing in the middle of the store, he seemed to tower over her tallest shelves and his shoulders seemed too wide for the suddenly narrow aisle. He seemed to take up all of the available space, not to mention the very air, that Kate had found it nearly impossible to breathe. Even now as he lay here sick and shivering, his body made her good-size mattress look no larger than a child's trundle bed.

"So you're back," she whispered, shivering a little herself, wondering—this time—how long he would stay.

"Katie."

Her head snapped up at the sound of her name. Kate blinked, and found herself caught in a dazzling and lucid turquoise gaze. Her heart thumped against her ribs. Her blood began singing in her ears. Warmth rushed through her like a summer wind. Don't, she told herself. Don't be so eager to be hurt. Breathe, damn you, breathe. She sat up straight, filling her lungs, fussing with the loose edges of her wrapper and stray locks of hair.

He moved his arm from beneath the quilt and held out his hand toward her. Open. Trembling. But for that, Kate might have held back. The moment she saw those tremors, her hand moved as of its own accord into his warm, encompassing grasp.

His voice was unsteady, too. "Aw, hell, Katie. I'm sorry."

She could think of a score of things for which he might apologize, beginning with buying her basket of apples back in Leavenworth City, but Kate didn't think that was what he meant. Why would the wind apologize for blowing? "For what?" she asked softly.

"This. For falling flat on my face this afternoon. For lying here flat on my back. I wanted...I want..."

"Hush. You're ill. Why don't you close your eyes and try to sleep."

He moved his head back and forth against the pillow, eyes closed, teeth clenched against another onslaught of shaking.

She squeezed his hand. "I'll go see if I can find another blanket." Kate moved to stand, but Race didn't release her hand. He gripped it tighter.

"Come hold me. Let me hold you. Let me hold on to you for a little while."

She stood there, gnawing on her lower lip. It would help, she knew. The warmth from another body was better than any blanket. That was how she saw little Nedda through a bout of fever a few months ago, by curling her own body around her daughter's and giving her that healing, human warmth. But this wasn't a two-year-old child in her bed. And if she held him—God help her—she'd never want to let him go.

The headboard rattling harder against the wall convinced her. Race required more warmth than another blanket could supply. She eased her hand from his and began to shrug out of her wrapper, then paused. "I'll just turn down the lamp."

No, he wanted to shout, but he bit down on the urge, swallowed the panic that surged in his throat. It was bad enough already to have her see him this way. Adding his damn fear of the dark was more than his pride could bear. Maybe more than Kate could bear.

He watched as she reached toward the lamp, as she twisted down the wick. He watched the light sink and felt the darkness rise up around him, inside him. And then, into that cold, clammy dark, there came the palpable warmth of Kate's nightgowned body sliding next to his. He turned on his side and slipped his arms around her, pulling her against his chest, tucking his knees into hers, pressing his lips into her hair.

"Better?" she whispered. "Does that help?"

Race could only nod into her fragrant tresses, knowing if he spoke his voice would shatter, if he opened his mouth at all only a broken sob would come forth. A sob of utter despair sailing on a note of pure relief. Dear Lord, he hadn't known just how empty and cold and desolate he had been until Kate filled him with warmth and hope. He was home.

Unable to see, he stroked his hand down Kate's smooth arm to reassure himself that her presence was real. He'd held her in his dreams this way at Belle Isle, at Andersonville. No dream, however, felt so silken and so warm.

Then, just as he'd put away his dreams of Kate during his imprisonment—because her heaven and his hell could not abide together—Race put away his nightmares and his fears. He was home. In heaven. And, by God, he meant to stay.

Chapter Sixteen

Kate hiked up her skirts and stepped as carefully as she could over and around the mud puddles behind the mercantile. Race's clothes had been hanging in the bright sunshine all morning. She knew because she had gone to the window at least a dozen times just to look at them, the same way she had climbed the stairs to peek into her room and look at who owned them. Each time she had looked at him—the last time sprawled diagonally and facedown—a tiny ripple of excitement had coursed through her. Each time, too, she reminded herself that even though Race was here—now—he would probably be gone tomorrow. If not tomorrow, then the day after that. Most likely, just as soon as he was feeling better, he'd be on his merry, saddle-tramping way.

He'd had such a terrible night. Even after she got into bed with him, the shaking had continued at least another two hours. It had been severe enough to rattle Kate's own teeth as she lay in his arms. Finally, toward dawn, he had lain still and his breath on her neck became cool and even.

She could have left him then, eased out of his embrace without waking him, but she didn't. She had remained, her eyes closed and all of her senses intensely attuned to him. To the heat radiating into her from his chest. To the moisture at the backs of her knees where his crooked into hers. To the big warm hand that had found its way to her breast, had curved and settled as if that were where it belonged.

It didn't, Kate reminded herself now as she jumped over the last puddle between her and the clothesline. No matter how good that hand had felt, it didn't belong. Or even if it did—and Lord, how could anything that felt so right not belong?—it wasn't going to stay. Race wasn't going to stay. She could depend on him about as much as she could depend on...

On the wind that was whipping at his shirt right this minute, she thought, as she reached up and plucked it from the line. She held the soft white cotton to her face a moment hoping to catch his male scent, but she breathed in only sunshine and the juniper wood smoke that was carried on the wind. Perhaps that was his true scent, she thought mournfully. Sunshine and wood smoke. The essence of drifter.

"Honestly, Kate." Althea's voice was crisp and belligerent, like the yapping of a little dog. "Why you persist in doing your own laundry is beyond me. Look at you, out here like a servant while that Fernanda woman is just lazing around inside the store. You really should consider who you are."

Kate turned to see her sister-in-law moving across the yard, her ice blue eyes so intent on the laundry that she walked right through every puddle in her path, then came to a stamping halt dead center in the deepest puddle of all. Kate swallowed a giggle, imagining the blonde's voluminous underskirts soaking up that muddy water, like so many wicks, all the way to the dainty straw hat that sat atop her yellow curls.

Althea stabbed a finger at the clothesline. "What are you doing now? Taking in other people's wash?" Her nose crinkled in disgust.

Kate gave Race's shirt a shake, snapping it like a whip between herself and the blonde. "Whose business is it but mine?" She snapped the shirt again, just missing Althea's turned-up nose. "And, if you don't mind my asking, Althea, just what are you doing here anyway? I'm sure it isn't for a friendly little chat."

"As a matter of fact, I came to relay some news." As she spoke, her pale blue eyes fastened on the shirt in Kate's hands. Her mouth twitched and her eyes flew to Kate's. "That's his, isn't it?"

Fanning the white cotton out over the front of her skirt, Kate began to smooth the wrinkles from it. "His? Well, I'd say it's a man's shirt, wouldn't you, judging from the size of it? Look at these nice broad shoulders and these long, ample sleeves."

Althea widened her stance and planted her hands on her hips. "I should have known he'd make a beeline for you. Just like a randy hound after a bitch in heat." She poked a finger at the shirt. "And I suppose it took you all of five seconds to tear that off him after he arrived." Her hot glare seared the trousers still on the line. "How long did it take you to get those off, Kate the Gate? And where is that damn saddle tramp now, I'd like to know? Upstairs, naked in your bed?"

Kate couldn't stifle a laugh. Yes, there was a naked man in her bed—shivering and pale and ill. She wondered if the whole truth would be a disappointment, considering Althea's lurid curiosity. She wondered if the woman would even believe her. Probably not, considering her reputation, and Race's, as well. And, quite frankly, Kate thought, she didn't care if Althea believed her or not.

With slow deliberation, Kate folded the shirt in half lengthways. "Who's in my bed and whether or not he's naked is none of your business, Mrs. Sikes."

"You're wrong about that, Mrs. Cassidy," the blonde retorted. "It's very much my business when my innocent little niece is living in a house with such despicable goings-on. She's a Cassidy, and I simply will not allow you to raise her as trash."

Kate's knuckles turned white now as she clenched the shirt in her fists. "Don't you ever use that word in reference to my daughter."

"And don't you forget," Althea shot back, "that *your* daughter is a Cassidy. It was my poor dead brother who gave her a name and kept her from being a bastard when Race Logan ran off and left you."

Kate's eyes narrowed on her sister-in-law's pinched, angry face. The woman was heartless. She had had no use for Ned when he was alive. She'd had no patience with his disabilities and no appreciation of his gentle and generous nature. Now, though, he was her *poor dead brother,* and she continually beat Kate over the head with his memory.

Her concern for Nedda was on a par with the concern she had had for Ned when he was alive. Nedda meant one thing to her Aunt Althea—money. The Cassidy money she couldn't get her greedy hands on any other way.

That's why she was so hysterical now that Race had returned! It didn't have anything to do with whether or not he was in Kate's bed, whether or not it further tarnished her dubious reputation.

"You're afraid he's going to claim her!" The words came out of Kate's mouth the second the realization formed in her brain. "You're afraid you're going to be kicked off your little gravy train."

Althea's pinched face slackened with shock. "How dare you say that? How dare you? After all I've done for you and that little brat!" She tore the folded shirt from Kate's hands, dashed it to the muddy ground, and stamped on it as her voice rose to a high, tremulous whine. "I won't stand for it. Do you hear me, Kate? I will not stand for it. That damn saddle tramp can't just ride back into my life and ruin it again. I won't allow it."

As she stood watching her sister-in-law's tantrum, Kate felt a wild, uncontrollable bubble of laughter rising in her throat. Didn't Althea know he wouldn't stay? Did she imagine Race Logan was solid rock and not the wayward zephyr that Kate knew him to be? How could this woman believe a daughter would make any difference to the wind?

Race woke slowly. As always, before he opened his eyes, there was that moment of despair, that tiny withering of his soul when he thought he was back in the stench and the muck of Andersonville. But now the sound of female voices drifted through his consciousness, and he became aware of the soft give of the mattress beneath him and the feel and fragrance of the pillow into which he was pressing his face.

The down of the pillow muffled his groan when he came fully awake. Every muscle, every sinew and nerve hurt. He felt as if he'd been dragged twenty rocky miles behind a mule team. Even his hair hurt. And then he remembered. The fever. Kate. Sweet Lord, he was in her bed—facedown, and from the feel of the mattress beneath him and the covers over his back, without a stitch of clothes on.

He breathed in her sweet scent on the pillow, soured now by his sweat. Well, hell, he thought. At least he was home. He was right where he wanted to be, even if he had missed his own damn homecoming.

Opening one eye to test the darkness, he realized the shutters were ajar, enough to let some light in. Enough to let him see. And what he saw made him suck in his breath. Two eyes so like his own he thought he was staring in a mirror. Dark hair. His dark hair. A face shaped like his own. But delicate. Different.

The little vision smiled at him then—his own tentative, lopsided grin, the one that had stared back at him in his shaving mirror all these years. The same. But feminine. Different.

Race lifted his throbbing head. The little vision blinked her big turquoise eyes. Her smile—that damn familiar grin—increased. Delicate. Different. Daughter.

He mirrored her smile. "Hello, honey."

The little girl reached out. She touched the tear that had loosened from his eye and was trickling down the side of his nose. Then she jumped back when an exasperated sigh came from the direction of the door.

"Aiee! There you are, *niña*. You come now. Shh. I will swat your backside if you..."

Race shot up in the bed, grabbing the quilt around him as he glowered toward the gray-haired woman in the door. "Nobody's going to be swatting my daughter's backside, lady."

Fernanda's mouth gaped momentarily, then broke into a wide grin. "*Sí, señor,*" she said. "*Bienvenido, señor.* Welcome home. You are feeling better now, no?"

He muttered a quiet curse, casting a bleak, apologetic glance toward the little girl who was now holding on to the Mexican woman's apron strings. "Sorry. I'm not used to..."

"I understand, *señor.* I am Fernanda. I have taken care of this *niña* since she was so big." Fernanda measured a score of inches with her hands. "The *señora,* too. Now I take care of you. First I will bring you a big cup of coffee."

Race nodded his gratitude. "You don't happen to know where my clothes are, do you?"

"*Sí, señor.*" She angled her head toward the window. "They are out in the sunshine. I will..."

"Thanks. I can get them myself. If you'll just fix me that coffee, I'd be grateful. The *señora* doesn't happen to have any whiskey around, does she?" He let his gaze fall once again on the little girl as his breath whistled in through his teeth. "Kind of a...a..."

"A surprise, *señor?*"

"Yeah. A surprise," he said softly, unable to take his eyes off his own small image. "A damn miracle is what she is."

Fernanda raised her eyes heavenward. "Sometimes I pray right, *señor.* This time, anyway. *Gracias a Dios.*"

"Good Lord!" Althea's eyes widened and her jaw slipped a notch.

Kate turned, and her jaw came unhinged as well when she saw Race—broad shouldered, bare chested, a quilt slung around his hips—ambling toward them across the backyard. Her heart lunged within her, and her first instinct was to run to him. Then she saw the hard glint in his eye and her next instinct was to pick up her skirts and run in the opposite direction.

A second after she saw Race, her gaze dropped to Nedda, who was trailing after him in and out of mud puddles, grinning from ear to ear. Wings of panic fluttered in Kate's chest. No. She had planned to keep them apart, she thought wildly. They weren't supposed to meet. At least not until Kate knew which way the wind was blowing.

Dear God! Nedda was absolutely glowing. Kate had never seen her daughter smiling so brightly. She was lit up like a little candle as she traipsed along behind Race. Behind the wind. And the wind would turn, would blow her out, would break her tiny heart.

Kate's hands curled into tight fists as Race came to a stop in front of her. "Get away from my daughter," she snarled, reaching for Nedda and shoving the little girl behind her skirts.

"Mama!" Nedda wailed.

"Shush," Althea snapped at the child. "Shut your little mouth."

As one, both Kate and Race leveled glares at the blonde. As one, they told her to shut up, but Race's deep growl was louder.

"Shut *your* little mouth, Mrs. Sikes."

Instead, Althea's mouth flew open, along with her pale blue eyes. "How dare you speak to me that way? Just who do you think you are, Race Logan, waltzing out here half-naked and ordering people around?"

Race ignored her. He turned his back on Althea. His eyes sought Kate's and his voice was plaintive, barely above a whisper, for her ears alone. "Katie, why didn't you tell me? My God, why didn't you tell me?"

"Just when was I supposed to tell you, Race?" she hissed. "When you didn't come back to Leavenworth that summer? Or maybe when you rode away from us right after Nedda was born? When, Race?" Hot tears welled in her eyes. "When would have been a good time to give you the news? When were you listening?"

He bit off a rough curse. "She's my child, Kate. For God's sake, I had a right to know. I'm her father."

"Ha!" Althea wedged herself between them, thrusting her chin up into Race's face. "You think you can come back after all this time, talking about your rights? You don't have any, you damn saddle tramp. Ned Cassidy was that child's father. All you did was sire her. It was Ned who gave her a name."

Race's eyes blazed, first at Althea, then at Kate. He looked angry enough that moment to strangle them both. Fleetingly, Kate was glad he was forced to use his hands to keep the quilt wrapped around him.

Althea, however, seemed oblivious to his wrath. She began poking her finger into his face. "Her name is Edwina Cassidy, mister, and don't you forget it. Kate named her for my brother. For her *father.* Didn't you, Kate?"

The last thing Kate ever imagined herself doing was taking Althea's side in an argument. Still, she found herself nodding her head now. It was true, after all. The name, the legitimacy had been so important. She had been so fearful for her child. She still was, but for different reasons. As if needing to touch her now, to reassure herself of Nedda's very existence, Kate reached behind her, pulling the little girl closer into her hip.

Althea was up on tiptoe now, shaking a fist in Race's face. "Her name's Edwina Cassidy," she bellowed. "Cassidy." She reached around Kate then, catching Nedda by the shoulder and wrenching her forward. "Tell this awful man what your name is, honey," she screeched.

Kate was about to push her sister-in-law's hand away, but Race did it almost before she could react. He gave the blonde a killing look, as he knelt down beside Nedda, who clambered up gleefully when he patted his quilt-covered knee.

He looked at the child solemnly and his voice was smooth and low. "I guess we better set this lady straight right now, huh? What's your name, honey?"

The little girl replied with equal solemnity, "Honey."

Race angled his head up toward the two astonished women. His sea-colored eyes glimmered with triumph. "Guess that answers that. My daughter's name is Honey. Miss Honey Logan."

"Miss Honey Logan," Kate muttered as she stood looking out the back window—again. She'd nearly worn a path from the front of the store to the back during the past half hour.

After Race's outrageous announcement, she had snatched Nedda by the wrist and stomped back into the mercantile. She had sent the child upstairs with Fernanda to remove her from the fray, and then Kate had stood—arms crossed, foot tapping, temper boiling—waiting. And waiting. Damn that man! He'd remained out back, arguing with Althea. As if that horrible blonde had any say in the matter at all.

And now—damn them both—they weren't even arguing. They were lingering out there like long-lost friends, whispering and plotting like two conspirators. Althea was rubbing up against him like a cat, and Race seemed to be enjoying every minute of it. Kate's mouth thinned to a severe line. Well, at least he wasn't draped in that awful quilt anymore. He was wearing a pair of denims Fernanda had whisked from a shelf in the mercantile.

"I can't afford to be giving pants away," Kate had screamed at the Mexican woman, trying to tug them out of her grasp.

Fernanda had looked at her then as if Kate had been trying to snatch food from a starving child.

"Oh, all right," she had snapped, "but you tell him he has to pay for them. I'm not running a charity here, Fernanda."

She had thought she was running an infirmary, she thought now as she glared out the window. Race looked anything but sick in those denims that fit him like a second skin. He looked hard and lean and not at all like the feverish wretch who had spent last night shivering against her.

"What the devil are they talking about?" Kate didn't realize she had spoken out loud until Fernanda replied.

"The *niña, señora.* I heard them when I took the clean pants out to the *señor.*"

Kate sniffed. They could stand out there in the mud all day, or till hell itself froze over for all the good it would do them in making plans for her daughter. *Her* daughter. If there was any planning to be done, she'd do it herself, thank you very much. And she aimed to start by figuring out how to keep that child's little heart from being blown to smithereens. She leaned her head against the window frame, eyes closed, wondering just how she was going to do that for Nedda when she couldn't even manage it for herself.

She didn't hear him moments later when he came up behind her. Kate nearly jumped out of her skin at the sound of his deep voice.

"Where's Honey?"

She whirled around, her face just a few inches from his bare chest. Kate felt her heart plummet to the pit of her stomach at the sight of those hard planes, and found herself suddenly mesmerized by the soft swirl of hair, the sweet chocolate color of his nipples. No wonder her sister-in-law had been rubbing against him like a deranged feline. She dragged her gaze up to his face, to those two brilliant jewels he used for eyes. "Where's who?"

"My daughter," he said softly.

Kate snapped out of her daze. She took a step back and forced a brisk tone. "Nedda's upstairs taking her nap. She won't be awake for hours."

"Damn. I wanted to tell her goodbye."

"Goodbye?" Kate's voice wasn't so brisk as she repeated his words. In fact, it faltered badly when she added, "So soon?" She ought to have been glad, she told herself. Glad, thrilled to death, and jumping for joy that he was leaving before he'd done any irreparable damage to Nedda's heart. Her own, she thought bleakly, was beyond repair. And it had only taken him a single hot summer night.

Kate shrugged listlessly now. "I'll send your clothes if you'd like. If you have any idea where you'll be."

"I know exactly where I'll be, Katie. In fact, you can probably just wad those clothes up in a ball and toss them to me at Juan Baca's place."

Her eyes widened. "The dance hall down the street?"

"Uh-huh." He chuckled deep in his chest, then reached out to tip her chin up. "I'm staying, Katie. Only not here in your place. A proper father has to be concerned with appearances, so I'll take a room down the street." He paused, his turquoise gaze sweeping her face. "And then I'm coming back every day with candy for my daughter and flowers for her mama. I'm going to woo both my women, Katie. And then I'm going to marry you."

Come with me, Katie. I want to take care of you. The words echoed in her head. Why did he say things he didn't mean?

"I don't believe you, Race." Her wide eyes narrowed now. "And I don't trust you. I won't trust you with my child's heart. You can't just breeze through here, breeze through both our lives with candy and flowers and..."

He raised his other hand, anchoring her face for his jeweled, penetrating gaze. "You didn't hear me right, Mrs. Cassidy. I said I'm staying. I've got plans for us. For you and me, and for Honey."

Kate tried to jerk from his grasp. "I know all about your plans, Race." Hot tears welled in her eyes. "I trusted you and your damn plans when I was a foolish girl who didn't know any better. But I know better now. And I won't let you break my daughter's heart with a lot of plans and dreams that won't be coming true." She stamped her foot. "And don't be calling her Honey. Her name's Edwina Cassidy, in memory of Ned."

Race's fingers clasped harder around her head and his features tightened. His voice was harsh. "Let's talk about your dreams, Kate the Gate. All those high-flying dreams of a barefoot little schemer. Tell me. Did Ned Cassidy make them all come true after you sold yourself for his fine name?"

Kate lifted her hand to strike him, but Race caught her wrist in a crushing grip.

"Did he, Katie? Did Mr. Ned Respectable Cassidy make all your girlish dreams come true?"

"By God, he tried, Race. More than you ever did. You didn't even bother to come back."

"Well, I'm bothering now," he shouted, digging his fingers into her wrist. "And, by God, I'm back. And whether you like it or not, Mrs. Cassidy, I intend to be a father to my child. To *my* child. To Honey. I've lost two damn years of her life already and I don't intend to lose another single day. Do you understand?"

"I understand," Kate said through clenched teeth. "I've heard it before, Race. Remember?"

Chapter Seventeen

Race drained his whiskey glass, then set it on the table with a resounding thump. "I want a room, Baca. Just a room."

Juan Baca, the mustachioed dance hall owner, scooted forward in his chair, nodding agreeably. "*Sí,* Señor Logan. *Un cuarto.* And a woman." He gestured with a manicured hand toward the dozen or so dark-haired *señoritas* in assorted states of undress.

A whole new crop, Race noted, since the last time he'd been in here. Hell, it had been so long half of them probably hadn't even been born yet. He let out a sigh. "I don't want a woman," he said slowly and distinctly, thinking it was probably the first time that particular combination of words had been uttered in this particular place. Just as slowly, he added, "I want a room."

Baca nodded again, twitching his dark mustache. "*Sí.* I understand. You want a room. You look tired, Señor Logan. You need a little sleep, eh? I give you the room, then after you sleep, I will send up the woman. Which one do you want?" He pointed. "Rosa? Estella? How about Bonita, the little one over there with the big—''

''I just want a goddamned room,'' Race growled from between clenched teeth. His head was splitting and his backbone felt like a cold, twisted shaft of metal. The two slugs of whiskey he'd just knocked back were roiling in his gut. On top of all that, he felt like a heel for yelling at Kate the way he had a while ago. He'd been in a hell of a mood after listening to that simpering, yellow-haired she-cat, Althea Sikes, go on and on about her dear departed brother and her poor bereaved parents back in Kansas.

He'd finally just told her to get to the signature on the document. ''What the hell do you want, cat?'' he'd asked her. ''Money?'' At least she'd been honest enough to admit it. And he had told her just as honestly that he didn't give a mule's hind parts what she told her parents about Miss Edwina Cassidy. If she wanted to keep up the long-distance ruse and milk her folks of every cent they had, that was fine with him. He wouldn't get in her way.

She had blinked those watery blue eyes. ''Do you mean that?'' Of course he meant it. ''Just as long as you understand that she's mine now, cat. She's Honey Logan from this day on. She's not a Cassidy. And if I ever catch you anywhere near her, I'll skin you alive, Mrs. Sikes. Do we have a deal?''

The bitch had even tried to kiss him to seal the bargain. He probably shouldn't even have tried to talk to Kate right then. But he had tried, dammit, and he'd lost his temper when she had crooned about Mr. Ned

Respectable Cassidy, then had said she didn't trust Mr. Horace Saddle Tramp Logan as far as she could throw him. Didn't damn trust him not to hurt his very own daughter. He'd gone off like a shotgun, and wasn't even sure now what he'd said to her, although he had the sour feeling in his gut that he had called her Kate the Gate. He knew he'd made her cry. Then, as he was leaving, he'd flat out threatened her when he told her he'd be back tomorrow and, by God, she better be ready to go on a picnic, or else.

Her cheeks had been wet with tears and her whole body was shaking, but it hadn't kept her from sticking her sharp little chin right in his face. "Or else what, Race?"

"Damned if I know, Katie," he'd grunted. And damned if he knew now what he'd do tomorrow if she wasn't ready. And she wouldn't be. That had been obvious in her hot green eyes, in the way she'd slammed the mercantile door right in his face and yelled through the window, "Go to hell, Race."

"I've already been there, Kate," he'd yelled back. "I believe I'll just stick around here."

Damned if he even knew now why he wanted the little hellion the way he did. Except that he'd been besotted with her since the first time he'd laid eyes on her. Except that dreams of her were about all that had kept him going these last two years. Damnation! He even wanted her right this minute when he was mad as hell at her, when all he truly wanted to do was to lie down and close his eyes a while. Alone.

"Just let me have a room, Baca," he groaned. "I'll send word down when I want the woman, okay?"

The dance hall owner smiled broadly. He clapped Race on the back. "*Sí. Un cuarto* now, Señor Logan. A woman later." Baca winked. "You rest a while. You rest up for Bonita."

Kate shifted onto her side, trying not to wake Nedda, who—finally—slept soundly, her thumb tucked peacefully in her wet little mouth.

Drawing her knees up, Kate felt like sucking her own thumb, hoping to discover a little peace herself. Damn that man! He wanted to be a proper father, did he? Well, where was he all afternoon when Nedda glumly dragged around the mud-spattered quilt Race had worn? Where was he when she could barely eat her supper because her blue-green eyes kept darting toward the window, hoping to see his? Where was he tonight when his daughter cried out in her sleep?

Kate gnawed on a ragged cuticle. Promises! That's all he had to give. That's all he'd ever given her. Promises and dreams. *Come with me, Kate. I'll be your daddy, Kate. I'll take care of you.*

"No, thank you, Race." She said it softly, her lips barely moving. "No, thank you, Race. I can take care of myself." She said it now, the way she should have said it back in Kansas three years ago.

And she was prepared to say it again the next day at noon when he came swaggering through the front door of the mercantile, looking as if he owned the whole damn place along with the people in it. His eyes moved over the stock on the shelves as if he were taking inventory. Then they moved over Kate the same way.

"There's a buckboard and a picnic basket waiting out front, Kate."

She raised the hem of her apron to wipe pickle juice from her hands. Her voice was sharp as a tack. "I'm very busy today, Race. I can't just take off from the mercantile in the middle of the day."

One big hand moved to his hip, and for a second Kate believed he was going to draw his gun. That'd be just like him, she thought, taking what he wanted at gunpoint when his lazy, lopsided grin didn't work and those magnificent eyes failed to put his victim in a stupor.

But those sea-colored gems shifted to Fernanda, who was folding a bolt of cloth at the far end of the counter, and the lopsided grin was just for her. "You know all the ropes around here, Fernanda?" he drawled.

"Oh, *sí, señor.* The prices. The cash box. Everything."

Race's gaze cut back to Kate. "Well, there you go."

Kate crossed her arms and shoved her chin out. "I'm not—"

He moved so fast she barely knew what was happening, other than the fact that she was screaming and kicking as he hauled her over the counter and carried her out the door and plopped her onto the front seat of the buckboard, then vaulted up beside her.

"Race," she hissed.

"What, darlin'?" He slapped the reins over the paired bay geldings and they took off like a double shot.

Kate slammed back against the seat, the breath momentarily knocked out of her. Unable to speak, she lashed her foot out sideways, connecting with Race's ankle. Her hands balled into tight fists.

Race's voice was a barely audible growl above the fast clip of the horses' hooves. "I've got a length of rope back there, Kate. I'm warning you. If you hit me, I'll truss you up like a little heifer and drag you all the way to the river."

Her fists remained—tight and white—on her lap as she glared at him. "Just what in blazes do you think you're doing?"

"I'm courting you, goddammit. What the hell do you think I'm doing?" he yelled.

She couldn't help it. She laughed, seeing his mouth nearly white with rage and his black eyebrows all twisted together and his hands nearly strangling the reins.

"I'm glad you think it's funny, Kate," he muttered, staring straight ahead.

"It is funny." She tilted her face toward him. "But it isn't going to do you any good. Not one little bit."

All he did was raise an eyebrow and move his lips into one of those lazy, arrogant grins. But it was sufficient to make Kate swallow hard and to redouble all of her waning defenses.

Race pulled left on the reins when he saw just the spot he wanted—a grove of aspens where the Mora

River narrowed and rushed over a bed of rocks. He set the brake and twisted the reins around it, then jumped to the ground, wondering if he'd have to wrestle Kate out of the buckboard the way he had wrestled her into it.

Damn if she wasn't nearly as stubborn as he was. He had thought she was warming up when she laughed, but then she'd gone all frosty again, riding with her spine so stiff and brittle he thought it might just snap in two as the wagon rattled over the last hard mile of brush and chuckholes.

He raised his arms to help her down, fully prepared to deflect a blow from one of those balled-up little fists of hers.

When he clasped his hands around her waist, though, Race thought maybe he deserved to be punched right then and there for the hot rush of desire that shot through him, and the sudden, guilty knowledge that, because of his strength, he could satisfy those desires right here, right now, whether Kate was willing or not. Perhaps because of that guilt, he set her down with exquisite care and gentleness, removing his hands immediately and watching silently as she drew herself up like a major, as if she were the one in charge here. Well, hell, he supposed she was when it came right down to it.

He reached into the bed of the buckboard and grabbed the blanket and the double-handled picnic hamper, then strode to the riverbank where he snapped the blanket out and let it flutter to the ground. Kate plopped down immediately, glaring at him and crossing her arms. He sighed slightly as he knelt beside her.

"Hungry, Katie?"

She shook her head and bit her lower lip.

Race stretched out. "Well, I am. Why don't you pass me that picnic basket."

She snatched at it, but looked surprised when she couldn't lift it with one hand. "What's in here? Bricks?" With two hands and a little grunt, she placed the hamper between them.

"Open it," Race said quietly.

Kate leaned over and lifted the lid. Her breath caught in her throat. Apples! The basket was full to the brim with lovely green apples. Her gaze fluttered to Race's soft smile. "You remembered."

"I'm not likely to forget the most important day in my life, Katie. I remember every detail—from your high-buttoned white dress to your pretty little bare feet."

She took an apple, polished it with her apron and handed it to Race. When she took another, Kate held the ripe, warm fruit for a moment in the palm of her hand. She remembered, she thought. She remembered knowing the moment she saw this man that her life would never be the same. Only she had thought it would be full of warmth and joy, not the empty-hearted pain and yearning the last couple of years had brought.

"You're gonna rub all the color right off that apple, Katie." Race's voice was barely more than a whisper.

Kate blinked. "I was just…just remembering." She bit into the sweet fruit, warm from the brisk polishing. She chewed thoughtfully a moment. "I stole those apples, you know."

Race tossed a core over his shoulder, then reached into the basket for another. "You stole more than that, Katie. You stole my heart." He gave a little tug to the hem of her apron. "You've been carrying it around in your pocket ever since."

The deep and sensuous timbre of his voice throbbed in the pit of her stomach. Her heartbeat quickened. She struggled to reinforce her failing defenses, rearranging her apron, fidgeting with a loose thread. "Well, that explains it then."

He wiped a streak of apple juice from his chin with the back of his hand. "Explains what?"

"Why you've behaved so heartlessly and why you—"

"Don't start, Kate." Race sighed and lifted a hand toward the sky. "We've got a crystal blue sky, Katie, without a storm cloud in it. It's too fine a day to argue. Let's see if we can't find one square inch of common ground, one little patch of conversation that isn't mined with explosives. How about if we pretend we're old friends who are just a little bit glad to see each other?"

She bit off a chunk of apple. "All right," she replied casually. "How've you been, Race?"

"Awful. My leg was busted three years ago. My heart was broken when my girl married somebody else. Then the Rebels tossed me in jail and tried to bust what was left of me. How 'bout you?"

"I've been fine. Just fine. Making money hand over fist at the mercantile. I'm even considering expanding it. And Nedda—"

"Honey," he corrected.

Her green eyes grew hot. "Don't you start."

Race threw up his hands, and after a gruff curse, he stood and walked to the river.

Kate pitched her half-eaten apple at his back. What did he expect? They weren't old friends. They'd been lovers for a single night. All they had between them was a beautiful child and a lot of broken promises. Perhaps if she knew him better, she thought, if they were truly friends, she might understand his wandering and might even be able to forgive him for breaking all those promises. She shaded her eyes from the glint of the sun on the river and called out to him.

"You know what our problem is, Race. We don't know each other well enough to be friends. I mean, you really don't know the first thing about me. Not really. For instance, what's my favorite color?"

He turned, giving her a blank stare. "Hell, I don't know, Kate. Red? Blue? Who cares?"

"Friends do. And they know about things like that. What's yours?"

"What's my what?"

"Your favorite color," she snapped.

"I don't have one. I never thought about it. Damn!" Race ripped his fingers through his hair.

"Old friends don't curse at each other, either," Kate shouted.

"You drive me to it, Katie. I swear, you drive me to it. You want me to pick a favorite color. All right. Fine. How about black? Just like my mood."

Kate sniffed disdainfully. "You're impossible, Race Logan. How do you expect to find any common ground when you won't even answer a simple question?" She gathered up her skirts, stood and shook them out with a vengeance. "And, anyway," she shouted over her shoulder, "black's not a color."

That did it. Race covered the ground between the riverbank and the blanket in a few long strides, grabbed Kate by the shoulders and brought her hard against him. He bent his head and rasped at her ear. "You want colors, Katie? How about the blue of a sky on a hot July afternoon? Or the sweet, sweet green of a young girl's eyes when she was giving herself to me for the very first time? Those are my favorite colors. They're the only ones I even know anymore." His lips drifted over her soft, fragrant hair, and his harsh tone diminished to a whisper. "Maybe we can't be friends, Katie. Maybe we don't even know how. But, Lord Almighty, we once knew how to be lovers. We lit up the night with our loving."

She tipped her head back, drinking in the intensity of his gaze, reveling in his hard warmth, shivering when he dipped his head to tantalize a corner of her mouth with his lips.

"Do you remember, Katie?" he whispered, moving his hand into her hair, threading his fingers through it, drawing her head back farther so her mouth was directly beneath his own.

Her words were little more than breath. "I remember."

"So do I, love." His mouth slanted over hers with a searing heat. His tongue traced the seam of her lips.

If Race's arm hadn't slipped around her waist, Kate would have sagged to the ground. When she lifted her arms to encircle his neck, her mouth opened beneath his like a flower, and his deep, claiming kiss poured sunshine through her, lashed her senses with summer rain and hot lightning, and filled her with a wild and willful weather.

Race dragged his mouth from hers, crushing her small body against him, breathing in the rich warmth of her sunstruck hair, still tasting her ripe kiss, reeling from it. He'd meant to take it slow. He'd meant to. But now his heart was ramming against his ribs, and the rest of him was aching with a need so hard he thought he'd explode.

Not quite the way he'd planned it, he thought dismally. If she hadn't trusted him before, it was a pretty sure bet she wouldn't trust him after he'd tossed her onto a picnic blanket and taken her with all the slow deliberation of a firecracker. And considering that their one and only episode of lovemaking had resulted in little Honey, Race wasn't about to take that chance again. Not until he and Kate reached some kind of an understanding about their future, anyway. If they were going to start a new little Logan every time they came together, he wanted to make damn sure those children arrived safe and secure within the bonds of wedlock.

He drew in a ragged breath and reached up to slip her arms from around his neck.

"Katie. Darlin'. Let's go for a walk and cool off. Let's get to be friends."

She blinked as if she didn't know the meaning of the word, as if he had said something in a foreign language. Race moved his thumb across her mouth, still wet from his kiss. His own mouth hooked in a grin. "Colors, love. Come on. Let's ramble on about colors for a while."

Hours later, Kate gazed at the dwindling colors of the setting sun. The oranges had blazed out moments before. Now there were only soft pinks and a few bright threads of turquoise. She crooked her arm under her head, then studied the man who was sleeping beside her, wishing she could see his eyes, for, of all the colors in the universe, that particular blue was her favorite. Race's eyes. And Nedda's.

She smiled softly. They weren't quite friends yet, but they had made a little wary progress as they'd walked for miles this afternoon. Walked and talked and refrained from touching each other with anything but their glances. Then they'd eaten more apples, and Kate had fallen into an exhausted slumber. Judging from the sunset, she supposed she'd slept a good two hours.

Race, too, perhaps. She was glad of that, because she had noticed the dark shadows beneath his eyes as the day lagged on. When she'd asked, he claimed he'd slept the night before, but she didn't quite believe him. He'd told her a little about the rebel prisons this afternoon, told her enough for her to guess the agony and horror of what he wasn't telling her. It helped her understand him. Not completely, but better.

Sadly though, she didn't think he'd be around long enough to truly get to know him. He was putting on a good show with this courting business. Heaven knows he'd been a gentleman this afternoon, and had mustered more restraint than she had been able to during that sizzling kiss. She vowed to do better in the future. After all, it wouldn't be that long before he was riding off on one excuse or another.

She traced a finger along the shadowy line of his jaw, then laughed as he twitched and swatted her hand away. "Wake up, lazybones," she said. "The sun's going down. We best start back."

He opened one eye. Already it was hard to bring her pretty face into focus. Colors had already drained from his vision. Soon it would be shapes. And then... "Hell and damnation, Katie," he snarled. "Why didn't you wake me sooner?"

He got to his feet quickly and then bent to tug the blanket out from under her.

"Race, for goodness' sake!" Kate scrambled up as he was shaking the blanket out, then snapping it in half, then half again.

"Here." He thrust the folded blanket at her, then picked up the hamper and began walking quickly toward the buckboard.

Kate opened the blanket and began to refold it properly. If he was so damn anxious to get away from her, she muttered to herself, why'd he ever drag her out here in the first place?

"Will you hurry up?" he shouted back to her. Race slammed the basket into the back of the wagon, then squinted west. He could do it. They were just a few miles from town and if he ran the horses flat out, they could be back before it was completely dark. Even if it got pitch-black, he figured, the horses would find their way to the livery stable and their waiting bag of oats.

He pulled himself up into the seat and unhooked the reins from the brake. Hell, now he knew just how poor old Cinderella felt when she had to beat it away from the ball by the stroke of midnight. Only he didn't even have that much time. In about twenty minutes he was going to be blind as a bat, and if Kate couldn't bring herself to trust a sighted man, she sure as hell wasn't going to put her trust in a blind one.

He ought to just sit her down and tell her. "Katie, after the sun goes down and the lamps go out, I'm blind as a bat. It happened to a lot of prisoners. Scurvy. Damn rebs could barely feed themselves, much less thirty thousand starving Yanks. It's supposed to improve. That's what they tell me. It shouldn't make any difference. With us, I mean."

If Isaac were here, that's what he'd tell Race to do. "Just go on and tell her, Horace. It don't make no difference, anyhow."

Only it did—dammit. It did. All his notions about loving Kate were bound up with his pride, with his belief in his ability to take care of her and their daughter, and with his deep need for her to trust him completely. How could she trust him to care for her or little Honey if he couldn't even see his hand in front of his face?

The light was fading so fast now that the horses were mere shadows. Panic filled his chest, hardly allowing him to draw a clean breath, as Kate climbed up beside him.

They'd gone about a mile when she suddenly leaned against him, her fingers clamping on his thigh, her voice high and tight.

"The horses are drawing awfully close to the river, Race."

He pulled back on the reins, his teeth clenched so hard he could barely speak. "Fine, Kate. If you don't like the way I'm driving, why don't you just go ahead and do it." Race slapped the reins into her lap.

"I wasn't implying—"

"Let's just get going, all right?" he snarled.

"Fine." Kate snapped the reins over the horses' rumps, pulling them left and away from the dangerously close riverbank. All the way back to town she bit her tongue. It had been such a lovely day. She had felt their friendship blossoming. Until sunset, when Race seemed to close up like one of those flowers that turn in on itself toward the end of day.

She'd seen him gazing at the setting sun, and she'd watched those beautiful eyes of his fill with sadness and longing, probably wishing he were going wherever the sun was going—west, over the mountains, away. In a way, she thought, she didn't begrudge him. If she had been born a man, she might have had that same wanderlust in her. She might have been free as a breeze, too. But she wasn't. She wasn't a man. She was a woman. A woman with a child who needed deep, secure roots.

Race wasn't going to stay. Not when there was *going* to be done. She almost wished now that he'd just pick up and do it tomorrow. It was too painful having him try so hard to convince her he wasn't going to go.

The front of the mercantile was dark when Kate pulled the wagon to a halt.

"You needn't bother seeing me in," she said as she held out the reins to Race.

"All right," he said as he stared straight ahead.

Kate lifted the reins a few inches. "Here."

"Here what?"

"Take the reins, Race, unless you want these horses to..."

His head jerked toward her and his eyes seemed to focus just over her shoulder. "I'll take them."

Kate looked down at his open, waiting hand. In the faint light from a sliver of moon, his palm glistened with sweat. And he was still not quite looking at her. It reminded her of the way blind people's gazes were almost, but not quite, on target. She moved the leather straps a little farther away from him.

"Go ahead. Take them, Race," she said quietly.

His mouth twitched with irritation, then he reached for the reins and missed, clamping his fist around thin air. With a muttered curse, he reached again and this time caught a handful of Kate's skirt.

"All right, Kate," he growled. "You've had your fun. Now give me the goddamn reins." He opened his hand once more, wet palm up.

"You can't see!" She hadn't meant to exclaim it, but she could hardly catch her breath.

He sat there a moment, a muscle jerking in his cheek and his jawline rigid. "Fine. I can't see. I'm blind as a damn bat. I admit it. Does that make you happy, Kate?"

"Oh, Race." Kate slid her hand into his, barely able to see now herself because of the tears that welled up in her eyes. She could barely speak for the sobs that were choking her. Dear God, she thought, it did make her happy. It filled her with a terrible, unforgivable joy, because now she knew he would stay.

Chapter Eighteen

A single lantern cast a soft yellow light on the haystrewn floor of the livery as Kate guided the team and wagon through the open doors.

Gilly Johnston, the stable keeper, peered out from a back door. A napkin was tucked into the open collar of his shirt and his mouth was full of biscuit. "Evenin', Miz Cassidy. Logan. You can leave 'em right there. I'll get to 'em soon's I finish up my supper."

"That will be fine, Mr. Johnston," Kate said.

"Just set the brake, if you will, ma'am."

"All right," she said. But before she could respond, Race reached for the wooden lever, jerking it up viciously.

"That'll do it," Johnston said. "Thanks, folks. I'll just get back to my meal now if you don't mind."

When the stable keeper disappeared, Kate glanced at Race. He was staring straight ahead, his mouth drawn into a tight, hard line. "Here," she said softly, offering him the reins that he hadn't been able to see before.

He took them now without hesitation and looped them easily over the brake. He sat there then, silent as a stone.

Kate bunched up her skirts, climbed down and walked around the back of the wagon. She lifted the lantern from its hook on a stall door. "Mind if I borrow your lamp to see us across the street, Mr. Johnston?" she called.

"Help yourself" was the garbled reply.

Slowly then, the way she would have approached a wounded animal, she walked to Race's side of the wagon. If she blew the lantern out, Kate thought, she could plunge him into darkness once more. He would hardly be able to get down from the wagon without her help. He was forced now to depend on others. How he must hate it!

And, heaven help her, how she loved it. But she couldn't let him know that. She had to find the right words. Men didn't take comfort easily from women. Even Ned, who had needed it so, had found her care and comfort hard to bear. And Race Logan had more pride and pure stubbornness in his little finger than Ned had had in his whole poor body.

Kate stood beside him quietly a moment, then lifted the lantern so its light shone between them. "Marry me, Race."

He turned slowly, looking down at her from the seat. His eyes were like sapphires in the lantern's light. There was more than a little suspicion in them, and the leeriness of a cornered animal.

"Marry me," Kate said again, a little more urgently this time. "Come be with me and Ne...with Honey."

Race didn't say a word. He merely stared at her, his jeweled eyes hooded now.

Kate lifted her chin. "Did you hear me?"

"I heard you, Katie." His voice was low and rife with suspicion.

"Well?"

He shook his head slightly. "Why now?" he asked, reaching out to touch a lock of her hair. A note of bewilderment crept into his voice as he let her hair sift through his fingers. "You wouldn't have me when you thought I was in pretty fair shape. Now you know I'm not and you're saying you want to marry me." His mouth slid into a mournful grin. "Maybe that night blindness has addled my brain along with my eyes, Kate, but I can't even pretend to understand what's going on in your head."

"It's not my head, Race. It's my heart. I...I trust you now."

He raised his eyes to the ceiling above. "She trusts me!" he muttered, then glared again at Kate. "Because I'm blind and useless half the damn time?"

"No. Because I believe you now. I believe you when you say you'll stay."

Again he shook his head in bewilderment. "That's a hell of a note, Katie." He laughed softly. "In a single breath you've just called me a liar, as well as a feeble sap who can't get a mile down the road alone anymore. If you're doing this just because you feel sorry for me—"

"Sorry's the last thing I feel, Race," she shot back. "Love's what I feel. I always have."

One dark eyebrow arched. "But you love me a little better now that I'm hobbled, is that it?"

"No," she protested. "That isn't it at all. It's..." Tears gathered in her eyes, and she lifted her shoulders in helpless frustration.

Race sighed roughly. Then, in what seemed like a single movement, he got down from the wagon, put the lantern on the seat and drew Kate into his arms, hard against his chest. "It's all right, darlin'. Hell, I feel sorry for myself. Why shouldn't you? It's not easy for a man like me. I try to tell myself I was lucky just to get out of those prisons alive. But I'm not all that grateful sometimes when I get to shaking like a baby's rattle, or when night comes and turns me clumsy and incompetent, as well as blind."

She slid her arms around his waist, pressing her cheek to the solid beat of his heart. "I feel awful, Race, for looking at your trials as my blessings. But I can't help it." She sniffed. "I'd bless just about anything I thought would keep you here."

He tipped her face up. "Loving you is going to keep me here, Katie, only you won't believe that."

"Maybe it doesn't matter why you stay," she whispered, "just as long as you do. Come home with me, Race. Love me tonight."

He touched his lips to a corner of her mouth. "Tonight. Tomorrow. Forever, love."

Kate reached for the lantern, but Race stopped her. "Leave it," he said. "I don't need it. I've got you to light up my night."

She threaded her arm through his. "You'll tell me if I'm helping wrong or just plain fussing too much, won't you?"

"Count on it, Katie." He laughed. "Right now I've got to admit it sounds pretty good though. Come fuss over me, love."

The interior of the mercantile was brightly lit when they walked in.

Fernanda yawned. "I go now. Shall I walk with you, Señor Logan?"

Kate was sure she saw the color rise in Race's cheeks as he looked to her for an answer. "He's staying, Fernanda," she said.

The woman grinned as she wrapped her shawl around her shoulders. "I come early tomorrow to care for the *niña.*" She looked from Kate to Race, then back. You sleep late, *señora.* You, too, *señor.* Late as you want. I will open the store for you."

While Kate locked up, Race carried a candle and the sleepy two-year-old up the stairs. Then, after Kate tucked her into bed, Race knelt beside the child a moment, smoothing her hair back from her face and adjusting the covers under her chin. "Sleep well, little Honey. I'll be here in the morning when you awake. I'll be here from now on."

The child blinked, then planted her thumb in the middle of her smile and whispered around it. "Night-night, Papa."

Race looked over his shoulder. His eyes were wide and glistening. "Did you hear that, Katie? She called me 'papa.'"

Kate smiled and nodded as she smoothed her hands over his broad shoulders. "I heard." She'd heard her daughter call almost every man in Loma Parda "papa," too, but she wasn't going to spoil Race's moment of joy by telling him. Besides, she thought happily, this time her daughter got it right.

The candle flame flickered as Race set it on the table beside Kate's bed. For a moment their two shadows danced and wavered on the wall.

Race lowered himself onto the edge of the bed to pull his boots off.

"Let me." Kate knelt before him.

Her head was bent to the task of taking off his boots, and Race watched as her hair fell like burnished silk over her shoulders. There wasn't enough light for him to see the color. Only the luster where the candlelight caressed it. He let his fingers drift over one rich wave as he watched the play of shadow and light on her face as it lengthened her lashes against her cheeks and glistened on the sweet curve of her mouth.

For a man who hadn't made love in three years, he thought, he felt an inordinate amount of patience. Or was it just that he was tamping down so hard on his need? He didn't want to rush. Dear God, he wanted this moment to last a lifetime if possible. He wanted to savor every second, every touch, every single inch of this beautiful woman who was at last his for the taking. And, more importantly, for the keeping.

If he kept watching her so intently, though, his control wouldn't be worth a plugged nickel. Race lifted his eyes and gazed around the dimly lit room and the candlelit shapes it contained. A square dresser. An arch of mirror above it. An oval frame... and within that frame the roundness of a vague but familiar face. Cassidy. The only man Race had ever wanted to kill. Now, though, there was no murder in his soul. No anger. Maybe, Race thought, there was even a little grudging gratitude for the man who would have cared for his woman and his child if...

She felt the change in him, heard his indrawn breath and felt the tension—like lightning—charging the long muscles of his legs. Kate looked up and saw the direction of Race's intense gaze. She put his boots aside, stood, and walked to the dresser where the tintype stared out from its metal frame.

Kate stood there a moment, Ned's image in her hands. Ned, who had loved her. Whom she had loved like a brother, like a gentle friend. But now there was Race. There had always been Race. She had wondered, those long nights lying beside Ned back in Kansas, what she would have done if the wind had called to her, had tempted her away from her husband and her vows. Kate thought she knew the answer, but she was glad, nevertheless, that she had never been forced to choose. "He was a good man," she said quietly, "but we never... with the baby coming... and he was so ill..."

"Shh. It doesn't matter, Katie. You were mine then just like you are now. Just like you will always be."

She opened a drawer and tucked the frame between the folds of a linen sheet, then closed the drawer soundlessly. Kate lifted her eyes to seek Race's reflection in the mirror.

"This is right, Katie. It's our time now. We're going to start all over again, you and I. Come let me love you, Katie." Race leaned forward and with one quick breath blew out the candle. "I don't even want a sliver of light to come between us tonight."

Darkness descended on him then, but this time it covered him like warm velvet as Kate moved close beside him. The sudden panic that always ripped through him was absent now, or replaced by a desire so complete it seemed to leave no room for any other emotion. And as his hands moved slowly, finding and then undoing the buttons of Kate's dress, Race felt as if he were seeing with his fingertips. Seeing perhaps more clearly than ever before in his life. He slipped her dress from her shoulders, then bent to taste the sweet skin in the hollow of her neck and to feel the wild pulse of her heart against his lips.

Then Kate's small hands—trembling and tentative at first, then eager, urgent—began undressing him, and her lips brushed over his skin with fire. A heat unlike any Race had ever known rushed through him. He felt a keen hunger, a thirst so profound it seemed unquenchable. A wanting so piercing there could never be an end to it.

He couldn't kiss her deeply enough then, couldn't touch her everywhere at once the way he needed to. He couldn't draw enough sweet succor from her breast to fill his need or to put out the fire that raged in him.

"Katie." His voice was hoarse and ragged as he swept her body beneath his and entered her, blindly, desperately, hard and deep.

Kate wrapped her legs around him as she cradled Race's head in her shoulder, welcomed his fierce desire deep inside her while she sheathed him in her own intense heat. There was nothing to separate them now—not time or distance or even a sliver of light. And when she felt Race's body draw tight as a bowstring, she lifted her hips and took him deeper, claiming his release with every muscle and nerve of her body, every beat of her heart, and every shimmering wisp of her soul.

Race shifted onto his side, pulling her into him, surrounding her with his arms. He sighed as he smoothed her tangled hair back from her cheek and her neck. "My hands are shaking, Katie," he whispered. "I'm afraid I'm going to wake up and find this was just a dream. I'm so used to dreaming...."

She brought his trembling hand to her lips. "Maybe it is a dream, Race. But it's a real one. And we're dreaming it together now."

He did wake a while later—eyes wide in the drenching, shapeless, colorless dark. In that panic-stricken moment, Race didn't know where he was. Only that it was dark and he had to find light. His hand snaked out, brushing over Kate's warm flank.

"What?" she murmured in her sleep.

"Nothing, love. Just sleep." He sucked in a cleansing breath, then let it go in a tattered sigh. His light was beside him, and he touched her again, smoothing his hand over her bed-warm hip, just to reassure himself. Like a cold man warming himself by a fire. Like a blind man finding comfort in the dark.

He lay awake then, just listening to Kate breathe. He heard the faint rustle of covers across the hall in his daughter's room. The contented night song of a mockingbird drifted through the open window. Then there was just Kate—her warmth beside him, the soft spill of her hair over his arm, her sweet, even breath.

And then from the window came another sound. At first Race thought it was a cat on the prowl, but then the yowling became distinct.

"Ka-ate."

"Don't be late, Kate the Gate."

With infinite care, he moved the covers, lifting and arranging them to shield Kate's ears. How long, he wondered, had she had to lie here and listen to that? Years. Her whole young life back in Kansas. His heart squeezed tight as he pictured her on that Fourth of July—a barefoot beauty standing up to face a whole damn town and claim her basket of stolen apples. He remembered, too, the way he'd taken her that night—with rough impatience, as if a hundred lovers had preceded him. Best, he remembered her green, forgiving eyes.

God, all he'd ever wanted was to protect her from her useless father, from the town that held her in such contempt, from everyone and everything. And in the end, he'd been the one she needed protection from the most—protection from his harsh loving and from the promises he hadn't been able to keep. Not that he'd done any of it on purpose, he thought bleakly. Lord knows he'd meant well when he'd broken his leg and when he'd "volunteered" for a reb prison. His reasons hardly mattered though where Kate was concerned. The simple fact was that he hadn't come back.

Race couldn't think of a blessed thing that would tempt him away from her. Well, Katie, he thought now, for what it was worth, he was back. Here, lying beside her, using her like a fragile candle to light his way through the brutal night, unable to fight her battles for her because he couldn't see the enemy. Not the cats yowling in the dark, anyway.

What he could do, though, was take her away. To Santa Fe. The way he'd meant to do three years ago. The way he'd planned before he'd followed those blasted wagons to Mississippi.

He closed his eyes, deepening the darkness. This time there wouldn't be any broken promises. This time there was no one, nothing to take him away. This time he meant to stay.

Chapter Nineteen

Kate stretched lazily. It was late morning, judging from the light, but she didn't want to get up. Not just yet. All she wanted to do was lie in bed and savor the memories of the night before. She rolled over, burying her face in Race's pillow, breathing in his windblown scent, wishing he were still in bed so she could fill her lungs with the real thing.

She felt . . . complete. Rolling onto her back, she clutched the pillow to her stomach, wondering if she were pregnant, and smiling at the notion. It had only taken one time before, and if her overwhelming feeling of completeness during their lovemaking the previous night was any indication, then she thought most definitely Race's seed had already taken root inside her.

Her lips curved in a slow, sensuous smile. There was a bolt of pale blue satin downstairs that would make such a lovely maternity dress. The light color might make her look as big as a house, but she didn't care about that. If she were carrying Race's baby, she didn't care if she looked as big as the whole mercantile. She'd be so proud and...

Her smile dissipated and her eyebrows drew together. If she was carrying his child, Race might not want to make love. Ned was her sole experience, and she wasn't sure whether he had refrained from touching her because of the baby or if it had been for some other reason.

Kate's teeth dragged on her lower lip. Here she was, twenty years old, possibly pregnant for the second time in her life, and she didn't know the rules. Holy hellfire, when it came right down to it, she didn't know very much about love. She'd only done it twice. But, oh, those times! Her insides warmed now just thinking about Race's hands and his mouth.

Her smile returned. If it was like this when she didn't even know what she was doing, imagine what was to come when she had a little practice. The smile widened. A lot of practice.

An hour later, after washing up and dressing and brushing out her hair, Kate came bounding down the stairs, but paused when she heard Race's voice in the store. It took her only a moment to recognize the second voice she heard. It was Gilly Johnston's wife. Race was obviously trying to help out in the store, but he was ramming his head against a brick wall when it came to Mrs. Johnston, who came in every week to peruse the merchandise, to finger bolts of fabric and waste Kate's time. Usually she'd unroll a particular bolt of calico, mash a few yards against her ample bosom, get her big fingerprints all over it, not to mention wrinkles, then put it back on the counter.

Kate grinned and sat down on the stairs, anxious to hear how the legend of the Santa Fe Trail, Mr. Race Logan, handled his first hard lesson in salesmanship at the tight fists of one Mrs. Gilly Johnston.

The woman was hemming and hawing as usual. "Oh, I don't know. It's nice, but..."

Then Race's deep voice, unusually smooth and beguiling now. "More than nice, Mrs. Johnston. That's a fine calico, and the little touches of yellow in it kind of pick up those bits of gold dust in your eyes."

On the stairs, Kate rolled her own eyes.

There was a note in the woman's voice now Kate had never heard before. The stable keeper's wife sounded like a weak-kneed sixteen-year-old girl when she said, "You're just joshing me, trying to make a sale."

"No, ma'am. Why I've already sold a whole day's quota of calico and more than a week's worth of pickles. Besides, I never lie about a lady's fine qualities. Not a married lady, anyway. What would be the point?"

Indeed, thought Kate. There was no point other than Race's seemingly inborn ability and natural inclination to sweep a female—any female—right off her feet. She could imagine the way Mrs. Johnston's heart was pumping right now, and could envision the flush of color on the woman's doughy cheeks. Still, Kate was pretty certain even Race's flattery wouldn't get this cheap woman to part with a single coin.

"I'll take twelve yards," Mrs. Johnston said.

"I'll be damned," muttered Kate. And she found herself muttering the same oath again when Mrs. Johnston coughed up an additional seventy-five cents for the IOU that Race kindly—though it must have pained him something fierce—reminded Mrs. Johnston that she owed. The old bat even simpered about what a pleasure it had been doing business with him. Kate heard her call as she went out the door, "I'm looking forward to buying more cloth from you, Mr. Logan."

"Best buy it fast, ma'am," Race answered. "In a day or so, I'll be on my way to Santa Fe."

On the stairs, Kate shot to her feet, but her heart felt trapped somewhere in the vicinity of her stomach. She walked into the store just as Mrs. Johnston went out the front door.

Race leaned his elbows on the counter. "'Morning, love."

Kate tried to take in enough breath to speak, but even when she did, her voice was thready. "When are you leaving, Race?"

He winced as if she had slapped him. "What . . . ?"

Jerking a thumb toward the door, Kate said, "I heard what you told Mrs. Johnston. About Santa Fe." She stiffened her shoulders and tried to subdue her quivering lips while telling herself she should be boiling with rage right now rather than just melting with sorrow inside.

Race came around the counter, and she didn't even have the strength to push him away when he drew her against him, or possess enough will to angle her head from his lips as they brushed over her ear.

"Do you always wake up this wrongheaded, Katie?"

"But you said..."

"I said I was going to Santa Fe. And I am. With you, with Honey." He laughed softly. "Even with Fernanda if she decides she can leave some old gent she's got by the short hairs."

Kate's whole body went still within the circle of his arms. "What are you saying?"

"I'm saying I'm moving my family to Santa Fe. Tomorrow. The next day. Just as soon as you can get packed up."

"All of us?"

"The whole kit and caboodle. Isaac, too, as soon as he gets back. He's family, too." He laughed again. "You can even take your friend, Mrs. Johnston, if you want."

"And then what?" she asked suspiciously.

Race leaned back, his palms cupping her face, his gaze intense. "And then we find us a preacher. And after that we just live, Katie." He kissed her nose. "And love. The way we did last night. The way I intend to every night from here on out."

Kate slid her arms around his waist, burying her face in the folds of his shirt. "You frightened me, Race. I guess, in spite of what I said, I still can't quite believe..."

He rocked her in his embrace the way he would have if he were reassuring his daughter. "Believe it, love. I'm not going anywhere. At least not without you."

Relief. She seemed to breathe it now. Yet, somewhere in all that sweet relief, there was a tiny and not-so-sweet prickle of resentment. Kate disengaged herself from Race's warm embrace, then walked behind the counter to stand where he had been earlier.

"I can't just pick up and go, Race. It's not that simple." As she spoke, Kate lifted the lid of the cash box, noting that it actually contained that valued commodity this morning in the form of a few silver coins and several neatly folded bills. It wasn't Race's salesmanship she resented, though. It was the fact that he was making decisions—enormous decisions—without even so much as a whisper in her direction.

He slung a hip up onto the counter. "Seems simple enough to me. What's so complicated, Katie?"

"This." She gestured to indicate the whole room. "I am running a business, you know."

Race tipped the cash box in his direction. "You've got more IOUs in here than a tree has leaves, love. Seems to me you're running a benevolent society instead."

She sniffed. "I still can't just walk away. I own this building, for your information."

"Juan Baca's going to give you four thousand dollars for the building and the inventory. If that's not as much as you want for it, then name the price and I'll make up the difference."

"Just like that?" Kate snapped her fingers.

"Just like that. Like I said, it's simple enough. If it's the business you're so attached to, then I'll set you up with another one in Santa Fe. I'm still a rich man, Kate. I've worked hard and saved most of my money for twenty years." He winked. "That's one of the benefits of being a saddle tramp. And if running a store in Santa Fe is what you want, then all you have to do is say so. Although—" he reached for her hand and brought it to his lips "—I was hoping we'd be having babies come along at such a clip you wouldn't have time for anything else."

She snatched her hand back. "Don't I have any say in all of this? Maybe I don't want to be having babies left and right." She crossed her arms. "Maybe," she added, "you could discuss some of this with me before you go selling my building out from under me."

Race swung his legs over the counter, pulling her between them, locking her in the grip of his thighs. He leaned forward, pressing his forehead against hers with a deep sigh. He had done just what she accused him of. He had sold her building out from under her. And he had hoped he could get away with it without having to discuss his reason for such high-handedness or the reason he wanted to see the last of this two-bit town.

"I want us to start over, Kate. Start fresh and clean. Especially...especially you, love."

"Oh," she said softly. "You heard. I was hoping..."

"I heard," Race whispered. "I'll tell you one thing. I won't have my daughter growing up listening to her mama being called names. And I intend to see you get the respectability you've always wanted, Kate. The respectability you deserve."

She slid her arms around his waist and said wistfully, "That name hounded me all eight hundred miles from Kansas, Race. What's to prevent it from dogging me another eighty miles or so to Santa Fe?"

"Me, Katie. The fine house I'm going to put you in. The fancy carriage and clothes. I'm going to build a wall around you and fairly smother you in respectability." He stroked her hair. "It's what you always wanted, isn't it?"

She nodded, not wanting to disappoint him, unwilling to diminish the sincerity of his intentions or the generosity of his gifts, and barely able to speak now because his warm mouth was moving over her ear.

"All I want is you, Katie," Race breathed as his hand moved to the front of her dress and began unbuttoning it. "Now. All of you."

"Now?"

He nodded and grinned wickedly as he continued undoing buttons.

"It's—it's broad daylight."

Race's only response was a throaty murmur as his hand slipped inside the open bodice of her dress.

Kate's head dropped back. His touch flooded her with warmth and wanting. "Oh, Lord," she said, sighing. "We'd better flip over the Open sign on the front door."

* * *

Upstairs, in Kate's bed, their lovemaking took on the same urgency it had the night before.

"One of these days," Race said, and sighed as he shifted onto his back beside Kate, "we're going to take it slow and easy. Katie! God, you light me up like a rocket. But I want it to be so good for you."

She sat up, the sheet bunched around her and her damp hair drifting over her shoulders. "I don't know if I could stand anything better than that, Race. For a minute there I thought it was nighttime and I was seeing stars."

He chuckled softly, his fingers plying a long lock of her hair. "I'm glad, darlin'." Then he feathered the lock across her breast, bringing her nipple to a tight rosy peak. "That's my favorite color. I like making love to you in the daylight, Katie. I like seeing all your pretty colors." His gaze roamed to her face. "I like watching your cheeks turn apple red the way they're doing now."

She tugged the sheet up to cover herself more. "I'm just not used to..."

"You will be," he murmured, tracing her lips with the tip of a finger. "Daylight and dark and everything in between."

Kate leaned toward him, propping herself on an elbow. A smile twitched at the corners of her mouth. "I like watching the way your eyes change color. First they're all sea green and cool. Then they turn such a wild and stormy shade of blue. I wonder if all our babies will have your eyes. I think we should have at least a dozen, don't you?"

"As many as you want, love," he whispered.

She sighed. "I believe I'm better at babies than I am at running a store. It's just that I can't stand to see anybody going without."

"That's something you won't ever have to do again. I promise you that."

"It'll take me a few days to get packed up. To leave for Santa Fe, I mean." Kate traced the line of his jaw. "There are a few loose ends that need tying up."

The backs of his fingers feathered up and down her arm. "Like what?"

"Cassidy business. I need to speak with Althea about..."

Race shoved up on his elbow. There was a heat in his eyes now unrelated to their earlier passion. "The Cassidy business is closed, Kate. Over and done with. Another week and you'll be Kate Logan, and then I don't ever want to hear that name again."

"Don't say that, Race. I owe Edmund and Hortense Cassidy—"

"Nothing," he shot back. "You don't owe those people the time of day."

"I owe them their granddaughter, Race," she said quietly, and when he opened his mouth to protest, Kate stilled his lips with her finger. "Listen to me. Ned's parents were kind to me. Not at first." She clucked her tongue. "At first, they figured me for a money-grubbing little schemer and offered to pay me to get out of their son's life. But when they found out about the baby—the baby they believed was their grandchild—they came around."

"Ha," Race sniffed.

"I know it wasn't me they were being kind to so much as it was the child inside me, but they were still kind." Her eyes filled with tears. "There hasn't been all that much kindness in my life, Race, for me to fail to appreciate it, no matter the circumstances."

"Katie," he whispered, "You deserve—"

She cut him off with an exaggerated groan. "What a person deserves and what she gets aren't always the same. You know that as well as I do."

He shook his head sadly as he smoothed the hair back from her face. "That's true, darlin'. No, they're not."

"I can't just rip that child out of the Cassidys' lives. They've never seen her, but they love her all the same. She's their future, Race. And she's their link to Ned. It would tear their hearts out to lose her. And, since Althea doesn't have any babies, there's no one to replace Nedda in their hopes and dreams."

"Well, I'm sure that's not from any lack of trying on Althea's part," Race said with a grimace as he dropped back onto the mattress. "Hell, a Sikes baby would elbow your daughter out of the way so fast she'd never know what hit her. You and your damn loyalty Kate. I swear..."

"It's important to me Race. I realize the Cassidys have to know the truth eventually, but maybe by that time Althea and Frederick will have given them a true grandchild and the loss won't be so difficult to bear."

Race shrugged helplessly. "Between you deceiving them out of love and their daughter doing the same out of greed, I half feel sorry for those people."

"*I* haven't used any of their money. Every cent is locked in a box I keep on a back shelf downstairs. And when the time comes for them to know the truth, I plan to give all the money back. I just want to talk things out with Althea before we leave. I just need to make sure she understands how things are."

He sighed. "She probably understands a whole lot better than you think, Katie. I hate to have you get even within spitting distance of that she-cat. The woman would just as soon claw your eyes out as look at you."

"Well, I've got claws, too, you know." She demonstrated by drawing a fingernail slowly across his chest.

"I know you do, darlin'," Race murmured lazily as he clasped his hands around her head and drew her mouth to his for a tantalizing kiss. "I want to feel those sharp little claws of yours on my back again, too, Katie. Now."

Chapter Twenty

The following afternoon, as the buckboard jounced up the long grassy rise that led to Fort Union, Kate glanced at her daughter, whose tiny feet didn't even reach the floorboards from her seat between her parents. Honey. The name seemed to fit her, Kate thought. Edwina had been such a sober name; even the nickname, Nedda, didn't reflect the child's innate sweetness or, for that matter, her stubborn stickiness.

"Honey." Kate said it softly, almost wistfully, and at the sound of it, two pairs of brilliant turquoise eyes turned to her. Honey's lifted round and quizzical, while Race's slanted sidelong and shimmered from beneath raised eyebrows.

"I was just talking to myself," Kate said, angling her head to press her cheek against her daughter's dark, sun-warmed hair. "You're being such a good girl." She opened the drawstring of her reticule. "I'll bet I have a peppermint stick in here for you."

The child squealed with delight, then sat in contented silence as she sucked on the bright striped candy.

Race grinned. "Got one of those for me, Katie? I've been good, too. At least that's what you told me last night when . . ."

"Hush," Kate snapped with a quick glance toward Honey. "Little pitchers have big ears, Race."

He gently nudged the little girl. "Why's Mama's face getting all red, Honey? Too much sun, I guess."

"Too much something," Kate muttered, trying to cool her blush, wondering if there would ever come a time—a night or a day—when Race's hands could ever touch her too much. Heavens, she barely knew the meaning of those words anymore. "Here." She whisked another peppermint from her bag and stuck it right in the middle of Race's grin. "That ought to keep you quiet for a while."

He laughed and waggled the candy rakishly between his teeth before returning his attention to the horses and the road.

Kate produced a third peppermint stick. There you go again, eating up the inventory, she berated herself before recalling that it didn't matter anymore. In a few days she'd be leaving the mercantile along with all its inventory. Nothing much mattered now except that she and Race were together. And they'd be together tomorrow and all the tomorrows after that. Forever. She knew the meaning of that, she thought, and it would never be too much.

Ahead, the fort's new brick and adobe buildings were the color of rust beneath the hot July sun. Kate remembered her arrival two years back when the hilltop had been white with tents and the air had been abuzz with hammers and saws and the racket of construction. She'd been weak then from childbirth. Weak and frightened and so unsure of her future. Isaac had sensed her fears and apprehensions, and had caught her up in one of his big, bearish embraces.

"You gonna do just fine, Miz Kate," he'd said. "Everything's gonna be just fine. 'Specially when Horace gets back."

She hadn't believed him, even then, but Isaac turned out to be right. 'Specially about Horace, she thought.

Kate eased Honey onto her lap, then leaned against Race. "I love you, Horace."

He shifted the reins into one hand, then wrapped his arm around her. "I love you, too, Kate. Funny you should call me that. I was just thinking about Isaac. I want to ask you something."

"Ask away."

"Well, I was just thinking about that big old bear and how he's been like a daddy to me." Race paused to angle his head toward their daughter, then said, "Cover the little pitcher's ears, Katie."

Looking surprised, Kate immediately clapped her hands over Honey's ears. "What in the world are you going to ask me, Race?"

"Isaac left just a few days ago. That'll put him back here maybe late September or early October." He shot a quick glance at Honey's covered ears before continuing. "If you'd consider living in *s-i-n* for a month or two, I'd like to postpone our wedding till then so I can have Isaac stand up for me. It'd mean a lot to him, Kate. To me, too."

Her reply was immediate and brusque. "Absolutely not."

And then it was Race's turn to look surprised.

Kate laughed. "That big old bear is the closest thing I have to a daddy now, and he can't be standing up for you, Race, because he's going to be walking me down the aisle."

He breathed a small sigh of relief as he clasped her more tightly against him. "Let me ask you something else now, darlin'," he drawled.

"What?"

"Are you ever going to just say yes without arguing about it first?"

Kate rested her head on his shoulder. "I guess you'll just have to hang around for fifty or sixty years and see."

Race had pulled up the wagon beside a water trough, and he leaned against its wooden side now, watching Kate wring out her handkerchief and then apply it with vigor to Honey's face.

He tipped his hat back with his thumb. "Katie, you're going to rub that baby's lips right off her face."

"I'm just making her presentable." She combed her fingers through the little girl's dark hair now. "I don't want her to look like a Gypsy when we visit the Sikeses for the very first time."

"Are you telling me that in two years that woman never once invited you inside her house?"

Kate dipped her handkerchief back into the trough and wrung it out again. "That's right," she said stiffly.

"And you're worried about looking proper," he grumbled. "If I were you, I'd be more concerned with some of the things I'm tempted to say to the fine and elegant Mrs. Sikes."

Snatching up Honey's hands, Kate swabbed them with the damp linen. "Be as rude as you want, Race. It doesn't make any difference to me." Kate knelt down and took her daughter's chin in her hand. "Now I don't want you to touch anything in Aunt Althea's house, Honey. Do you hear me?"

"God forbid," Race muttered as his daughter nodded solemnly. "And if the notion strikes you to kick your precious aunt in the behind, you just hold back, Honey. Daddy'll do it for you."

Once more Kate clapped her hands over Honey's ears. "That's a fine thing to be telling your daughter, Race Logan. Just what do you intend to do if she goes ahead and does it?"

"I intend to laugh, Katie, love," he said. Then he raised a wicked eyebrow. "And I dare you not to laugh yourself."

"I will not." She bit on her lower lip.

"Not even this much?" Race measured off half an inch with his fingers. "Not even a little snicker?"

Kate bit harder on her lip, trying to stifle a giggle.

He moved his fingers together. "This much?"

She shook her head.

"How 'bout just a little ladylike smirk then?"

Kate exploded with laughter.

As they followed the flagstone path that led to the officers' quarters, Kate's attention was drawn to the activity on the parade ground where scores of soldiers were saddling horses or tending their rifles. The giggles she'd been trying to suppress subsided instantly. Her gaze shot to Race, who was intently watching the scene.

"What?" she asked him. "What's happening?"

"Trouble," he said, his tone low and distracted. "Indians more than likely."

She knew immediately what was going on behind that hard blue-green gaze. Isaac had left only a few days before, heading north through hostile territory. Kate put her hand on Race's arm, not certain if she meant to reassure him or to steady herself.

"I'm sure he'll be all right," she said.

Race didn't reply. He merely nodded, then pressed his hand to her back to guide her farther along the walk.

A feeling of dread welled up inside her, but Kate didn't have time to truly comprehend it, because the next minute Race was knocking on the Sikeses' front door, and a moment after that she found herself in a parlor that more closely resembled a museum whose every table was topped by dozens of porcelain figures, glass paperweights, fragile china boxes and delicate vases.

Kate suddenly felt like a bull in a china shop—a bull

with a curious two-year-old calf. She clamped Honey's small hand in a death grip. "Don't touch," she whispered to her daughter, tempted to add, "Don't even breathe."

Althea had greeted them coolly, then swept ahead of them into the parlor. She turned now, her blue eyes as pale as frost and an icy smile on her lips.

"Well, this is certainly a surprise. To what do I owe the unexpected pleasure of your company, Kate?"

Kate opened her mouth to reply, but Race cut her off.

"It's the last time you'll have that pleasure, Mrs. Sikes. Kate came to tell you goodbye, but she's polite enough that she'll probably lead up to it gently."

Althea flinched perceptibly and one hand flitted up to touch a yellow curl.

"You take all the time you want, Katie," he continued. "I'm going to take Honey outside before she gets into trouble with all these gewgaws in here." He cast a meaningful look around the cluttered room as he picked the little girl up in his arms and strode to the door.

"So," Althea said, patting her curls again, "you finally got him. I hope you haven't come here to gloat."

Kate sighed. Somehow she had imagined her sister-in-law's disposition would soften with this leave-taking. It appeared, however, that Althea's chilly heart was impervious to any sort of warmth. "I didn't just come to say goodbye, Althea. I wanted to thank you, too, for not saying anything to your mother and father about Honey...Edwina, I mean...and about Ned not being her father. It was a comfort to me, even if you didn't do it out of affection or loyalty."

Althea offered a sniff in reply.

"About your parents," Kate continued. "I'm worried that they'll feel they're losing their granddaughter. I know how much Honey...Edwina...means to them."

"*Meant* to them."

Kate blinked. "I beg your pardon."

The blonde slid her hand over the silk gathers of her skirt. "My monthly is late. Four days now." A brittle smile formed on her lips. "I'm never late."

Instinctively reacting to the news, Kate gave a happy little gasp and reached for her sister-in-law's hand. "That's wonderful news, Althea. Frederick must be so happy."

Althea snatched her hand back. "I haven't told him yet. Frankly, I don't care if he's happy or not. What matters is that my mother and father will be happy."

"And generous," Kate said softly, already feeling sorry for the child who was coming into this world merely to claim an inheritance.

Althea readjusted the gathers of her skirt, smoothing them over her still-flat abdomen. "I don't plan to tell them until after the baby is born. Your little...what's that awful name Race gave her? Sweetie? Honey?"

"Honey," Kate replied.

"Well, your little Honey is still an heiress. For a few more months, anyway. Quite plainly, Kate, I need the little brat, at least till my own brat comes along. I mean, if I told them about her true origins and then something went wrong with my baby, it would be rather like cutting off my nose to spite my own face, wouldn't it?"

Kate felt ill suddenly. She turned toward the door, then faced the blonde again. "I hope it goes well for you, Althea. I truly do. And I hope when you finally hold your baby in your arms you'll love him for himself and not..."

"For the Cassidy money?" Althea laughed sharply. "Kate, you really are a fool. Maybe it's because you never had anything so you don't know what there is to be had in this world. I want fine clothes." She swept her hand around the room. "I appreciate nice things. I want that money. I need it. And, believe me, if I could have thought of another way to get it, I would have. You don't really think I want to give up my figure for a year and go around looking like an elephant, do you?"

Tears gathered in Kate's eyes as she gazed around the cluttered parlor. "You'll have to put most of these things out of reach of tiny little hands," she said, her voice wavering. "Especially the glass. It could cut..."

Althea linked her arm through Kate's and moved her brusquely toward the door. "I appreciate the sweet maternal advice, but I believe I'll know how to manage properly when the time comes." She opened the door. "Goodbye, Kate. Have a nice life. Oh, and congratulations on getting Race after all this time. Now all you have to do is worry about keeping him."

She gave Kate a little shove that sent her across the threshold, then she closed the door firmly behind her.

Kate walked slowly across the parade ground. She felt bruised, as if her sister-in-law had slapped her. She ached for the tiny life that had been conceived solely in greed, yet she knew there was nothing she could do. For a moment, though she knew it was wrong, she almost hoped that that poor baby would never be born. What kind of life could he ever have when all he meant to his mother was the prospect of money, when the woman regarded him as a dreadful but necessary inconvenience?

She swiped the tears from her eyes, then looked across the busy parade ground to see Race with Honey settled on one broad shoulder. The ache in her heart gave way to a flood of love. Now, there was a child who was loved, Kate thought. And not just by her mama. She watched as Race's big gentle hand reached up to spread protectively across his daughter's back.

It wasn't until Kate was closer that she realized Race was deep in conversation with a captain of the cavalry. And it wasn't until she reached them that she heard, with dull anguish, the words "Kiowas" and "a few day's north from here."

Her heart held still when she saw the hard set of Race's jaw and the storm color in his eyes. Isaac was in trouble. Kate didn't even have to ask. And so was she. Oh, God, so was she.

They walked back to the wagon in silence—Honey riding Race's shoulder and Kate tucked into the bend of his arm—and they kept silent until they were a mile down the road to Loma Parda, when Kate grabbed the reins from Race's hands and pulled the wagon to a halt.

"What are you doing, Kate? Lord, you nearly broke the horses' necks not to mention nearly knocked the baby right off the seat." He resettled Honey between them.

"Go on," she snapped.

"What?"

Her green eyes were wide and wet. Her hands fumbled with the reins as if they were suddenly too hot to hold. "Just go on, Race. I can't say this all soft and sweet because it hurts too much. It hurts so much it's almost killing me." She drew in enough air to continue. "Just go. Please. I'm not asking you to stay."

In a single, smooth motion he took the reins, then grasped both Kate's hands in his. His voice was warm and low. "I wasn't asking to go, Katie." His turquoise gaze searched her face, then delved deeply into her eyes. "What are you saying to me, love?"

"Damn you," she swore as the tears began to stream down her cheeks. "You knew you didn't have to ask. You know that I love you and, because of that, I can't keep you from being what you are."

He tightened his grip on her hands. "Katie, darlin'..."

Kate glared at him now through her tears. "I love you so much, but sometimes, Race, I swear I hate that part of you that will go anywhere or risk anything when somebody you care about is in trouble."

"Isaac's in big trouble, Kate."

"I know."

His mouth tautened. "It might be too late. I might not be able to do anything, but I have to try."

"I know that, too." She sniffed.

And now it was Race's eyes that were suddenly swamped with tears. "Aw, hell."

Kate lifted a hand and pressed her palm to his cheek. "I wish I could go with you," she said, trying to keep her voice from breaking while her heart felt as if it was doing just that. Telling him to leave her was the last thing Kate ever thought she'd do. She heard her own words as if someone else were speaking them.

"You be careful. Especially at night. And when the sun goes down, you stay close to a fire. Or find somebody to latch on to. That captain seemed like a decent man. You tell him you can't see at night and let him be your eyes for you."

She smoothed her hand along the shoulder seam of his shirt then, like a mother sending her only son off to his first day of school. "Don't you be too proud to ask for help when you need it, Race. Do you hear me?"

He nodded.

Kate laughed a little wildly then. She lifted Honey onto her lap and wrapped her arms around the little girl, burying her face in her hair for a moment. "I can't believe I'm doing this."

Race shifted his arms to encompass them both. "Shh. It'll be all right, Katie. I promise you."

"I have to believe that or I could never let you go," she whispered. "There's one more thing I have to tell you and I want you to listen like you've never listened before in your life. I love you. I'll always love you, Race Logan. And I trust you." Her voice wavered as she lifted her gaze to his and watched a tear spring loose from his eye. "I guess I know something now that I wasn't sure of before."

"What's that, love?"

"It doesn't matter how often you leave me or how far you go. All that matters is that you'll come back. And I know you always will."

Chapter Twenty-One

July 4, 1880

Kate and Isaac sat side by side in the shade beneath the big green awning of Logan Savings and Loan, watching the festivities in the crowded plaza before them. Though statehood was still a distant dream for the territory of New Mexico, there were enough Americans in Santa Fe now to make Independence Day a celebration, indeed. Even the venerable adobe Governor's Palace was draped in red, white and blue bunting.

"We ain't exactly the life of this here party, Miz Kate," Isaac noted sleepily.

Kate laughed. "No, I guess we're not." Her hand moved to her swollen belly. "But I'm six months gone with my fifth baby, Isaac. What's your excuse?"

"At my age, Miz Kate, I don't need no excuse to sit with a pretty lady in the shade."

"I'm glad you're here," she said. Kate reached over to pat his gnarled hand, her fingers just brushing his empty sleeve. He wouldn't be here with her now, she thought, if she had kept Race from riding north that day fifteen years before. The cavalry had taken care of the Indian raiding party, but it was Race who had bullied the badly wounded Isaac into staying alive after he'd given up all hope of rescue. Once Race had brought him back, however, the big bear of a man recovered quickly, despite the loss of his arm. By late autumn, he had been on his feet again—first walking Kate down the aisle and then standing up for Race during the wedding ceremony.

"You're not having those ghost pains anymore, are you, Isaac?" she asked him as she leaned toward him and carefully repinned the loose fold of the sleeve.

"You mean the one where I feel the finger I ain't got on the trigger that ain't there?" He rubbed his jaw with his left hand. "I prob'ly haven't felt one of those in two or three years now, Miz Kate. Seems like it was about the last time Horace was struck down by the shakes." He grinned. "I 'spect we're both improving."

Kate sat back in her chair. "I'm glad to hear that. I do have a bone to pick with you, though, about the way you use your remaining arm to teach your namesake to shoot a pistol. I know the two of you think I don't know how you sneak out in the hills south of here with all those empty bottles and tins. But I do know, Isaac. And I don't approve. Zack's too young..."

"Young Isaac's fourteen now. By that age his daddy was pretty near a man. And the boy's a fine shot, too. A fine shot." The old man arched a salt-and-pepper eyebrow. "He gonna do it anyway, Miz Kate. Best he be learning from me."

She sighed with resignation. "My babies are growing up too fast, Isaac." Kate patted her stomach. "Before we know it, this little one will be fourteen, too." Her gaze idled on the crowded plaza. "Where do you suppose they've all gone off to, those babies of mine?"

Isaac pointed toward the edge of the crowd. "There's your yellow-haired baby coming back to you right now."

As the old man spoke, Kate caught sight of her other fourteen-year-old son. Her Cassidy child. Althea's son. She felt a small hitch in her breath at the sight of his lanky build and his tousled, wheat-colored hair. "It's like seeing a ghost sometimes, isn't it, Isaac?"

The black man nodded. "He do resemble Mr. Ned. Good-hearted like Mr. Ned, too. Not like his natural mama."

Such a sad irony, Kate thought, that her sister-in-law, who had been intent on bleeding her parents dry of their fortune, had instead bled to death herself after giving birth to the boy. Frederick Sikes had brought the baby to Santa Fe then, left him in Kate's arms, saying he made a better soldier than a father. And not that good a soldier, Kate thought now, for he had died not long after that when his rifle misfired.

Sad for the Cassidys, too. Both Edmund and Hortense passed away within a month of hearing of their daughter's death. Instead of a great fortune, the couple had left a pile of debts. Kate imagined that somewhere—heaven or hell—Althea was ranting and raving about the futility and unfairness of it all.

Ah, but Althea had left a beautiful little boy. Kate loved him so, and Race, who'd been so determined not to even look at "a pale, pasty-faced Cassidy" purely doted on the blond, gentle boy who was so different from the wilder, dark-haired sons.

The boy loped toward them, arriving only slightly out of breath. It was like seeing Ned again—happy and in robust good health—like having him tell her their brief, unprovidential marriage had been blessed after all and destined to bring good into lives other than their own.

Kate smiled at her son. "I was just thinking about you, Cass." She reached out and combed the ragged hank of hair from his forehead. "Where are your brothers?"

"Zack's helping out with the fireworks. The last time I saw Creel and Aitch, Fernanda was stuffing them with tortillas and sweet peppers." He puffed out his chest proudly. "And I sold all those penny flags for two cents each, so I thought I'd just come rest a while with you and think about how I'm going to invest my profits."

Kate slanted a grin toward Isaac. "This boy has mercantile in his blood, doesn't he?" She patted the arm of her chair. "Sit. Rest a while."

Cass sat, then sighed—long and loud. "Well, I don't know if anybody's going to get any rest now.

Here comes Honey and she looks like she's got a hornet up her skirt."

Kate echoed his sigh, only hers was longer, louder and better practiced. "Honey's always got a hornet up her skirt about something. I swear she gets more like her daddy every day. I'm glad my boys all get their dispositions from me. They're cool and calm like their mama."

"Oh, yes, ma'am." Isaac's mouth sloped in a grin.

"Well, I am," Kate insisted. "Most of the time."

Isaac and Cass both mumbled an uh-huh just as seventeen-year-old Honey stomped up on the sidewalk. There was murder in her turquoise eyes.

"Mama, if you don't come get Daddy right this minute, I swear I'm going home to get a gun and then I'm going to blast him from one side of the plaza to the other." She stood with her hands plastered to her slim hips and one foot furiously drumming on the boards of the sidewalk. Her long dark hair was barely restrained by a wide black velvet ribbon as it tumbled over her shoulders and down her back like a Spanish mantilla.

Kate folded her hands in her lap as she gazed calmly up at her daughter. "What's Daddy done now, Honey?"

"He's bidding on my supper basket," the girl wailed.

"You're lucky somebody is," Cass said just under his breath, earning himself a scalding glare from his sister.

"Well, I think that's sweet," said Kate.

"Sweet! How can you say that, Mama? It's just awful. This is the worst day of my whole life." Honey plopped down onto the sidewalk, scrunching up her bustle in back.

"Your daddy loves you, Honey," Kate said. "Of course he's making some bids on your basket."

"He's trying to buy it, Mama," the irate girl snorted. "Lord, it's so embarrassing. Lieutenant Cleary's on one side of the plaza and Daddy's on the other, and they're glaring at each other and shouting one sum after another. All my other beaux ran out of money half an hour ago."

Young Cass shook his head, then leaned over to kiss the top of Kate's head. "Mama, I believe I'll just go rest someplace a little quieter," he said, standing and sauntering back toward the plaza after giving his sister a disgusted scowl.

"How much is that basket of yours worth now, Miss Honey?" Isaac asked.

"A hundred and seventy-five dollars!"

"Oh, for heaven's sake!" Kate struggled up out of her chair. "What does that man think he's doing?"

Honey jumped up, too. "See, Mama. I told you. Daddy's just ruining my day. And he's driving Lieutenant Cleary into the poorhouse, too."

With a frown creasing her forehead, Kate stared into the crowd. "Where is he, Honey?"

"Right over there." She jabbed a finger toward the east side of the plaza. "See him?"

"Where?" Kate shaded her eyes against the brilliant sunlight.

"Right there, Mama, leaning against the hitching rail, looking like he thinks he owns the whole blasted town."

"He damn near does," murmured Isaac, still sitting behind them.

When Kate's eyes lit on her husband, her heart—as always—beat a little faster and a tiny stitch of desire tugged in the pit of her stomach. Aren't you a handsome devil, Race Logan? she thought. Fifteen years had silvered his hair and deepened the rugged lines in his face. He never wore buckskin anymore, but dressed like the banker that he was now, in rich, imported wools, the softest cottons, and the finest silks. Somehow, though, Kate always pictured him as she had first seen him that day in Kansas—in tawny buckskins, a tomcat on the prowl.

"Are you coming, Mama?" Honey asked impatiently.

The little grin that had been playing about Kate's lips flattened out now. Handsome devil or not, it was time for Race Logan to be taken down a notch or two where his only daughter was concerned. Kate grabbed two fistfuls of skirt, ready to march across the plaza and confront him.

"Did you forget something, Miz Kate?" Isaac asked.

Kate looked over her shoulder at him. "What's that, Isaac?"

The older man arched an eyebrow and aimed his gaze at the bare toes peeking out from beneath Kate's rucked-up skirt.

"Damnation! I did forget. You know I can't get my shoes on when I'm so far along, Isaac."

"Mama," Honey called.

Kate threw up her hands. "All right. I'm coming." She winked at Isaac. "What do you suppose everybody'll say about the banker's barefoot wife?"

Grinning, Isaac leaned back in his chair. "Knowing the banker as I do, Miz Kate, I don't suppose anybody'd even breathe one little word."

If looks could kill, Race's black scowl should have brought the young lieutenant to his knees half an hour ago. Instead, the son of a bitch just kept upping his bid.

"Two hundred twenty," Race called out now.

"Two twenty-one," Lieutenant Cleary promptly responded.

Goddamn young pup didn't know when to quit, Race thought. Well, hell! He'd stand out here all day and all night, too, if he had to. There was no way he was going to let his daughter...

"Three hundred dollars." Kate's voice rang loud and clear across the plaza. Heads turned and elbows shot out as everyone watched the obviously pregnant Mrs. Horace Logan, Jr., stride toward her husband.

Once beside him, she crossed her arms and leaned a hip against the hitching post, mirroring Race's pose.

"What are you doing, Katie?"

"I'm bidding for Honey's basket," she said calmly. "I'm going to buy it and then I'm going to give it to that nice young Lieutenant Cleary."

"The hell you are," Race growled.

"The hell I am."

"Three twenty-five," he called out.

Kate smiled up at him. "Three-fifty," she yelled.

Race scraped his hat from his head and slapped it against his thigh. He glowered down on his wife. "Do you want your daughter taking off someplace with that...that...?"

"That polite young officer? Yes, I do, Race."

"Three seventy-five," he yelled.

"Four hundred," Kate countered.

Race's mouth tautened. "That's my goddamn money you're bidding with, woman."

Kate's eyes narrowed. Then she cupped her hands to her mouth to call even louder. "Four twenty-five."

"My daughter is not going off with—"

"Four-fifty," Kate yelled.

"—some heavy-breathing, fast-handed—"

"Four seventy-five."

"—lieutenant who only wants—"

"Five hundred."

"Katie," Race said through clenched teeth.

There was fire in Kate's eyes now and her voice was menacing and low. "He only wants to share a supper basket with her, Race. He's not some saddle bum in town for a day and hell-bent on having a hot time with the town tramp."

Race glanced at the crowd that had gathered around them and was edging closer now, whispering and smirking behind their hands. He ripped his fingers through his hair. "C'mon, Katie! What's this all about?"

Kate blinked, suddenly aware that this confrontation wasn't about Honey at all. It had nothing to do with today, but went back years and miles to another Fourth of July, to another time and place. It was about a handsome devil named Race Logan and a young girl called Kate the Gate. Most of all, it was about her own notions of respectability.

"Our daughter is a beautiful, bright, good girl, Race. Trust her to do what's right. To do what's right for her." Kate bit her lower lip to keep back the tears that were suddenly brimming in her eyes. She, too, had been, if not beautiful, at least bright and good when Race Logan happened to her like a hot summer storm. She had barely known him when she had given him her innocence that night, and though Kate had no regrets, she wondered now if perhaps Race didn't harbor just a shred of contempt for that. After all, look how he was going on about Honey.

"Katie?"

Race's soft inquiry nudged her from her reverie. His lake-colored eyes washed over her face with gentle concern.

"Honey, are you feeling all right?" he asked.

"Did I win the bidding?" Kate asked him archly.

Race sighed. "I guess you did. You can tell the auctioneer I'll get the money to him as soon as the bank opens tomorrow."

"Fine." On that curt note, Kate pushed away from the hitching rail and walked toward the table where the supper baskets were on display. "I'll take Honey Logan's basket," she said briskly, "and for five hundred dollars you can throw in my basket, too. It's the one with the red-checkered cover. There." Kate pointed.

With a basket over each arm then, she strode toward Lieutenant Cleary, who was deep in conversation with Honey.

"I believe this is what you wanted, Lieutenant," Kate said, offering him the basket. "Please have my daughter home at a reasonable hour."

The tall, sandy-haired officer grinned. "Yes, ma'am."

"Mama, what'd you say to Daddy?" Honey whispered frantically. "He's on his way over here and he looks like he's chewing half a dozen hornets."

The lieutenant stood taller as Race Logan's shadow fell across all three of them. "Afternoon, sir," he said.

"I want my daughter home at a reasonable hour, Lieutenant," Race said.

Kate glared over her shoulder at her husband. "I've already told him, Race."

Honey linked her arm through the young lieutenant's, tugging him away. "Well, we're off. Don't look so worried, Daddy." She laughed brightly. "I won't do anything Mama wouldn't do."

Kate was halfway home when Race caught up with her. If she hadn't been carrying an extra ten or fifteen pounds around her middle, he thought, and if the walk had been downhill instead of up, she would have been home already, judging from the way she had stalked away from the plaza.

He slowed now, measuring his strides to stay just behind her. Until he figured out what was going on inside her head, he didn't want to get too close. Kate had a way of going for his shins that he had learned to avoid over the years.

"I'd be happy to carry that basket for you, Kate," he called out now, then watched her shoulders stiffen as she refused his aid.

"No, thank you, Race. I'm managing."

He fell silent, staying behind her, watching the sunset light up her hair, enjoying the proud set of her shoulders and the slight sway of her bustled backside. She was walking with such determination he was surprised he couldn't hear the clop of her heels on the street.

"Are you wearing shoes, Katie?" he called up to her.

She stopped, staring straight ahead, steaming. "No, I'm not, Race. I realize it's not very dignified or respectable for a banker's wife, but then I guess I'm just not a very dignified or respectable person."

"Good." He swung an arm under her knees and lifted her high against his chest, then grinned down into her startled face. "Because I have some very undignified plans for you now that we've got the whole house to ourselves."

"Put me down this minute," Kate protested as he strode toward the adobe wall that hid their house from the street. She pushed against his chest, but it was as unyielding as the wall.

"Quit bashing me in the side with that basket," he groaned, opening the gate and carrying her into the courtyard of the sprawling adobe structure. "What've you got in there, anyway? Bricks?"

"Apples," she said softly, a little sadly.

Race halted. "What?"

"It was a surprise. I thought you'd bid on *my* basket, but you were too busy being distraught over Honey and her lieutenant."

Race closed his eyes and shook his head. "Katie, Katie. I'm sorry. I went a little crazy when all those young bucks started bidding."

"You went a lot crazy," she corrected. "You can't keep her in a gilded cage, you know. Even if you try, she won't stay there."

His mouth thinned to a severe line as he set Kate down. "Is that why you're angry? You think I'm being too strict? Am I wrong trying to protect my little girl?"

Kate shifted the basket onto her other arm, then lifted her chin to meet her husband's quizzical gaze. "Who protected me from you, Race Logan?"

She smiled victoriously at his stunned expression, then turned and walked into the house.

Kate was sitting on the edge of the bed, too tired to get up and undress, too distressed to lie down. It was silly to have lost her temper that way, she knew, but sometimes it just plain nettled her when Race was so overprotective of their daughter. And it stung her that he couldn't see how that made her feel about her own behavior that hot summer night back in Kansas.

Race entered their room, and from behind his back he produced a shining green apple and held it out to Kate in a gesture of peace. Without a word she took it from him and proceeded to take a bite.

He stood there a moment, as if testing her mood, then said, "I just hope to hell your daughter had something sensible in that basket of hers." Race grinned then as he sat beside her and used his thumb to catch the drop of apple juice at the corner of her mouth.

"Roast pork," Kate replied.

"Well, that sets my mind at ease." His grin widened briefly, then turned serious. A warm light flickered deep in his eyes. "It happened fast for us, Katie. Like fireworks. Remember?"

"I remember."

Race's fingers moved to the high collar of her dress and began slipping the small pearl buttons. "So do I, love. And if it's half as good for our Honey when her time comes, I'll be happy. Our sons, too. I hope they get struck by the same lightning that struck me when I first laid eyes on you."

He parted the lace collar and bent to kiss the delicate skin his hand uncovered. He whispered against Kate's throat. "Nobody could have protected you from me, love. Nobody. You were mine that day. You'll always be mine. My barefoot beauty."

"Barefoot, but respectable," she corrected, arching her neck beneath the beguiling warmth of his mouth.

His fingers continued to undo the buttons on her dress as his lips drifted over the swollen mounds of her breasts.

"Infinitely respectable, Mrs. Logan," he murmured, his breath warm and moist against her skin as he braced her back to lower her gently onto the bed. Race claimed her mouth then with a deep, sweet kiss.

"Katie, Katie," he said with a sigh. "You taste like apples, again."

* * * * *

Where do you find hot Texas nights, smooth Texas charm and dangerously sexy cowboys?

Crystal Creek reverberates with the exciting rhythm of Texas. Each story features the rugged individuals who live and love in the Lone Star State.

"...Crystal Creek wonderfully evokes the hot days and steamy nights of a small Texas community...impossible to put down until the last page is turned."
—*Romantic Times*

"...a series that should hook any romance reader. Outstanding."
—*Rendezvous*

Praise for Margot Dalton's *Even the Nights Are Better*

"...every bit as engrossing as the others. Ms. Dalton wraps you in sentiment...this is a book you don't just read, you feel."
—*Rendezvous*

Don't miss the next book in this exciting series. Look for SOUTHERN NIGHTS by Margot Dalton

Available in June wherever Harlequin books are sold.

CC-16